HER
FEAR

HER
FEAR

THE AMISH OF HART COUNTY

Shelley Shepard Gray

AVON
INSPIRE
An Imprint of HarperCollins*Publishers*

P.S.™ is a trademark of HarperCollins Publishers.

HER FEAR. Copyright © 2018 by Shelley Shepard Gray. All rights reserved. Printed in the United States of America. No part of this book may be used or reproduced in any manner whatsoever without written permission except in the case of brief quotations embodied in critical articles and reviews. For information, address HarperCollins Publishers, 195 Broadway, New York, NY 10007.

HarperCollins books may be purchased for educational, business, or sales promotional use. For information, please email the Special Markets Department at SPsales@harpercollins.com.

FIRST EDITION

Designed by Diahann Sturge

Library of Congress Cataloging-in-Publication Data has been applied for.

ISBN 978-0-06-246921-2 (paperback)
ISBN 978-0-06-284609-9 (library edition)

18 19 20 21 22   LSC   10 9 8 7 6 5 4 3 2 1

To Erika, with my heartfelt thanks and gratitude.
Erika, you embraced my idea for a suspenseful
Amish series set in Kentucky and encouraged me to
run with it. All authors should be so blessed.

We can say with confidence, "The Lord is my helper, so I will have no fear. What can mere people do to me?"

HEBREWS 13:6

Do what you can with what you have where you are.

AMISH PROVERB

NOTE TO THE READER

While *Her Fear* is set against the real backdrop of Hart County, Kentucky, the characters are purely fictional. In writing this work of fiction, I've taken artistic license in some areas so that I may create the necessary situations for my characters. Therefore, any resemblance between the characters in this book and any real members of the Amish and Mennonite communities are coincidental and unintentional, and are completely due to fictional license.

Shelley Shepard Gray

PROLOGUE

Until that moment, Sadie Detweiler hadn't thought mere words could hurt so badly. But as Harlan continued to speak, each word cutting her as deeply as if it were a shard of glass, Sadie felt her heart was bleeding. For a moment, she even wished she was feeling her father's cane on the backs of her thighs instead. That pain, at least, was familiar and fleeting.

Harlan Mast's words would haunt her for the rest of her life.

"Are you positive you are pregnant?" Harlan asked for at least the third time. He scanned her body slowly, obviously searching for changes in her shape. "Maybe you are mistaken."

If Sadie was bolder, she would have told him about her missed periods, about the early-morning nausea, even about her English friend Ana buying her a pregnancy test at a pharmacy two towns over. But Sadie could no more have told Harlan such personal information than she could have pulled off her *kapp* and started dancing in the middle of Sunday's church service.

All she could give Harlan was her honesty. "*Jah*. I am sure. I am going to have a *boppli*. I'm gonna have our baby, Harlan."

His eyes narrowed. "How do you know for sure that I'm the father?"

The pain in her heart got worse. "How could you ask me such a thing?"

"What? It's a fair question." He was looking like a stranger now. Nothing like the man who'd been courting her for months, who had whispered sweet things while they'd kissed. Who'd murmured fierce promises just before he'd led her into his barn late one night.

Unable to look him in the eye, Sadie stared down at her feet. "You—you know that you were my first."

He made an impatient sound, as if the moment that had changed her life meant nothing to him. "That was ages ago."

"*Nee*, that was nine weeks ago."

"How am I supposed to know for sure that you haven't been with someone else since then?"

Stunned, she lifted her head again. Stared at him.

Harlan was looking at her like she was a stranger. *Nee*, as if she were a pest. Vermin. Something akin to her being a fuzzy green caterpillar on an ear of corn he was about to eat.

The blue eyes she'd once thought looked so perfect were now distant and cold. His hands, those hands that once couldn't stop touching her, were now clenched by his sides.

And she'd at last come to terms with the truth. He wasn't going to hold her, beam with pride that their babe was growing inside her, or even ask her to marry him. But he had to be confused or in shock. Too dazed by her news to know what to say or to make plans.

She was going to have to be the strong one.

Clearing her throat, Sadie attempted to keep her voice calm and steady. "When should we tell our parents? I was thinking maybe it would be best to do it today. That way it's out in the open and we won't have to worry about their reaction."

He shook his head. "I'm not going to tell my parents anything."

"*Nee?* Well, they're going to be mighty surprised when we get married and have a baby right away."

"I ain't marrying you, Sadie."

"But I'm pregnant."

He waved a hand. "Maybe. And *maybe* with my baby."

"But—but we've been courting. Everyone would expect it . . ." She expected it.

"I can't have you now."

"But—"

"Sadie, I know you've heard the rumors. Our church district has grown so much that the bishop said we need another preacher. Men are going to draw for the lot soon. More than one of the elders has asked me to consider putting my name in. That won't happen if I'm associated with this."

She knew he was speaking about the tradition of a few chosen men entering their names in order to be selected for a lead position in their church community. The men chosen for the lot would each pull a hymnal. The man who found a scripture verse nestled inside would be selected for the position.

"But my father is one of the men who wants you to join the lot." Didn't Harlan see how misguided his words were? Why, he was acting as if only one of them had a good reputation and was from a good family.

"Your father is well respected and he respects me, too. He won't, though, if he finds out that we were making babies in my barn when you were supposed to be at home and in bed."

Sadie felt a bolt of triumph. Finally, he was admitting what they'd done. But then his words registered.

None of what he was saying had much to do with her, or their future. He was talking about things that didn't really matter. And as if they had a choice about their future.

Once again, she attempted to bring his focus back to reality. "This baby ain't going to disappear. It's coming in about seven months. We need to make plans."

He drew in a sharp breath. "You could get rid of it. Then no one would ever know."

She stepped back, reeling from what he was saying. "I would know, and so would you! Besides, I could never do that."

"If that's the case, then you're on your own."

She was on her own?

When he turned away, she rushed forward and gripped the sleeve of his shirt. "Harlan, I know you're upset, but I have to tell my parents. And you know what will happen then. My father will pay a visit to you. Think what will happen!"

He smiled. "You tell them what you want, but I know what I'm going to say."

"What?"

"That I don't know who you behaved wantonly with, but it surely wasn't me."

Ignoring the pain that each word caused, she whispered, "If you do that, I'll tell them you're lying."

"Will you?" He smiled softly. "Sadie, *jah*, you do that. Go ahead and tell them what you want. Say whatever you want about me, but I think we both know who is going to be believed."

When he turned and walked away, she finally allowed the tears to fall down her cheeks. She was very afraid that he would be right.

THE NEXT MORNING, sitting gingerly in the buggy with a cloth tote bag on her lap, Sadie swallowed past the hard lump that had formed in her throat and seemed content to dwell there for the upcoming journey. Harlan had not been wrong.

She'd gone home, told the news to her parents, and been subjected to both her father's vicious words and two strikes from his cane. Then they locked her in her room while they went to go speak to Harlan.

She'd waited anxiously, sure that Harlan's lies would be discovered and that they'd return home with a wedding date. But even as she heard the front door open and her parents' footsteps on the stairs, neither came to her door.

Instead, at five o'clock that morning, her mother rushed into her room and told her to hurriedly dress and to pack all of her belongings.

She was being sent away.

"Willis and Verba are the worst sort of Amish," her father said almost laconically about his in-laws as he drove her in their buggy to the bus stop. "They have loose morals and live in the middle of Kentucky. But they are family, so they'll likely take you in."

Likely? He wasn't even sure? "I don't want to go," she blurted. Honestly, she would rather get beaten with a cane again than be alone and afraid in the middle of a strange place.

Without a second's pause, her father pulled over the buggy to the side of the road. "Then get out."

"What?"

"You've embarrassed and shamed me enough," he said, his expression thunderous. "As far as I'm concerned, you ain't no kin of mine. Not any longer. I can only blame it on the devil that is lurking inside of you, since you are continuing to lie to me about who the father of the baby you're carrying really is."

"I didn't lie about Harlan. He really is the father."

"He's got no reason to lie, girl."

"But—"

"Don't argue with me. Now, either get out here or get on the bus to Willis and Verba. Make your decision."

She had no choice. No matter what life was like in Kentucky, it couldn't be worse than attempting to survive by herself. "I'll get on the bus, Father."

His body stiffened as he guided the horse back onto the road. "Don't call me that ever again. I'm not your father. You are nothing to me."

Sadie didn't say another word during the rest of the journey. Or when he bought her a bus ticket and grudgingly gave her five dollars in case she needed something to eat or drink.

All she could think about when she sat on the warm bus, surrounded by strangers, the majority of whom were English, was that she finally understood what fear really was.

Fear was being alone. Fear was feeling abandoned.

Fear was realizing that anyone could lie, hurt, and betray her. Anyone at all.

Sadie made a vow right then and there that she would never forget that again.

CHAPTER 1

June 29

W hat are you doing to her?" Willis Stauffer demanded.
"Don't touch her like that." This time he punctuated his
words by gripping the sleeve of Noah's EMT uniform. His
fingers dug in like claws, tight enough to rend the fabric.

Alarmed, Noah eyed the man's gnarled hand before allowing his gaze to drift to Mr. Stauffer's face. Dark eyes, half
hidden by prominent wrinkles, peered back suspiciously.

The animosity that flowed through the older man's expression caught Noah off guard. After all, he and his two
partners were there to try to save the woman lying on the
living room floor of the run-down farmhouse. Why would
this man, this woman's husband, be acting as if they were
there to harm instead of help?

"*English*, is she going to be all right?"

That slur was intentional, and both Noah and Willis knew
it. Noah might be wearing an EMT uniform, but he was as
Amish as the family living in this house.

Though his first reaction was to correct the man, Noah's training enabled him to hold his tongue. It wasn't his job to change people's perceptions of him—or to try to explain why he had chosen such a job when the rest of his family farmed.

No, he was there to help those in need and, in this case, to assist Chad and Mitch in saving Verba Stauffer's life.

After ascertaining that the other men had things in hand, Noah turned his head slightly so that he could meet Mr. Stauffer's cloudy eyes. "I don't know if she's going to be all right or not," he said honestly. "I hope and pray she will."

The vulnerability that had slipped into the man's expression abruptly vanished. "That tells me nothing."

"I know," Noah said as he rose and gently pried his arm from Willis Stauffer's grasp. "I realize this ain't easy to watch, but rest assured that my partners here are *gut* men."

"You sure?"

"I am certain of it." Turning to watch as Chad was taking the woman's pulse and entering the information into his iPad, Noah continued. "They are doing their best, *jah*?"

But as he feared, Noah's attempt to soothe was rebuffed. Mr. Stauffer sent him a look of scorn before turning back to his son, Stephen.

Stephen, Verba and Willis's only child, was a widower and the parent of Esther and Monroe, who stood nearby, lurking in the doorway.

"Noah," Chad said, motioning downward with his chin.

Immediately, Noah knelt down again next to his partner. "*Jah*?"

"Mitch is outside calling the hospital. We're going to bring her in. Keep an eye on her vitals while I secure the IV."

"Sure thing." Because Noah had only recently finished training, he was only regulated to support the other EMTs, which suited him fine. The more he learned, the more he realized he didn't know.

Mitch and Chad always made sure to include him, though, which made him feel worthwhile.

They also made sure to let him know that his presence in the Amish homes helped tremendously, and this call was no exception. When they first arrived, Verba was near hysterical, complaining of severe cramping, dizziness, and nausea. Noah had knelt on the floor and spoke to her quietly in Pennsylvania Dutch. As she calmed, he stepped out of the way to respond to her husband and so Mitch and Chad could take her vitals and get the woman's health history.

Mrs. Stauffer's eyes were closed now. Her pulse was slow but steady. That said, she really didn't look good. As Chad finished taping an IV line, Noah glanced back at the family. Each stood silent and wary.

All looked uneasy, almost as if they resented the medics being there.

Well, all but one of them.

A woman standing apart from everyone else, watching Chad work intently from the doorway of one of the bedrooms. To Noah she looked as if she yearned to help but didn't dare budge from her spot.

He recalled Willis telling Mitch that her name was Sadie Detweiler when they'd first arrived. Mitch had been asking questions about family health history, and Willis stated that the girl wasn't part of his family, at least not this immediate one.

Glancing at her again, Noah couldn't help but think that she didn't look like she fit in. Why was she even there?

While the other members had an exhausted and run-down

look about them, Sadie, with her light-brown hair and hopeful expression, seemed out of place.

Chad got to his feet and turned to Mr. Stauffer. "We're going to take her to the hospital and let the doctors run some tests."

Stephen stepped forward. "Is she still awake?"

Noah answered as he helped Chad lift Verba onto a stretcher. "*Jah*. But she's weak. You were right to call for help."

"I'm real glad the first vehicle I flagged down stopped and called 911 for me."

"Me, too," Noah said, though he was surprised to realize that the family didn't have access to a phone shanty. They really were on their own here in the outskirts of Munfordville.

"Whether she lives or dies, it's in the Lord's hands now," Willis murmured, obviously resigned.

Normally, Noah would agree. They might be trained in saving lives, but they were not miracle workers. They could only do their best and hope the Lord would do the rest. Still, there was something alarming in the man's sudden stoic behavior.

When they first arrived, Willis was desperate and demanding. Now? He stood off to the side. It could have been Noah's imagination—that the man seemed to have an abrupt change of heart—but what *had* changed for him?

"The Lord is our savior; that is true. But we canna give up hope. Ain't so?" Noah murmured gently.

"Let's go," Mitch called out.

Chad gripped the front of the stretcher and started walking. Lifting the back, Noah scanned the room. "We're taking her to Caverna Hospital. It's on South Dixie Street, over in Horse Cave," he said in Deutsch. "You can meet us there."

Looking anxious, Stephen rushed to their side. "Can't one of us go with you?"

"There's no room. Sorry," Chad said as he began to lead the way, stretcher in hand, out of the front door.

"But that don't seem fair," Stephen protested. "Someone needs to be with my mother."

"I will be in the ambulance," Noah said. "I'll also ask for a patrol car to come out to pick you up."

Willis frowned. Before he could fuss, Noah added, "One should be here before too long. I promise." Mentally, he kicked himself. He knew better to promise anything.

Five faces stared back at him in various expressions of dismay and anger. But Noah couldn't let that sway him. If Mitch or Chad didn't want any family member to ride along, there was a good reason for that.

He was glad. Every once in a while, when they did allow another person in the ambulance, sometimes the concerned family member was harder to deal with than the patient.

Just before Noah looked away, he watched Stephen exchange a glance with his father. Then Noah caught sight of Sadie staring at him with such a look of fear that he felt chilled to the skin. Was she simply concerned . . . or was she in trouble?

Or was his imagination simply getting carried away?

And for that matter, what was going on in that house? He'd been on over a hundred house calls since he'd started eight months ago, and rarely did the people act as wary as this family. Were they hiding something?

"You got her?" Chad asked.

Returning his attention back to where it needed to be, Noah answered. "Yes."

"All right, then. Let's get on our way."

They reached the ambulance and both climbed into the back, pulling the stretcher inside. The moment he closed the door, Noah turned to Mitch, who was driving.

"Would you see if Deputy Beck or somebody can swing by and take the family to the hospital?"

"I'm on it," he called back.

Relieved that was going to be taken care of, Noah tried to focus on Verba but felt like he was still in that living room amid the thick tension.

"You okay there, Amish?" Chad joked as Mitch sped down the highway.

"Yeah."

"Why did that man call you 'English'?"

"You caught that?"

"Couldn't help it. He sounded ticked that we were in his house in the first place." Chad shook his head in dismay. "It never fails to surprise me how people react in situations like this. I've seen whole families in tears, others completely silent, still others acting angry and lashing out at us."

As Noah worked on the handheld machine to make a tag for the woman's wrist, he said carefully, "I guess some people don't know how to handle situations that are out of their control."

"Do you think that was what was happening inside that house?"

"I don't know. Just because they are Amish, it doesn't mean I understand how they think. They might just be wary of outsiders."

"Maybe you're right. For what it's worth, you handled them real well. You're doing a good job."

The praise wasn't lightly given, and meant the world to Noah. "Thank you."

After seeing that Verba was resting comfortably, Chad lowered his voice. "Not to be mean, but that family seemed like an odd lot."

"I was just thinking that."

"Did you notice the pretty gal in the back of the room? Her eyes were so blue they looked violet."

"I noticed."

A shiver raced through him as he remembered what else he'd noticed. That she was scared.

But of what?

Chilled, he rubbed his arms.

"You sure you're okay?" Chad asked again, his voice filled with concern.

"I'm fine." Feeling sheepish, he said, "I guess a ghost just walked on my path."

Chad grinned in appreciation. "Tell it to stay far away from me, okay? I don't intend to lose this woman."

"I'll do my best," he said as Mitch continued to speed down the highway, sirens and flashing lights encouraging everyone in their path to stop and pull out of the way.

Even the occasional horse and buggy.

CHAPTER 2

June 29

When the front door closed behind the emergency workers with a decided click and they had driven off, the flashing lights that had been shining into the house vanished.

It was rather symbolic.

Now Sadie was surrounded, again, by only dim light peeking through the sheer curtains of the two windows in the middle of the dark-paneled room. Though she was used to living in rooms with no electricity, she couldn't help but feel that her cousins' home was darker than most.

Perhaps it was because of the constant state of anxiety that filled the air. It permeated every decision in the Stauffer household and led to a tension so thick that Sadie felt like she could grasp hold of it. In her more fanciful moments, Sadie imagined that each member wore their burdens like badges of honor. It was a worrisome habit, given that not one of them seemed eager to divest themselves of any weight.

Those feelings seemed to weigh them all down, almost as if they had extra burdens to carry with them at all times.

Though Sadie had only lived with them for three weeks,

she knew by now to keep out of the way. Everyone in the household seemed to have a specific place—and her spot, for now at least, was to be in the background.

Stephen rapped his knuckle against the door in frustration. "I canna believe they didn't allow even one of us in that ambulance."

"The worker said a patrol car would come, Daed," Esther pointed out. "I bet it will be here any minute."

Sadie watched Stephen and his son, Monroe, exchange glances. The two of them looked so very different. Stephen had brown hair and grayish-blue eyes while Monroe had golden-blond hair and mesmerizing hazel eyes.

"We need to get ready, then," Willis said. "Stephen, you and Monroe go make sure the cellar door is locked, in case someone really does show up."

Without a word, Monroe and his father walked outside.

After they left, Willis turned to Sadie and his grandchild Esther. "When the police come, I want you girls to stay in the *haus*. Do you understand?"

"*Jah*, Dawdi," Esther said while Sadie nodded.

He looked like he was about to say more when a sheriff's cruiser pulled up. "We'll be going now."

"I hope *Mommi* will be all right," Esther said.

"Only the Lord knows what will happen, Esther."

"Yes, Dawdi."

After Willis opened the door and called for Stephen and Monroe to meet him at the sheriff's car, he turned back to them. "Will you women be able to get supper ready while we are gone?"

Sadie gaped at him, having a difficult time believing that Willis was worried about supper when his own wife was near death. But Esther nodded obediently.

"*Jah*, Dawdi. We'll see to supper."

For the first time since his wife had collapsed on the ground, his expression softened. "*Danke*, child," Willis said before walking outside to join the other men by the car.

Sadie watched through the glass as a young man in a tan uniform shook Stephen's hand, then gestured the three of them into the vehicle. Stephen got up front in the passenger side while Willis climbed into the back with Monroe.

Minutes later, the car disappeared down the street.

When they were alone in the house, Esther exhaled. "Come on, Sadie. Let's go sit for a spell."

Sadie followed her into the small kitchen and watched as her cousin sat down on one of the stools that lined the back counter. She matched Monroe in looks—all blond hair and hazel eyes. But that was where their similarities ended. While Monroe exuded confidence and constant good humor, Esther was far more reflective.

Now that Esther was facing another loss, Sadie wasn't sure how her cousin was going to react. Was Esther about to burst into tears? Would she start pacing and fretting?

"Can I get you anything?" Sadie asked.

"Some water sounds good."

Happy to be of use, Sadie poured them two glasses. "Here you go."

After drinking almost half of her glass's contents, Esther wiped her brow. "What a day, huh?"

It had been quite a day. A terrible one, to be sure. Verba had collapsed just minutes after their noon meal. Stephen had tried to revive her for several minutes, and Monroe had run down the street to find an Englisher willing to stop and call for the ambulance.

She and Esther had prayed while Stephen knelt beside his mother and wiped her brow.

Willis, in contrast, stared out the window with a blank expression on his face. Sadie hadn't been able to figure out if he was too upset to tend to his wife, was watching for Monroe to return, or was worried about something she couldn't fathom.

"What do you think happened?" she asked, now realizing that Esther wasn't about to start crying. "Your grandmother seemed okay at breakfast, didn't you think?"

"I thought she was all right." She took another sip of water. "But maybe she wasn't."

The comment seemed too pat. "Why do you say that? Had she been complaining of aches and pains?"

"Of course not. Mommi wouldn't complain."

"I wish she would have. Then we could have been able to tell the emergency workers something of worth," Sadie said, remembering how the EMT named Mitch asked for Verba's medical history. Both Willis and Stephen had acted like he was prying. Sadie frowned. "I hope Verba hasn't been ailing for a while but didn't tell you all anything. Or that your grandfather knew something was wrong but wanted to keep it private."

Something flashed in Esther's eyes before she shrugged. "I couldn't begin to guess what happened to my grandmother, Sadie. Maybe we'll never know."

Confused by her cousin's tone, Sadie backpedaled. "Oh, of course. Forgive me, I didn't mean to be intrusive."

Esther got to her feet. "You ain't. It's simply that I have no idea what happened to Mommi."

"I hope she is already doing much better."

"Me, too." Opening the ancient refrigerator, Esther spoke

again, this time her voice sounding warm and familiar. "Speaking of keeping aches and pains to oneself, how are you feeling?"

"I guess I deserved that," Sadie said with a sheepish smile. "I'm all right. The babe seems to be finally settling down." She'd been so very sick and queasy at the beginning of her pregnancy. Now that she'd just hit thirteen weeks, she was having more good days than bad.

She'd also gotten adept at keeping her discomforts to herself. Of course, she'd learned to do that on account of her own family history.

"I think we might as well start cooking. At least then it will be done while we wait for the men to return."

"All right. I can do that."

"I know you didn't feel too good this morning. Do you feel able to help me fry chicken?"

"Of course I can." Sadie almost changed her mind when she was handed a freshly slaughtered chicken, a cutting board, and a knife. Just the thought of hacking the bird into pieces made her ache to take back her promise.

But, then, all she had to do was remember what her life had been like before she moved to Kentucky.

Back in Millersburg, she not only had to cut up the chicken, she often had to help kill it and pluck the feathers before preparing the meal.

While the idea of cutting up a bunch of raw chicken made her already-sensitive stomach queasy, it wasn't anything too awful. Her father calling her a liar, and being estranged from her family, was worse. Much worse.

Resolutely, she washed her hands, slipped an apron over her expanded waistline, and picked up the knife. Nothing would get done if she didn't get started. Steeling herself, she cut off a wing and set it to the side.

Esther cracked two eggs, added some buttermilk to the dish, then mixed up flour and spices while Sadie continued to work on the chicken. Then Esther poured oil into a cast-iron skillet and set the gas burner on low.

Sadie began soaking her chicken pieces in the buttermilk concoction, then washed the cutting board and knife. Esther, by this time, had started peeling potatoes. She glanced Sadie's way and smiled. "We're a *gut* team, ain't we?"

"*Jah*. Between us, we have made this supper a couple dozen times now," Sadie agreed.

"At least." Glancing over at her, Esther said, "When did you start helping in the kitchen? I started when I was ten, or thereabouts."

Sadie paused to think about that. "I remember learning how to snap peas when I was five or six, so I've been helping out in the kitchen for a long time."

"Do you like it?"

"You know, I never thought about whether I liked it or not. I simply did what I was supposed to do. We didn't have much choice in the matter. What about you?"

"I haven't had much choice, either, now that I think about it," Esther replied with a grin. "But that don't bother me. I like cooking all right." After glancing at the door, she added, "I'd rather spend my days sewing, though."

Sadie, in the midst now of frying the buttermilk-soaked pieces, looked around at all the dishes—and felt the sweat dripping down her back, thanks to frying a whole chicken in the middle of a hot summer day with the door closed. Sadie smiled. "Sewing is *much* cooler."

"And cleaner."

"*Jah*." Sadie agreed. "That, too."

They continued to work in silence for almost another half

hour. As Esther had mentioned, they had made this meal several times already—and were able to smoothly share the small workspace. It made Sadie think of her sisters—Grace, Faith, and Emma.

They'd often tried to help her, but more often than not the girls only succeeded in creating more work for her—additional to her efforts to shield them from the worst of their father's abuse.

But they, in turn, gave her so much love. When they were all younger, her little sisters often reminded Sadie of a litter of kittens. Whenever their parents weren't around, the girls would joke and tease each other. Then, come nightfall, at least one of them would knock on her door and ask to sleep by her side.

She knew she'd given them a sense of security, just as they'd made her life so much happier. She missed them.

She wondered if she was ever going to see them again. During moments like this, she hoped so. At night, though, when she felt so alone and uncomfortable on her cot in the kitchen, she was sure that she would never see them again.

"Do you ever want to do something else but work at home?" Esther asked.

Sadie put down the slotted spoon she'd been using to flip the chicken over in the hot grease. "I don't know what you mean."

"Come on. Lots of Amish girls around here work in shops or in greenhouses. I have to imagine it's the same up in Ohio."

"It is. Many Amish girls work outside the home up in Holmes County. I've seen them work in restaurants and bakeries." She smiled. "They get paid to cook and clean."

"See, that's what I mean. Haven't you ever wanted to do a job like that?"

"My family is Swartzentruber Amish, Esther. Women aren't permitted to work outside the home."

"Their rules are so strict. Was abiding by them so hard?"

"Oh, sometimes," she lied. Actually, she had wanted to get out of her house more than anything. Yearned for a change in a schedule that never seemed to deviate—and was desperate to have even a little bit of money of her own, too.

She'd tried to push all those dreams away. Then Harlan started courting her. She'd told herself that it wasn't that she disliked her church's rules, it was that she was so unhappy in her father's strict household.

Now that she'd gained some distance, she thought that was probably the case. It wasn't that she didn't want to follow the rules—get married, have children, take care of her family—she wanted to be respected, too. As she was falling in love with Harlan, she realized that she was confronted with the terms of her life and her future.

But then? Well, the Lord had other plans.

She suddenly got everything she'd ever wanted . . . but at a terrible price. Now she was out of her house. Her routine had been shaken up, and she knew she needed to find a way to support herself . . . because in a few months she was going to have someone else to care for.

Esther stopped peeling and had begun slicing the potatoes. She stared at her. "Sadie, you really never thought about doing anything else, have you?"

Feeling awkward, Sadie took a breath. "To be honest, I used to want to make crafts or maybe sew dresses or clothing for other people, but I eventually discarded that idea."

"Can you sew that well?"

"*Jah*." She felt herself flush. "I know I shouldn't brag . . ."

"You aren't bragging, Sadie," Esther said with a sweet smile. "You're celebrating your worth."

Hating that she felt so tentative, she said, "Do you really think that way?"

"I do. I mean, the Lord made us all special, don't you think?" When Sadie nodded, Esther looked at her curiously. "I haven't seen you sew since you've been here. If you enjoy it, you are welcome to use my mother's old sewing machine."

"Would your father mind?"

"Not at all! He especially wouldn't mind if you offered to make him a new shirt," she said with a wink.

"Well, then, maybe I will do that." Sadie took another breath as reality returned. "As soon as your grandmother gets better."

Esther looked pensive as she went back to her potatoes. "*Jah*. As soon as she gets better."

Thinking that Esther needed time alone with her thoughts, Sadie started washing dishes. The hot, soapy water felt soothing on her hands. The ease of the chore, one she'd done more times than she could count, calmed her insides, too. She was feeling at ease here, working side by side with Esther.

So different than how she'd mostly felt at home.

At last Esther broke the silence. "Hey, Sadie?"

"*Jah*?"

"Things were difficult at your house, weren't they? I mean, even before you found out you were pregnant."

Sadie pressed her hands deeper in the water, letting the hot water slide up past her wrists. Finally she spoke. "My father was strict. Very strict. We had roles in our *haus* that he demanded we adhere to."

"Ah."

"My father would have never allowed any of us to get a job outside of the house. That is why I stopped sewing." There. That was the truth. It just wasn't the whole truth.

"You would have gotten in a lot of trouble, huh?"

"*Jah*," she said lightly. She would have been punished without a doubt. "I guess I was too afraid to do anything I wasn't supposed to."

"When you say things like that, I don't know whether I'm more shocked about you getting pregnant . . . or that you didn't do it earlier."

"Esther!"

"I'm sorry. But, Sadie, your life there sounds so sad. I would've done whatever I could to leave."

There was something about the way Esther was talking that made her uneasy. She almost felt like her cousin was hinting about something more than just Sadie's strict upbringing. She pulled her hands out of the water and dried them. "I didn't do anything on purpose. I trusted Harlan. I never expected he would lie about what we had done."

"I canna believe your parents believed him instead of you."

"I couldn't believe it either at first." Unable to stop the torrent of words, she continued. "My mother refused to believe that a handsome, wealthy, and upstanding man like Harlan would ever lie. No matter how I tried to get her to understand my side, she didn't listen. They even locked me in my room until they decided what to do with me."

"How did you get out?" Esther asked as she went over to continue where Sadie left off, turning again each piece of chicken in the oil.

"I told them I would run away." Lowering her voice, she said, "Sometimes, I think that they wanted me to do that.

To just leave." Taking a deep breath, she concluded her sad story. "They eventually decided to send me down here. And here I am."

Esther's eyes widened. "Does Harlan know what happened to you?"

"I imagine he does. My parents wouldn't keep my disobedience a secret. They have other children to raise and keep in line."

"One day everyone will realize that you were right and he was wrong."

Just as Sadie was about to nod, she caught herself. "I used to hope for nothing more. But now? Well, I don't think it even matters."

Uneasy again, she joined Esther at the skillet. The chicken looked done. Together they removed the pieces, then Sadie wrapped a towel around the handle of the pot and pulled it away from the burner.

Esther put a pot of water for potatoes on the stove. "What would you do if Harlan came here to find you, and he apologized?"

"I canna imagine him doing such a thing."

"But if he does?"

"If he does, I don't think I will care."

Esther gaped at her. "But he is your baby's father."

"I know. But he didn't want the child. And neither did my parents. Now, though, I have no idea what will happen next, it feels like it is too late. They might have pushed me out of their lives, but what's done is done. I've already left and I'm not going back."

Esther hugged her, and they went back to preparing supper, waiting for news about Verba. But when the men still hadn't returned hours later, some of their hopefulness began to falter. Eventually, Esther fell asleep on the couch. Sadie covered her up with a quilt, sat in the wooden rocking chair, and stared out the window.

Worried that their worst fears had been realized.

CHAPTER 3

June 29, 6:00 P.M.

Almost immediately after bringing Verba Stauffer to the emergency department, Noah's team was called out again, this time to a near drowning at an Englisher's pool. A young child had fallen in. Chad performed CPR and revived the child, much to everyone's relief.

After they brought that child to the hospital for observation, they returned to the firehouse and spent the next two hours carefully cleaning the ambulance, restocking supplies, and submitting reports.

When they got called out to the hospital again, they discovered that Verba Stauffer had died soon after they'd dropped her off.

Noah was stunned. When they returned to the firehouse, he brought it up again. "Chad, you spoke to more people than I did. What was the cause of death? Did anyone tell you?"

Chad shook his head. "The doctors think she might have eaten something that didn't agree with her. Maybe she had an allergic reaction."

"Maybe." It didn't seem like she'd been having an allergic reaction, though.

"We won't know anything for sure until they get toxicology results from the lab," Chad commented before going back to the report he was working on.

Though he was disappointed with the way his partner was speaking so matter-of-factly, Noah understood that Chad wasn't being disrespectful. He was simply trying to keep his distance.

Noah had learned back during his first month on the job how difficult it was to take home all the pain and hurting he witnessed while working. He was hired to help save lives, not change them.

That had been a difficult thing to wrap his head around, but eventually he learned to do the same thing. Otherwise, all the worry and stress would get him was a bunch of sleepless nights. He'd come to understand that even prayer wouldn't heal every person or soothe the men and women who were burdened with addiction or suffering from disease.

So even though Chad tried to keep his distance, it didn't mean that he didn't care. "Did she look near death to you?"

Chad looked startled by the question. But in his typical way, he considered it thoughtfully before answering. "Honestly? No. If I were to take a guess, I thought maybe she had a burst appendix. She was complaining of awful stomach pain."

"I wish we could have done more."

He sighed. "Noah, we try to save lives, but we aren't miracle workers."

This was true. Noah knew if his father was standing close, he would remind him that their fates were ultimately in the Lord's hands.

"You are right," he said at last to Chad. "We aren't miracle workers, nor do we need to be. May she rest in peace."

"Amen." Chad waited a moment, then said, "Since she's Amish, will you attend her service?"

"*Nee*. We are in different church communities. I didn't know them."

"Sorry. Do you hate it when I say things like that? When I assume that all the Amish know each other?"

Noah couldn't help but grin. "I don't hate it, Chad." Thinking about his big family and how many Amish men and women there were, he said, "I probably do know most of the Plain people in the area. However, the Stauffers are different. I don't think they associate with many people, Amish or English."

"So they're living off the grid."

Noah smiled again. He wouldn't have described them that way, but it wasn't a bad description. "*Jah*. They are." Returning to the original question, he said, "Even if I did know them, I probably wouldn't attend Verba's funeral anyway. I think they might blame me for her death."

"You know that would be wrong. Remember what I've been telling you since you first started. We do the best we can. That's all we can do."

Noah nodded. There wasn't anything Chad could say to help him, and fixating on Verba's death wasn't going to help his peace of mind, either.

Pointing to the clock, Chad said, "Let's get out of here. Our twelve-hour shift is done."

Noah smiled. "I won't argue with that."

Chad's steps slowed as they walked out of the room. "You going to be okay? You do such a good job, I keep forgetting that days like this, when one of our patients dies, are new for you. Do you want some time off or anything?"

It was offers like that that made Noah know he had a lot to be grateful for. Chad McGovern was a good man and a good mentor. "Thanks, but I'll be fine." He hoped he would, at least. Chad slapped him on the shoulder, then headed out. Noah went to the locker room.

After washing up, he strode to his locker and took off his dark-blue ball cap with the Hart County EMT logo blazoned across the front of it and his black work boots. He set them in his locker, then removed his uniform shirt and trousers and folded them into his backpack. He would take them home to wash and hang on the line.

In their places, he slipped on a pair of dark-gray trousers and a light-blue short-sleeved shirt. Then he sat down and pulled on a pair of dark boots that fit him so well they felt almost like a part of his body.

Finally, he put on the straw hat that he'd placed neatly on top of his boots when he'd started his shift twelve hours ago.

Feeling satisfied that he was once again dressed Plain, he closed his eyes and took a moment to give thanks for his blessings. Even the hardest ones to accept.

This prayer was part of his normal routine. When he started working as an EMT, he'd made a promise to himself to always take a moment at the beginning and end of his workday to remind himself of who he was.

With a renewed sense of peace, he hiked the backpack onto one of his shoulders and walked out of the locker room and through the rec room and kitchen.

Mitch, his immediate supervisor, was sitting at one of the tables, sipping coffee and eating a turkey sandwich. "You getting out of here?"

"Yeah. I guess you aren't?"

"Nah. George's boy is pitching tonight. He asked if I could

stay an extra three hours so he could watch the baseball game."

"That was nice of you."

Mitch shrugged. "Tamara said she didn't care. She's out running errands."

"Hopefully you won't get called out again."

"It's almost July fourth. We'll get called out."

Noah grinned as he tipped his hat and left. Mitch wasn't wrong. Even though they hadn't had much rain and there were warnings about setting off firecrackers in the dry heat, people still did. And got hurt while doing it.

After exiting the firehouse, he walked the mile home to the small house that he shared with his older brother. They lived right next door to their parents, and just a block away from their sister and her husband. Though many of their parents' friends enjoyed living in a *dawdi haus* in back of one of their children's homes, Noah had often gotten the impression that their parents liked having their bit of privacy. He and Silas sure did.

While it wasn't that the two of them ever did anything too outlandish, they both had demanding jobs. He worked as an EMT and Silas owned his own construction company. They both enjoyed the freedom of being able to come and go without being questioned—and to sit around and do nothing in the evening if that was what they desired.

Chances were good that if they still lived with their parents, they would be expected to spend at least a few hours each evening talking with them.

On days like today, even that small amount of time felt like a burden.

When he walked into the house, Silas was sprawled out on

the couch in the living room. His black hair was damp, his white shirt was untucked, and his feet were bare.

"Hey," Noah said. "Long day?"

"*Jah*. And hot," he murmured, not even bothering to open his eyes. "Next year, remind me to go on vacation in the middle of summer. It's too hot to build houses in the sun."

"I'll make a note of it," he said sarcastically as he sat down in their father's old lounge chair. It was rickety and threadbare. Noah also happened to think it was the most comfortable chair in the world.

When he worked the squeaky lever to recline the chair, Silas grinned. "It's sounding worse than ever. I tell ya, one day you're gonna force that chair back and it's gonna fall apart."

"Probably. Hope it's not today, though."

Silas finally opened his eyes and studied him with concern. "You sound almost as tired as I feel. What's going on with you? There wasn't a fire today, was there?"

"*Nee*." After debating for a moment about how much to share, he said, "We did have a real difficult call today, though. An Amish woman collapsed at home. She later died."

"Who was it?" he asked as he sat up.

He didn't usually feel comfortable talking about people's private injuries or problems; the Amish community was real small. Likely, he and his brother wouldn't know this family, but word would spread about the woman's death.

"Verba Stauffer. Do you know her?"

Silas's expression grew even more confused. "I've never heard of her. What was she like? Young? Old?"

"Old. She collapsed and was lying on the floor when we got there. Mitch and Chad tried to get her stable when we arrived, but I guess it wasn't any use."

"If she was old, maybe it was her time?" Silas said after a while. "I mean, sorry, I know it is hard, but the Lord don't intend for us to live forever."

That had been what their grandmother was fond of saying. Hearing it would upset their *mamm* to no end, but Noah and Silas always kind of thought Mommi's matter-of-fact view on death was a comfort.

"I should probably take that saying to heart," he said at last. "But I can't shake the feeling that maybe it wasn't Verba's time."

"What are you saying?"

"I don't know. I know I'm still learning, and am no doctor, but her dying so quickly was surprising. The whole thing seemed off, somehow."

Silas was still staring at him intently. "Off how?"

"I don't know. Her pain, well, it seemed like she had kidney stones or a bad appendix or something." He shrugged. "And that house, it was a real mess."

"Noah, look around you."

"*Nee*, it wasn't a matter of dishes in the sink or dirt on the floor. I mean, the house had a feeling about it that spoke of neglect." Thinking of the woman off near the bedroom, and of the men watching him, Mitch, and Chad with angry expressions, he continued. "There is something peculiar going on there."

"Like what?"

"I canna put my finger on it exactly, but it was disturbing. There was a tension in the house that you could feel from the minute you stepped inside," he continued, remembering the way Stephen and Willis Stauffer kept exchanging glances with each other. "Then, well, there was a girl there, a woman really. She was a cousin or some such."

"Nothing too peculiar about that."

"True, but she acted like she wasn't even sure where to stand. She lurked in the back of the room, gripping a doorframe like it was a lifeline. She didn't say a word and hardly moved a muscle."

"You sure got a good look at her for someone responding to an emergency."

Feeling himself flush, Noah said, "Anyone would have noticed her. She was ill at ease and frightened. I . . . well, I can't stop thinking about her."

Silas sat up and studied Noah more closely. "You're serious."

"I am. She seemed scared; and then, like I said, the whole situation felt off."

Silas looked at him curiously. "How so?"

"I don't know. It might have been my imagination, but it kind of seemed like the whole family was on edge. Not from fear about their relative, but for another reason."

"Like what?"

"Like . . . Oh, I don't know. Like maybe someone had something to do with the woman's illness."

Silas's voice hardened. "Do you hear what you are saying?"

"*Jah*. And yes, I know I shouldn't even be thinking such things."

"I think you're jumping to conclusions."

Noah heard the warning in his brother's tone. Silas was right. It was sinful for him to even be contemplating such things. But even if he was stepping over the line, it sure didn't feel right to keep these thoughts to himself. "Maybe they didn't mean for her to die. Maybe it simply went terribly wrong. But all I do know is that Verba didn't get deathly ill on her own."

"What are you going to do?"

"I don't know," he replied, glad again that his older brother was the type of man who always went right to the point. "I'm an EMT in training, and Amish to boot. There ain't a person in either the medical field or in law enforcement who's going to listen to a single word I say."

Worry flared in Silas's eyes. "But, bruder, if you don't say a word . . ."

Though Silas's voice dropped off, Noah didn't need to be a mind reader to finish his thought. "If I don't say a word, then there will be no justice for Verba . . . and it could very well happen again."

CHAPTER 4

Friday, July 6

That lingering sensation of feeling that something was suspicious about Verba Stauffer's death stayed with Noah for days. It cast a dark haze over his mood, and he did everything he could to shake it off.

He prayed for Verba's soul every evening. Tried to convince himself that he had an overeager imagination. He even tried to push his concerns about her—and her uneasy relatives—out of his mind.

Nothing worked.

Finally, after a whole week passed, he resigned himself to the fact that the Lord wanted him to focus on it. He didn't know why and he wasn't sure if he could make a difference, but the new responsibility eased him. He began keeping his eyes and ears open whenever someone mentioned Verba in passing.

He even cast aside his worries about being taken seriously and mentioned his concerns to Mitch one evening. To Noah's relief, Mitch had listened to him intently. But after Noah said his piece, his supervisor pushed aside his worries.

"What's happening to you is perfectly normal," Mitch had said. "All of us at one time or another find ourselves getting too caught up in a case. You need to give yourself some distance, man."

Not wanting to directly disagree, Noah nodded and promised to drop his fears.

But he found it impossible.

Finally, not being able to help himself anymore, he rode his bike back to that house. Feeling like he needed a reason to visit, he brought with him a small first aid kit that they often gave out to classrooms when he and the firemen visited schools. It wasn't much, but most people seemed appreciative of the gift of some basic medical supplies.

As he rode, he tried to imagine how he would be greeted. He had no idea what to expect. Would everyone be in mourning and too upset to receive visitors? Were they going to be curious as to why he was there, maybe even willing to talk to him about the woman's death?

Or, maybe instead, they were going to be resentful of his presence. Mitch had told him that it had happened to him when another patient had died. Since he was the last to come in contact with the departed, the very sight of him brought back terrible feelings of anger and loss for the family.

A chill ran up Noah's spine as he contemplated that happening. Unfortunately, he could absolutely imagine receiving that kind of reaction. He'd felt something inside of that house. He'd felt it and had been taken aback enough to still be thinking about them and wondering what had happened there.

Realizing he was already standing on their front lawn, and simply staring at the front door, he shook himself out of his reverie, grabbed the white-and-red first aid kit, and strode to the door. Mentally preparing himself for whatever was on the other side, he knocked on the door.

When no one immediately answered, he knocked again. "Hello?" he called out. "Anyone there?"

Again, silence. Now what?

He stared at the first aid kit in his hand. He supposed he could leave it at the door, but it would be better if a note accompanied it. It was too bad he hadn't thought that far ahead and brought a pen and piece of paper with him.

Feeling vaguely foolish, he set the kit down. So much for his good deed.

"No one is in there," a feminine voice called out. "But I guess you realized that by now."

He spun and swallowed hard when he realized that it was the very woman he'd come to see. Sadie. "How long have you been standing there?" Aware that he sounded angry, he cleared his throat. "I mean, I'm surprised to see you standing here."

"Are you?" She looked puzzled. "Well, I haven't been here long." She gestured around the corner. "I was hanging up laundry. It took me a minute to realize someone was knocking at the door. We don't get many visitors."

"Ah. Well, I don't know if you remember me, but my name is Noah Freeman. I was one of the EMTs the other day."

"I remember you."

"And your name is Sadie, right?" he asked even though he knew for sure that it was.

"I am." Gesturing to the doormat, she said, "What did you drop off?"

"That? Oh, it's a first aid kit." When she continued to stare at him in confusion, he said, "We give those out to schools and such."

"Did you think if we had one of these it might have saved Verba's life?"

He tried not to flinch. "*Nee*, she was *verra* ill." Feeling more uncomfortable by the second, he mumbled, "Boy, you're direct." Suddenly, a new thought occurred to him. "Or were you being sarcastic?"

She looked down at her feet, then covered her middle with her hands. "I wasn't being sarcastic at all. Forgive me. Sometimes I say and do things without thinking about the consequences. I guess this is one of those times."

This was a very odd conversation. Or maybe she was simply a mighty odd girl. Absolutely regretting his decision to visit her, he stepped away. "To be honest, I don't give out first aid kits to people I've met during calls."

"You don't?"

"I never have before. I guess . . . well, I was looking for a reason to stop by and this seemed as good as any. I didn't want to show up empty-handed." He picked up the plastic container and snapped open the box. "Just so you know, there's lots of useful items inside. Bandages, gauze, salve . . ."

"*Danke*. I'll, uh, ask my relatives what to do with it." After examining the insides for herself, she set it back down by the doorstep.

He stood where he was, unable to stop watching her. She was barefoot. Her feet were slender and feminine. He supposed one could say they were pretty. Actually, she was pretty. Very pretty.

But he'd noticed that from the very first.

He liked her light-brown hair, so tightly confined under her *kapp*. He liked the color of her eyes. He didn't know if he'd ever seen blue eyes that exact shade before. But more than that, she appealed to him because she seemed so out of place. Noah realized then that was the key.

He understood how it felt to feel out of place. Knew what it felt like to know that he would never completely blend in because his very presence was at odds with the surroundings.

"I'm sorry for sounding so confused," Sadie finally said. "I'm new here."

Instead of dwelling on their combined awkwardness, Noah focused on the information she'd just shared. "Where did you move from?"

"Ohio."

"That's far."

"It is." She looked down at her bare feet. "On some days it feels like I've come a long way, indeed."

That sounded cryptic. Wanting to know more, he fired off another question. "What made you decide to move here?"

"A lot of things." She pursed her lips, then continued. "I . . . um, well, I got in a disagreement with my parents and I had to leave. *Mei onkle* Stephen is my mother's younger *bruder*, you see."

Noah wasn't sure if he did "see," but her situation was becoming clearer. She had to leave her home because she was kicked out.

Though he wanted to know more about why a sweet girl like her would be asked to leave her home, he wasn't going to make her share any more of her situation. "It's *gut* your uncle Stephen and his family had a place for you."

She made a face. "Oh, they didn't. I mean, they don't. Not really." Looking at the house, she continued. "I'm sleeping on a cot next to Esther in the kitchen at night."

"You don't have a bedroom to sleep in?"

She shook her head. "Verba and Willis have a room." She

bit her lip. "I mean, Willis does now. Stephen shares the only other room in the house with his son, Monroe."

It was a cramped household, and it sounded as if she and her cousin Esther got the worst of it. For a moment, he thought about that, thinking that his father would have made him and Silas do the sleeping in the kitchen so their sisters could have a room, but maybe it didn't really matter one way or another.

When he realized that Sadie was watching him, awaiting his response, he attempted to lighten things up. "I hope you and Esther get along."

"So far we do. We don't know each other real well yet."

She hardly knew her relatives. He felt sorry for her . . . and was growing more concerned about her, too. She seemed so alone.

"It's real hot out. Would you like to take a walk down to the creek? It's pretty shady, and we could put our feet in the water."

She glanced over to where he was pointing, seemed to stare longingly at the narrow dirt patch that peeked out, then shook her head. "I can't. I've still got more laundry to hang up."

"All right, then." But just as he was about to wish her good day and turn around, he found himself blurting something else. "May I help ya?"

Her eyes widened. "With the laundry?"

For a moment, he was brought up short. Sadie was acting as if his offer was a big deal. Thinking about all of the times his mother had wrangled all of the kids to help her hang clothes on the line, and put them away, he felt a burst of pity for Sadie. Things were obviously much different in this home.

Hoping that she wouldn't notice how deeply her words were affecting him, he shrugged. "Well, *jah*. It ain't anything." When she still hesitated, he started walking around the house. "Come on, or I'll do it without you."

When she hurried to his side, he grinned.

She caught that. "I'm amusing you."

"Only a little bit," he said as he saw the pile of laundry in a large wicker basket. Beside it was another basket, this one holding clothespins. Picking up a sheet, he shook out the wrinkles. "How would you like to do this? Want me to hand you items or do you want me to hang them on this clothesline while you take the other one?"

"Whatever you want."

"It's your line, Sadie."

She exhaled, as if she had just come to a very important decision. "Would you mind handing me each item? That will help me the most."

"I can do that." Walking over to her, he handed her the sheet and even held it while she secured the pins. When the white sheet was fluttering in the hot sun, he smiled at her. "See, that wasn't so bad."

She smiled. "You're funny, Noah."

"I get that a lot." It was a fib, of course. He couldn't think of anyone who thought he was particularly funny. Most of the time, they simply concentrated on how he was so different than the rest of his family.

He pulled out another sheet and handed it to her. "I bet this won't take us long now."

"Maybe not."

It ended up taking over an hour to get all the laundry fluttering in the faint breeze. The basket seemed to keep filling up with clothes. There was far more inside it than he had imagined.

The wet laundry was heavy, too. He found himself wondering how a slight girl like her had carried it outside in the first place. "Where is your washing machine? In the basement?"

"*Nee*. My relatives don't have a gas washing machine. We wash our clothes by hand in the tub over there."

He stared at the twin metal pails, the kettle that had obviously held hot water, and the wringer. When he thought of how much his mother complained about hanging up laundry on Mondays, he couldn't imagine how she would feel if she'd had to wash everything without a washing machine.

"Someone should have been helping you."

"I don't mind. I did laundry this way back in Ohio, too."

Just as he was about to comment on that, her cousins and their father walked up from the lane.

"Sadie, what is going on?" Stephen asked when they came to their sides.

Sadie gripped her hands tightly behind her back. "Nothing, Onkle. Noah came to deliver a first aid kit."

Though Esther didn't seem concerned by Noah's visit, Monroe did. He was staring at Noah like he should've known better than to stop by without an invitation. However, it was Stephen who marched over, picked up the first aid kit, and thrust it toward Noah. "We don't need this. You can take it with you."

Noah held up his hands. "It only holds gauze, bandages, salve, and a few other things. Nothing untoward."

"But still, it's nothing we need here. You may go now."

Now was definitely not the time to fight. "All right," he said as he took hold of the first aid kit. "Sadie, I'll be seeing ya."

She didn't answer, however. Instead, her face had become an expressionless mask.

Almost as if she hadn't heard him.

Feeling more disturbed than ever about the things that were going on in the Stauffer household, Noah put the kit in his backpack and got on his bicycle.

As he rode away, he knew something was very wrong here. What he didn't know was what he was going to do about it.

CHAPTER 5

Friday, July 6

The moment Noah was out of sight, Uncle Stephen marched up to her. "What were you thinking, inviting that man into our yard?"

Sadie felt her insides churn the very same way they did when her father berated her.

Though Stephen hadn't raised his voice, she still felt the sting of each word. His accusing glare, combined with the way he was biting out each word, didn't feel all that different than the times her father struck her with a cane.

Instinctively, she shrank from him. "I'm sorry, Onkle."

He froze, then took two steps back. "I ain't going to hurt you, Sadie. I would never do that." His voice was hurt and, perhaps, slightly shocked.

She forced herself to lift her chin and gather her thoughts. She could do this. She could defend her actions like a grown woman. She was going to be a mother soon. She needed to learn to stand up for herself.

"I didn't invite Noah here," she replied at last. "Like he

said, he showed up with the first aid kit. I couldn't very well ignore him."

"That may be what happened, but it don't change the fact that you deliberately disobeyed us. You know we don't want or need strangers around here."

Though he wasn't touching her and he was obviously taking care to speak evenly, her uncle's words still alarmed her. She had to obey him, to obey their rules. She couldn't get kicked out of their house. She needed a place to stay. She *had* to have a place to stay.

"I'm sorry," she said quickly. "I won't do anything like that again."

"I hope not. Remember, you promised to abide by our rules."

Sadie glanced at Esther and Monroe. They were standing side by side, a mixture of pity and frustration on their faces. With a sinking feeling, she realized that neither was going to stand up to their father.

She shouldn't have expected that they would. After all, hadn't she kept her mouth shut when her own father yelled at one of her siblings?

"I will, Onkle," she said quietly. "You know how grateful I am to be here. I will try harder to remember your rules, I promise."

Maybe it was her heartfelt apology, or maybe it was that he'd allowed his temper to cool, but Stephen seemed to relax a bit. "I'm sorry, Sadie. *Mei frau* told me more than once I sometimes speak and act without thinking." Looking sheepish, he continued. "Evidently, she wasn't wrong. Did I scare you? Are you all right?"

"*Jah*, Onkle. I am fine."

He eyed her more closely, from her bare feet to the wisps of hair that had come loose from their pins under her *kapp*.

"Perhaps you should go sit down for a spell? It is a warm one today."

"*Jah*. Um, maybe I will." She was tired and her ankles were swollen, but, as she was discovering, this condition would be a part of her life until the baby arrived.

"All right." Turning his head to include his children, Stephen said, "Don't either of you tell your *dawdi* about him being here. It's a blessing he wanted to go to town by himself today."

"You want us to lie?" Monroe asked, sounding almost sarcastic.

"I want you to say nothing. If he happens to ask if anyone came over today, then you may answer. But until then, there's no need for your grandfather to know. All it will do is make him upset."

Monroe folded his arms across his chest. "We ought to talk about this, though. What we're doing ain't—"

"We don't speak of this in front of the women, Monroe," Stephen interrupted.

"All right, but it ain't like they don't know."

"We won't say a word, Daed," Esther interjected before Monroe could protest again.

"*Danke*, child." Stephen sighed again before turning toward the cellar. "Come with me now, son. We have work to do."

Without a word, Monroe followed.

After the cellar door was closed, Sadie turned to her cousin. "Do you think your father really did forgive me?"

"Daed? Oh, sure. He wasn't that upset."

"*Nee*, he was."

Esther's eyes shone with amusement. "I suppose he was. But you saw how his temper blew over. That's the *gut* thing about Daed, you see. He has a great bark, but his bite ain't all that bad. And even when he does bite, it's not all that painful."

Sadie thought her cousin had a point. Yes, her uncle's anger had scared her for a bit, but his concern for her had been confusing. She couldn't recall either of her parents ever apologizing for any of their words or actions.

Part of her was thinking that maybe Stephen had been lying to her. That later tonight he would start yelling at her the minute her guard was down.

"I hope he doesn't bring it up again."

"He won't. It's forgotten now."

Sadie doubted that. But she'd learned by now to keep much of her opinions to herself. They all had secrets, lots and lots of secrets, and she was constantly at a loss of what to do about that. The problem with a secret wasn't that it was hidden, it was the fact that it was always there, lingering in the background of everything she said or did. Secrets did not change reality—they only made reality more difficult to deal with.

Crossing the yard to the laundry basket, Sadie said, "I'll finish putting this up, and then take your father's advice. I think I really do need to sit down for a while."

"I think you should sit down now," Esther said as she hurried over and pulled the basket her way. "You shouldn't be lifting heavy wet things anyway."

Unable to stop herself, Sadie said, "I've never met an Amish woman who wasn't expected to do her share, baby or no baby on the way."

Esther shrugged. "Maybe that's right. But how about this? I've never met a woman—Amish or not—who wouldn't accept a helping hand when it was offered."

"You have a point there." Feeling a twinge in her belly, she said, "When you put it that way, I'll just say thank you."

"You're welcome. Are you feeling bad? You look a little peaked."

"I'm just tired."

"Instead of going in the house, you should take that blanket off the line and go lie down in the shade."

Just imagining how nice it would be to give both her back and her swollen ankles an hour's break in the middle of the day sounded heavenly. "Are you sure no one will mind?"

"Of course not. You need to take care of yourself and the *boppli*, Sadie. That is what is most important."

Overcome by exhaustion, she nodded. After grabbing a quilt from the line, she carried it to the edge of their property. Then, under the shade of a trio of apple trees, she stretched out. The grass was soft underneath the warm quilt, creating a welcome cushion. In the distance, she could hear squirrels chattering as they chased each other in the woods.

Lying on her back, she gazed up at the clouds, remembering when she was a young child and spent hours imagining figures and shapes in the puffy wisps of cotton overhead.

Oh, but she'd used to enjoy those stolen moments so much. She'd discovered if she concentrated on the clouds overhead, the feel of the breeze on her skin, and the faint scent of her mother's rosebushes, she could ignore everything else.

And there had been so much that she'd wanted to ignore.

Staring up at the sky, Sadie tried to recreate those carefree moments. She watched the soft clouds drift above, tried to imagine them as shapes—and blocked out Harlan's lies, her father's anger, and her mother's expertise in pretending that everything was always okay.

Tried to forget the tension in the air and the way Verba had cried out in alarm before she collapsed on the floor.

Attempted to ignore how Noah's kindness had affected her.

Blocked out as best she could the many other disturbing thoughts that were running through her head.

Little by little, her body relaxed. She felt her eyes begin to close. And finally, allowing herself to drift off to sleep, she could feel that it was going to be very hard to find the will to wake up.

CHAPTER 6

Tuesday, July 10

He was forty years old and had nothing to show for it. Inwardly, Stephen winced, hating himself for feeling so pitiful.

Then, too, there were some who would say his statement was a terrible exaggeration. Maybe even blatantly false.

After all, he did have something to show for his life, and that was two wonderful-*gut* children.

Now *that* was not an exaggeration. They really were wonderful. Monroe was handsome and smart. He'd always been popular with the other *kinner* in school and had often had the top marks in math and spelling. Now he was just as popular in the community. He was the type of man who could make the best of any situation. Stephen had no doubt that Monroe would get asked to be a part of the lot the next time they needed to call for a preacher.

That would have made his mother, Jean, so proud.

She would have been just as proud of their Esther, who was loyal and happy and comfortable—and would make any man a worthy wife. Stephen figured that the young men in the area would come courting soon, too. He'd had a feeling they were simply biding their time until she was of age. Now they were no doubt waiting until several months passed after Esther's grandmother's death.

As Stephen aimlessly walked along the aisles of the bulk-food store, scanning labels without actually reading them, he wondered why he wasn't feeling the need to grieve. Was it because he now felt numb to almost any kind of pain?

Or was he feeling mostly relief?

The thought both shamed and scared him.

Everything he was feeling was so different than when he'd lost his sweet Jean. She'd accidentally drowned when Monroe was nine and Esther was eight. They'd been at the Green River, and she'd gotten caught up in an undertow and had died before he could get to her side. He'd never forget that frantic swim, his lungs burning as he tried so hard to get to her faster, all the while seeing her vanish from his sight.

Some said it wasn't his fault. Perhaps when he died, the Lord would say the same thing, too.

But her parents had never been shy about placing the blame firmly on his shoulders. He'd vowed to care for Jean and he'd failed.

He had accepted the blame, though he'd soon discovered that it didn't really matter. Jean was gone, and Esther and Monroe had been left without a mother.

And that was when everything in his life had started falling apart. First he'd sold the house and moved in with his parents so he could still farm. Then he'd discovered that his parents were low on money, so he loaned them most of it.

By the time he fully understood where that money was going, he was stuck. He was out of savings and out of choices.

Soon, he was helping his father in the cellar and making runs. Lying to everyone from the sheriff to the bishop.

And then someone started blackmailing them, and the profits that they made were eaten up again.

Now he found himself stuck in the middle of a topsy-turvy cycle, feeling like he was a bit of laundry getting spun and wrung out but never getting a chance to rest, dry, and be put to use.

Thinking of the metaphor for his life, Stephen grimaced, both at his flight of fancy and that he was even allowing himself to dwell on self-pity.

"You know, I've often felt like groaning at these shelves myself," a woman said from his right.

He turned, then flushed. Because, of course, it had to be Daisy Lapp. Daisy had been Jean's best friend growing up, but he and her had never been close. Though she'd never actually said anything, he'd gotten the feeling that she didn't approve of him.

A tiny part of him now realized that she had been justified in her feelings.

"Sorry. I didn't see you there, Daisy." The moment he blurted his words, he wished he could take them back. He'd sounded rude.

"There's no need to apologize. I just walked up."

Her perky, immediate reply was a good example of why he'd never trusted her. Daisy had an answer for everything. Always.

Jean had often found her girlfriend's quips funny. He, on the other hand, felt that her constant need to have the last word was the reason why she was an old maid.

Now, though? He was finding her smile strangely comforting.

When Daisy smiled at him again, her wide-set brown eyes filled with kindness and laughter, Stephen was tempted to smile back. And maybe notice that she'd kept her girlish figure and looked far younger than her age.

Which was something else he shouldn't be noticing.

He was ready for her to get whatever she'd come for and leave him in peace. "Am I in your way?"

For a second, hurt flashed in her eyes before she covered it up. "*Nee.*" Reaching out, Daisy grabbed a plastic container of pecans and placed it in her shopping basket. "I know I already told you this at the funeral, but I am sorry about Verba."

"*Danke.*"

"How is Willis doing?"

"About as well as a man can expect to be, given that his wife is dead."

She inhaled sharply. "I'm sorry I asked."

And now he was sorry he was behaving like such a bully. Practically feeling Jean's long index finger jabbing him in between his shoulder blades, he exhaled. "Daisy, I am the one who should be apologizing. I have no excuse for talking to you like that. Please forgive me."

To his shame, she gazed at him closely, as if she was trying to figure out if he was telling the truth or not.

Whatever she saw in his face must have given her comfort, because she simply shrugged. "Don't worry about it. I'll, ah, get out of your way now."

Her voice was thick. Husky. His insides sank as he realized that she was attempting to fight off tears. Feeling alarmed, he reached for her. "Daisy, I was sincere. I truly am sorry." Somehow, whether on purpose or because he was destined to make a mess of it all, he ended up grasping her hand and not her arm.

And then her fingers clasped his own and held on tight.

Daisy looked just as startled as he did by their sudden connection. She let go.

"Don't mind me. I'm simply having a bad day." She made an effort to smile, but it failed.

Which caused something inside him to hurt. "What's the matter?" he asked quickly. "Is there anything I can do?"

"*Nee*, I just haven't been feeling like myself lately." She rolled her eyes. "Or for quite a while. I'll be okay."

"What has been wrong?"

"I've been tired. Real tired. My joints have been hurting, and I've been experiencing a couple of other things. First, I went to the chiropractor, but he referred me to a physician over at the clinic." She sighed. "Today one of his assistants called Mrs. Cartwright, who told me that I now have to go see a specialist."

"So something is really wrong."

"Maybe there is." She pointed to a faint rash that sprayed across her cheeks. "I canna believe it, but it's this awful rash that has people spun up." Daisy's bottom lip trembled. "I've got to go at the end of the week and get examined."

"But then you'll be all right?"

"I hope so." She looked at her basket. "And now my quick trip to the store for pecans has lasted much longer than I planned. I best get going."

Stephen started realizing that he really didn't know much about Daisy. He didn't know who Mrs. Cartwright was, didn't know where she lived, and didn't know if she was the type of woman to make light of things or exaggerate them.

He didn't even know if she had a sweetheart or some family members around. "Who are you going to the doctor with?"

"Mrs. Cartwright is going to take me."

"Who is she again?"

"She's my boss. I clean her *haus*, Stephen."

That didn't seem like the right person to sit by her side. "You don't have anyone else to help you? No one in your family lives nearby?"

She opened her mouth, then seemed to come to a decision. "Stephen, no offense, but I've known you for twenty years. My best friend in the world was your wife. We live in the same church district and I used to sit with Jean in your kitchen for hours at a time. All this time you've done your best to avoid me even though, for the life of me, I've never understood what I did to cause you so much pain. I think it's a little too late to be givin' you basic information about myself, don't you?"

Everything Daisy said was right. But that didn't mean his interest was wrong. He did care about her; certainly because Jean had cared so much about her. But there *was* something about Daisy Lapp that was good, and she deserved having people around, looking after her.

Part of him wanted to dispute her words, right there in the middle of the bulk-food aisle. But if he did that, Stephen knew he would be having that argument for himself, not her. And he had probably already been selfish enough where she was concerned.

"I understand," he finally said.

His easy acquiescence seemed to take the wind out her sails. "You do?"

"I'll see you at church, Daisy. You take care getting home."

"*Danke.*" She gave him a hesitant smile, confusion and maybe a bit of regret illuminating her eyes.

Stephen turned and started walking before he changed his

mind and said anything else. It was only when he got to the checkout register that he realized he had neglected to put a single thing in his basket.

An Amish teen who was standing next to him frowned at his empty basket. "Want me to help you find what you came looking in here for?" he asked.

"*Nee*. I don't think what I need is here after all," Stephen replied, setting his basket on the counter and walking away.

Once out the door and in the bright sunlight, he scanned the parking lot for Daisy, but didn't see any sign of her. She was either still in the store or long gone.

It seemed he'd been in the store for over an hour and had nothing to show for it except the stark feeling of guilt and disappointment.

CHAPTER 7

Tuesday, July 10

Try as he might, Noah couldn't get past the idea that there was something wrong at the Stauffer house. He couldn't put his finger on it, but he'd been in enough homes to understand when things weren't working.

Things definitely weren't working right in that home.

His problem—as far as he could tell, anyway—was that he had no idea why he cared. He didn't know the Stauffers and wasn't exactly sure he wanted to know them.

Though he would be lying if he didn't admit that there was actually only one member of that household whom he did care about. For some reason, Sadie had gotten under his skin and he couldn't stop thinking about her—not even when he napped. Last night, at the firehouse, she starred in his dreams. Over and over, he spied her in the distance and would approach. She looked as if she was trying to ask him something . . . but each time he got close enough to hear, she disappeared.

He didn't know what that dream meant about either her

or himself. All he knew was that she'd somehow snuck into his very being.

Now all he had to do was figure out what to do with his confusing feelings about her and her extended family. Did he want to chance visiting her again and risking her uncle's wrath? Or should he simply step away and give the family space? They'd just lost a family member after all. It was very likely that they were still mourning her loss.

He was stewing on that and eating an enormous breakfast after a twenty-four-hour shift when his mother knocked on his door. Letting her inside, she followed Noah into his kitchen.

"Look at you, eating eggs and bacon like it was six in the morning instead of six at night."

He shrugged as he sat back down at the table. "Can't help it. I like breakfast. It's easy for me to make, too."

After curving a hand around his cheek in that way she always had, since he was a little boy, his mother pulled up a chair. "I saw you walk by the house a few minutes ago. I thought I'd catch up before you went to sleep."

"I'm glad you did." He was, too. He was blessed with an easygoing mother who instinctively knew how to balance her interest in his life without intruding too much. He and Silas had talked more than once about how lucky they were to have her. So many of their friends were constantly trying to get a break from their parents. He and his siblings, on the other hand, enjoyed spending time with them.

"So, how was your shift?"

Thinking of the three calls, one to a nursing home, the second to a private house, and the third to a vehicle accident, he shrugged. "All right, I guess. Everyone is going to be okay."

"You do a lot of good work, son. Each time you go out, you help save lives. That's something to be proud of."

"You always say that."

"If I say it often, it's because it's the truth."

She sounded so sure. So sincere, which was a gift he knew he'd never take for granted. "You never make me feel bad about the job I chose to do, Mamm. I don't know if I've ever told you how much I appreciate that."

"There's no need for you to thank me. I know you, Noah." She chuckled. "Besides, would ya really want me to snipe at you?"

"Of course not. It's just that I have a feeling that you wish I was still farming."

"I birthed five *kinner*, Noah. Silas is a carpenter, Joanna married a farmer, and Harry enjoys farming next to your *daed*. I figure having only one black sheep is good odds."

He gaped at her before he realized she was making a joke. "Mamm, I canna believe you said that. But you didn't mention Mel."

"Our Melody is a little young yet."

"She ain't that young, Mamm. She's seventeen."

She laughed. "Funny you should mention that. Melody reminded me of that very same thing just a few hours ago."

"Oh? Why? What did she do?"

"Nothing for you to worry about. Finish your supper before it gets cold."

"Okay, but while I'm eating, you have to fill me in on my dutiful siblings."

"Everyone is the same . . . except Melody."

"So . . . what's going on with her?"

His mother, still so slim and pretty in her cranberry-colored short-sleeved dress, darted a glance around his kitchen, then finally blurted, "I think she has set her sights on Ben Zook."

Noah relaxed immediately. "Mamm, I think our Melody was born with her sights on Ben Zook. They've liked each other for years."

Looking pained, she wrinkled her nose. "That's what your father said."

"And?"

"And Joanna might have said the same thing, too." With a grumble, she added, "As did her Andrew."

"Even Joanna's husband was aware of Melody and Ben's relationship?"

His mother blushed. "No need to rub it in, Noah. Obviously, I was the last to know that there was something special between Melody and Ben."

"Ben Zook is a good man. He's just as smitten with our Melody as she is with him. They seem happy with each other. Melody could do far worse."

"Oh, I know," she said quickly.

Almost too quickly. "Mamm, what is bothering you? Do you know something about Ben that ain't *gut*?"

"*Nee*." She shifted in her chair, gazed out toward the street. "But sometimes I think she should look around a bit. She's only seventeen."

"What you're saying makes sense," he hedged. He didn't want to disagree with his mother, but he also was fairly sure that no good would come out of trying to tell Melody to ignore what she was feeling. "If Melody does ever want to change her mind about Ben, she's got plenty of time to do that."

"I don't think that's going to happen. She told me earlier this week that they intend to get engaged soon."

"Ah. What did Daed say?"

She waved a dismissive hand. "You know your father. Anything Melody says or does is wonderful-*gut*. She has him wrapped around her finger."

Though Noah was used to talking with his mother about his younger siblings and offering advice, in this case, he knew he was out of his element. He'd never been in love . . . but, of course, just in that moment an image of Sadie, smiling softly at him, flashed in his head.

What did that mean?

"Mamm, I think it might be best if you let Melody make her choice, just like you and Daed allowed me to make mine."

Looking aggrieved, his mother nodded. "Your father said something very much like that just this morning."

He winked. "I'm thinking that means it's *gut* advice."

"I just don't want her to make a mistake, or years from now wish she had taken her time."

"You know Melody as well as I do. She is as unwavering and steady as—" he looked around, trying to come up with the appropriate comparison and settled for the oak tree next to the window where they were sitting "—as this oak here."

"Noah, if that tree gets hit by lightning and falls down, I'm going to be mighty upset with you."

"I'll prepare myself." He stood up, put his plate to one side, and realized that maybe God had brought his mother over not just to talk about Melody. Maybe it was so he could talk about someone he'd been wrestling about as well.

Liking that idea, he made a decision. "Hey, Mamm?"

Her eyes perked up. "*Jah*?"

"Do you know anything about the Stauffers? They live out near Cub Run."

"Stauffer?" She bit her lip. Then frowned. "Isn't that the family who just lost the mother?"

"Uh-huh. Her name was Verba. Did you know her well?"

"Verba Stauffer? Not really," she murmured.

"I thought you knew everyone."

His mother's cheeks colored. "I do, but I've never gotten to know them."

"How come?"

"I couldn't say, not really." She looked away and started fiddling with the stack of paper napkins on the center of the table.

His mother was a lot of things. Shy and tentative she was not. "Mamm, you know something."

"Maybe."

"Won't you share at least some of it? I'm not just interested in gossip. This is important."

She turned back to him, her light-blue eyes clouding with concern. "I heard stories, but that don't mean anything. You know how people like to talk."

"What have you heard?"

"Noah, why is this family on your mind? Is it because you went on a call to their house when Verba took ill?"

"Partly. I mean, that is very sad and all . . ."

"Any death is sad, but I don't think she was in particularly good health, son. Every time I saw her at the market, her skin looked paper thin and kind of sallow." She flushed. "Sorry. That's unkind."

"There was a young woman living there. A distant relation. She's been on my mind."

"How distant?"

"I think she might be a cousin? Her name is Sadie. She's moved here recently from Ohio."

"Why are you thinking about her? Was she sick, too?"

"*Nee*. I mean, I don't think so." Boy, my mother must know

a doozy of a story for her to be sidestepping around what she knows about the family, Noah thought.

"So, she's a cousin who moved here recently. You are concerned about her but she's not ill . . ." Her eyes brightened. "Have you fallen in love, too?"

"*Nee!*"

Instead of fussing that he raised his voice to her, Mamm was staring at his face. "You like her, though."

"I'm worried about her. I went out to see Sadie again, and she was doing laundry by herself. She revealed that she sleeps on a makeshift bed in the kitchen."

Her eyebrows rose at the mention of his visit. After a moment, she said, "While that's too bad, that's nothing to be upset about."

"*Nee*, it's more than that. She made it sound like she had to leave Ohio, like she got kicked out. And now she is in this awful house. When her uncle came home, I overheard him yelling at her for talking to me."

Mamm looked dismayed but not surprised. "What are you going to do next?"

"I don't know. It's not like she asked me for help. I guess I need to keep looking out for Sadie, if that's possible."

"I'm not sure that's a good idea. I can't believe I'm saying this, but I'm starting to wish you had your own Ben Zook. Then I wouldn't be worried about you getting hurt, or involving yourself in situations that you can't escape."

Finally they were back to his original question. "What do you know, Mamm?"

"There are rumors that the men in the family have a moonshine business."

"Moonshine." He gaped at her. "But they're Amish." While

he realized some members of their church might have a glass of homemade wine from time to time, operating a still and selling liquor was something else altogether.

"Indeed, they are—but just because someone is Amish doesn't mean they don't have vices. And, well, it ain't like they drink it all themselves. People of all sorts buy it from them. At least, so I have heard."

"I'm thinking you know quite a bit about all of this." He was struggling to keep his voice even. It was difficult, though, because he'd always considered his mother was rather innocent.

It was something of a shock to realize that she knew more about the moonshine business than he did.

"A lot of people do. I'm certainly not the only one. It's just that no one talks about it."

Noah was tempted to find fault with that, but he knew he'd been guilty of that as well from time to time. Not all of his friends—English or Amish—always made the best decisions. Some had been bad enough that he'd wanted to tell someone, but he'd kept his mouth shut. No one wanted to be considered a tattletale or busybody. "I see."

Seemingly encouraged by his comment, she continued. "This business of theirs is all rather secretive and sneaky, at least according to your father."

"Daed knows about the moonshine, too?"

Her eyes lit up. "He does. I think most everyone knows something about it."

"I didn't!"

"Anyway, like I said, the family tries real hard to keep it under wraps. I've heard that the men lie about the amount of money they're making; and the women, well, I guess they pretend they don't know what their men do all day."

Noah was worldly enough to know that the Kentucky hills were practically littered with bourbon distilleries. Tourists flocked to them. During his *rumspringa*, he'd even visited one to see what all the fuss was about.

But a homemade still, hidden in a home or barn, was different. It was not only illegal, it could be dangerous.

In fact, the whole business sounded dangerous. "Do you think Sadie knows about the family business?"

"I would imagine so. I mean, how could she not? Your father said those stills are notoriously unstable. Maybe that's why she seemed uneasy."

"Maybe so."

"Now you look even more worried, son. Please don't be. The Stauffer family might not be my cup of tea, but it don't mean they're bad people."

"Maybe not, but I'm still worried about her. I just wish I knew what to do."

"If you aren't sure what the best course is, I think that means it's time for you to get some sleep." She picked up his plate. "Go on. I know you've been up for hours and hours. I'll wash your dishes for you before I go home."

"I don't need you washing my dishes."

"I'm sure you don't. But . . . maybe I need to do them from time to time."

Noah doubted that. But he didn't doubt how tired he suddenly was. Right now, even walking to his bedroom felt like a chore.

After giving his mother a quick hug and offering his thanks, he wandered toward his bedroom. When he and Silas first bought the house, Silas and his crew did some remodeling. Now both he and Silas had a bathroom connected to their own bedroom.

Last year, he'd spent almost a whole paycheck on a new king-sized bed and fresh sheets and blankets.

After taking a much-needed shower, he lay down on those new sheets and stretched out his legs. Allowed his eyes to drift shut, all while taking comfort in the fact that the room had dark shades and was blessedly cool.

This room, so comfortable and private, in a house that he shared with his brother and right next door to his parents, was everything he'd ever wanted. It soothed both his body and his soul.

It was vastly different than Sadie's circumstances. Living in a house filled with distant relatives. Sleeping on a cot in the center of a hot kitchen.

Living in fear of being caught, or the still exploding into flames.

And though he knew his mother was probably right, Noah's last thought was that someone had to look out for Sadie.

No, *he* needed to look out for her.

To his surprise, instead of making him wary, the decision only added to his sense of peace. He drifted off to sleep making plans.

CHAPTER 8

July 12

Sadie wasn't sure where the money came from, but when Uncle Stephen placed the fifty dollars in her hand and told her to use it for her fabric and other sewing supplies, she was so excited about the opportunity that she didn't argue.

She and Esther walked to town together, but then separated when Esther ran into one of her old classmates from school. Sadie didn't want to interfere with their time, and they agreed to meet near the coffee shop in an hour.

That was how she ended up alone in Ada's Fabrics, which Esther had said was the best fabric and notion store in the county.

It was a small place. Cramped but surprisingly cool, thanks to the fans overhead that were attached to the generator.

After surveying the space, Sadie made up her mind. She was no longer going to pretend that she wasn't with child. Instead, she decided to at last embrace the pregnancy. The matter-of-fact way that Esther had embraced it made Sadie realize she'd been foolish to try to keep her condition a secret. In about six months, she was going to be a mother for the rest of her life—so the rest of the world was just going to have to come to terms with that, too.

Feeling pleased with her new attitude, she decided to make a baby blanket out of various yellow and white prints. To her surprise, there were several bins of neatly rolled remnant fabric, each for just a couple of dollars. If she shopped smart, she would have plenty of money left over.

"You be needin' any help?" the woman who ran the store called out.

"*Danke*, but I think I have been finding everything all right."

The woman began walking toward Sadie. She had coffee-colored skin, short hair, and kind-looking brown eyes. She was wearing a long dress with short sleeves but no *kapp*. Sadie wondered if she was Mennonite, or just enjoyed dressing modestly.

"My name is Ada," she said in a sweet, melodic voice. "You're new around here, aren't you?"

"I am. My name is Sadie. I recently moved in with my cousins, the Stauffers."

"You're kin to them?" Ada said as she approached.

"I am." Sadie's smile faltered as a bit of her insides deflated. Here it was again . . . that almost judgmental look and tension that was sent her way whenever she either mentioned that she was living with the Stauffers or when she was seen walking beside one of them.

"How are things going? I'm real sorry about Verba."

"Thank you. My family is sad but is doing the best they can." Ada nodded slowly. "That's all you can do, right?"

"*Jah*. That is true." She glanced with longing at the fabric. She had hoped to make this outing a happy experience, not another uncomfortable hour.

"So you getting fabric for a specific project in mind?" Ada asked. "Or are you just looking around?" Before Sadie could answer, she held up a hand. "If you are just looking, that's all right with me. Lord knows, I spend a good amount of time in here just dreaming of projects to start."

Ada was making an effort to be kind. Sadie liked that. She liked how she wasn't acting like she knew everything there was to know about the Stauffers.

Maybe this was a sign that it was time to come out of her shell a little bit.

Feeling like she was jumping off a cliff, Sadie looked her in the eye. "I actually do have a project in mind. You see, I'm going to be making a baby blanket."

"I notice you're looking at yellow." Ada's smile widened. "Let me guess, you don't know whether the woman is having a boy or a girl?"

"That is the truth. I don't know if it will be a boy or a girl." She smiled, liking how that sounded.

Ada nodded, just as if Sadie's choice of fabrics was a very important decision. "How far along is she? If she's pretty far, you could ask. I'm only pushing because I see a lot of women wishing they had either bought pink or a blue material. Yellow ain't for everyone."

"I'm sure it isn't, but I'm fond of it." Exhaling, she said, "And because it's for me, I don't think I'll be changing my mind."

"You're gonna have a baby?"

"I am."

The woman's expression went slack before she pulled herself back together. "I see. Congratulations, then." Softly, she added, "A baby is a miracle, isn't it?"

Tears pricked Sadie's eyes. Had anyone actually referred to her babe as that? "It is, indeed."

Suddenly, she felt as if the Lord was walking with her, coaxing to believe in herself and in the baby, too. By pretending it didn't exist or that she wasn't experiencing all the emotions and physical reactions that took place with pregnancy, she'd been doing both her, the babe, and Him a disservice. After all, He had brought her this child for a reason.

As a tear fell, she swiped it with her hand. "I'm sorry. It's just . . . well, thank you for saying that."

After gazing at her another long moment, Ada sighed. And then pulled Sadie into a hug. "Oh, child. You've been having a time of it, haven't you?"

She nodded when Ada released her. "It hasn't been easy, but I'm okay."

"Are you going to be living here in Hart County?"

"Yes. I mean, I hope so."

"With the Stauffers, or with your man?"

"With the Stauffers." Figuring she might as well share some more, she admitted, "I . . . well, I don't have a man. He didn't want me or the babe." Since she'd already shared so much, Sadie continued. "I'm grateful for my cousins. My family didn't take the news well. I had to leave them."

A troubled expression entered Ada's eyes. "You poor thing. So you had to leave home and you're now living with relatives."

"They've been kind to me. I'm real glad I'm not alone anymore."

"I bet." She folded her arms over her chest. "To be real honest, your cousins don't have the best of reputations. I had always assumed that they didn't care about folks. But it seems like I was wrong, wasn't I?"

Sadie didn't know if Ada was wrong or not. Sometimes

she felt as if she was a terrible obligation to the Stauffers. Other times, she felt like she was forgotten, like a constant afterthought.

No matter what, it was probably a good time to move to a different topic. "I thought I'd make a starburst pattern. What do you think, four or six different patterns?"

"I think because it's going to be for a babe that four would be a good choice."

Holding out the pieces in her hand, she said, "I like these three together."

Ada knelt down, dug down deep into the scrap pile, then pulled out a pale-yellow polka-dot fabric. "How about this for the fourth?"

"I think it's mighty pretty. Now I just need some thread and needles. Oh, some pattern marker, too."

"Are you going to sew this by hand?"

"*Jah*." Maybe one day soon she'd feel comfortable using Verba's old treadle sewing machine.

"Okay, then, honey. Let's get you set up."

Ten minutes later, Sadie was stepping out of the shop with a shopping bag filled with everything she needed to begin her project. Though her hands were filled, her entire body felt lighter. It was amazing how the very act of sharing her burden had helped her whole disposition.

Just as she was scanning the area for Esther, she noticed Noah standing with her outside the coffee shop. At first she feared that something else had happened. But when she saw that the two of them were simply speaking together, her heart quieted.

When they spied her, both Noah and Esther stopped talking. They turned to watch her approach.

Uncomfortable with both their attention and the way Noah was now staring at her, she wondered if Esther had told him about the pregnancy.

Her steps slowed. What if Esther had told him? What would he think of her then? Would he suddenly turn away from her and act as if she wasn't good enough to befriend? Or, would he try to accept her and make an effort to understand her side of the story?

Did it even matter? She had no time or energy for another man in her life. Her future was too fragile and uncertain. And there was too much going on with the Stauffers for her to invite anyone into their fragile circle.

Esther raised a hand, smiled, and called out, "You coming, Sadie?"

Sadie paused, then took a deep breath and strode forward. It seemed today was a day to take chances and to believe in herself.

Hopefully things would go as well with Noah as they did with Ada.

CHAPTER 9

July 12

Sadie looked different. Maybe it was the smile on her face. Maybe it was because she was out in the open instead of on the Stauffers' property, which Noah privately thought tainted everything in its wake.

Whatever the reason, that glow of happiness surrounding her made her look even prettier, which he hadn't thought could be possible.

When she got close enough to greet, Noah stepped slightly away from Esther, with whom he'd been chatting. Earlier, after an awkward greeting, Esther had explained to him that she was waiting for Sadie, and then they started chatting—about the weather. Almost as if she hadn't witnessed her father making it very clear, just a few days ago, that Noah was a person unwelcome in, or even near, their home.

Because Noah wasn't going to pass up an opportunity to see Sadie, he'd chatted about the heat and the sunny skies, too.

And then, there she was.

"Hiya, Sadie," Noah said as she approached. He knew he sounded far too enthusiastic. "I can't believe we're both out in town at the same time."

"Hello, Noah," she said formally, wariness entering her expression right before his eyes. She turned to Esther. "I'm sorry that I ran late. Have you been waiting long?"

"No worries. I haven't been waiting long at all." Esther smiled. "Besides, I had someone to pass the time with. Noah showed up after I had been standing here only a minute or two."

Noah held up a canvas bag. "I needed to get some hardware supplies next door. When I saw Esther, I decided to say hello." Inwardly he cringed. He was saying far too much.

Holding her own bag close to her chest, Sadie swallowed. "Ah."

Esther smiled. "He caught me off guard, too. When he started talking, I looked around to double-check that he wasn't talking to some woman behind me."

"She's exaggerating," Noah said. "So . . . how are you?"

"I'm good." After another awkward moment passed, Sadie shook her head as if to clear it. "Have a nice afternoon, Noah. Me and my cousin were about to go inside."

Thinking of no way to keep her, he nodded. "I understand. Enjoy your meal."

"Wait, Noah," Esther said. "Actually, I was wondering . . . could you do me a favor?"

"Of course. What is it?"

"Well, you see, I just had such a good time talking to my friend Rachel that she wondered if I could stop by her *haus* and say hello to her mother." Esther frowned. "She's ailing, you see."

Noah wasn't following. "What do you need from me?"

"I think it would be real awkward if Sadie came along. I

was just going to go see her another day. But maybe, if you have time, you could take Sadie home for me?"

"What?" Sadie squeaked.

Noah thought Sadie looked like her cousin had just lost her mind. He didn't blame her. He was taken aback, too.

But not enough to pass up this opportunity. "I'll be happy to take her home."

"*Danke*," Esther said.

"Wait a minute!" Sadie interjected. "I can go home on my own."

"*Nee*, you can't," Noah said. "You're new here. It would be better for you to be walking with someone who knows the area."

"I'm afraid I have to agree," Esther said. "Please, Sadie?"

Lowering her voice, Sadie said to Esther, "Your father won't be happy."

"He'll be fine. Won't you do this for me?"

Sadie darted a look his way. "All right. But . . ."

"*Danke*. Tell Daed I'll be home by five, if he asks." And with that, she turned away and trotted off.

Sadie groaned. "I'm real sorry about this. I don't know why Esther was acting like that."

"I'm not upset."

"Are you sure? I feel like you've been taken advantage of."

"I don't. Not at all." He gestured to the restaurant. "Are you ready to go inside?"

"We don't have to do that."

Noah knew he needed to say something fast to set her at ease or he was going to lose her. "Ah, it looks like you went shopping at Ada's Fabrics."

"I did. How did you know where I was? Did Esther tell you?"

"*Nee*. I recognize the bright-yellow shopping bags. My mother has brought home her fair share over the years."

"Oh. It's a *gut* store. And the lady who runs it is nice."

"She is." He smiled at her again. "You know what? Penny's has really good pie. It would be a shame to be so close and not get a slice. Want to go in? I have it on good authority that pretty much everyone thinks she makes the best fruit pies around. What do you say?"

"Do you think she'll have peach?"

"In the middle of July? I reckon so."

"Well, all right."

There he went again, smiling like a fool. What was it about this woman that caused him to rethink everything he thought he was attracted to in a girl?

SADIE KNEW SHE shouldn't be standing with him.

She knew she should've started back home by herself. No matter what he or Esther said, she knew she wouldn't get lost and would be just fine.

But no matter what she thought she *ought* to do . . . here she was.

What was it about Noah Freeman that made her want to reexamine everything she thought she wanted or knew about men? Was it his looks? His ready smile? The fact that her first impression of him was of a rescuer?

Or maybe it was because he didn't know about her secret or her past and wasn't gazing at her through that lens. Being around him did make her feel fresh and easy. Almost like she used to be, before she'd realized just how narrow and confining her life had been destined to be.

"Hi, may I help you?" an English woman in her early thirties greeted them.

She had bright-pink hair, and was wearing a uniform like

a waitress back in the 1950s would have worn, along with high-top tennis shoes.

Sadie couldn't help but stare.

Noah, on the other hand, didn't seem to find her appearance strange at all. "A table for two," he said easily.

The hostess looked at them both and smiled. "I've got just the spot for y'all. Come right this way."

It was obvious that the woman thought they were on a date. Sadie glanced at Noah to see what his reaction was. He didn't look embarrassed.

She supposed she needed to stop being so skittish, too. It didn't matter what this woman thought of them. She certainly wasn't going to be running to her relatives' house to inform them of Sadie's latest indiscretion.

"Sadie, are you ready to sit down?" Noah called back.

With a start, she realized that she'd been standing there in the middle of the restaurant, lost in her own daydreams.

"*Jah*. Of course." Quickly, she crossed the restaurant and took a seat in the booth, opposite from Noah.

If the hostess thought her actions were strange, she didn't show it. Instead, she placed a mini chalkboard on the table in between them. "Penny makes pies every evening and morning, so everything is real fresh. We've got five to choose from today. Iced tea, lemonade, water, and coffee, too."

And with that, she turned and walked away. Sadie watched her for a moment before concentrating on the blackboard. Today's offerings were peach, strawberry, cherry, apple, and blackberry. "Which kind of pie are you going to get?"

"Cherry. What about you?"

"Peach?"

He tilted his head to one side. "Is that a question?"

"I'm not sure." Oh, but she was so bad at this. "I guess I'm not used to making decisions."

"Not even about what kind of pie to have?"

If she was bolder, she would have told him that that was especially what she wasn't used to doing. "Not even that."

"I've had their peach pie lots of times. They serve it warm with ice cream."

Her stomach growled. "Now I have even more decisions to make."

"Indeed you do."

When a young woman came to take their order, Sadie felt much more at ease. She was Amish and about their age.

"I'm Ida. What would you like?"

Noah leaned forward. "It's time, Sadie. What will you have?"

"Can I have peach pie and a scoop of vanilla ice cream, too?"

"What will you have to drink?"

"Water."

"Cherry, warmed, with vanilla ice cream—and water for me, too," Noah added.

"I'll be right back."

Sadie exhaled. She'd done it.

For the first time since they'd met up, Noah wasn't smiling. Instead, he was gazing at her in concern.

"Is something wrong?" she asked.

"*Jah*. Sadie, I've been sitting here, trying to come up with a whole bunch of reasons to explain why you are reacting to everything the way you are. But for the life of me, I simply can't figure it out."

"Figure out what?"

"Why are you so tentative? I know your uncle was mad

I was over. But Esther didn't seem to think me visiting you would be a problem. She would know, right?"

"*Jah*. I . . . you're right. I don't think my uncle Stephen will be too upset if I have pie here with you."

"Then why does it seem like you are afraid of something? You aren't afraid of me, are you?"

"No. I'm not afraid of you." She just felt afraid of everything else right at the moment.

"Then what is it?" Before she could reply, he said, "Is it your family here? Are you uncomfortable around them? Do you feel trapped or something?"

"Of course not."

"You need to be honest with someone."

He was no doubt right. She did need to be honest with someone about how uneasy she felt with her relatives. How alone she felt here in Kentucky.

How scared she was about her future.

And there was something about Noah Freeman that felt good and clean and special.

But if she shared her fears and told him the truth about the baby, he'd never look at her again.

Though that would probably be better in the long run, she was just weak enough to hate the thought of that happening.

"Noah, I agreed to come in and have pie and allow you to walk me home so Esther could see her friend's mother. That's it."

"I can help you, Sadie."

"But I don't want your help."

"You may not and that's your choice. It's just . . . well, I hope you don't one day regret keeping me at a distance."

She didn't say anything. But she was pretty sure that she already did.

CHAPTER 10

July 12

Daisy was in such a daze, the receptionist at the doctor's office had to ask her the question a second, then a third time. "Will next Tuesday work for you or not?"

Would it? Unable to make even that much of a decision, she froze.

Mrs. Cartwright tapped one manicured nail on the open calendar that was taped to the light-gray countertop. "You usually clean my house on Tuesdays so I think it will work, don't you? I'll be able to take you."

She knew what Mrs. Cartwright was saying. Instead of Daisy doing what she was paid to do, Mrs. Cartwright would be carting her around Hart County. Gratitude melded with frustration and singed her insides. "You wouldn't mind?"

"Of course not."

"All right, then." She exhaled deeply and looked back at the receptionist. "That day will work for me."

Looking relieved to get Daisy on her way and help the next person in line, the receptionist typed in the date on her computer screen and gave her an appointment card. "Here you go. Come fifteen minutes early. We'll need you to fill out paperwork."

"More paperwork?" It felt like she'd already told them everything she could about herself. What else would they need to know?

"We'll do that. Thank you," Mrs. Cartwright interjected crisply. "Let's go have some lunch, Daisy. My treat."

Daisy was so overcome by Mrs. Cartwright's generosity, she hardly knew how to respond. Eileen Cartwright had always been a nice woman, but Daisy had never imagined that her kindness would extend so far as it had over the last week. From the moment Daisy had mentioned that she was being sent to the specialist and was going to have to get more tests done, her employer had taken charge and gone above and beyond Daisy's expectations. "Thank you," she said at last.

After they got into her shiny black sedan, Mrs. Cartwright pulled onto Main. "I thought maybe we could go to Bill's Diner. Does that sound good to you?"

Bill's was a staple in Munfordville. In the whole county, actually. Bill and his wife specialized in wholesome comfort foods and ran a special every day that seemed to have no rhyme or reason beyond that it was what Bill felt like cooking.

"It sounds *gut*. I just hope the special ain't liver-and-onions."

"You and me both." Mrs. Cartwright wrinkled her nose. "I'm always surprised whenever I see so many people order that. I've never been a fan."

"Me, neither, though I had a girlfriend once who enjoyed it more than anything."

"Once? What happened to her?"

"She passed away a few years ago. It was Jean Stauffer."
She paused, half expecting Mrs. Cartwright to grimace.
The Stauffers' reputation wasn't too good. Actually, it was
so bad that almost everyone had an opinion about them. Jean
had been a good woman, though. One of the best.

"I didn't know her."

"She was Amish." Daisy exhaled. She felt guilty, like
she was being disloyal to Jean, but she simply didn't have
the energy to try to defend the Stauffers when she'd never
agreed with Jean's choice of a husband in the first place.
Jean had been a delicate sort, prone to sickness. Stephen, so
robust and, well, masculine, the opposite of that. "Jean and
I grew up together."

"I'm sorry you lost her."

"I am, too."

They drove on, Mrs. Cartwright with both hands on the
steering wheel and Daisy holding tightly to the stack of
papers the nurse in the office had handed her about lupus in
her lap. The papers felt unnaturally heavy, like their contents
contained a great burden.

She knew she was no doubt going to have to study the
information carefully, and then probably have to read it all
again.

Then she remembered her manners. "Thank you for your
help today. And for next week, too. I don't know what I
would do without you."

Eileen glanced at her, her kind eyes shining through her
glasses. "Like I said when I picked you up this morning, I'm
glad to help. You've been helping me with my house for
fifteen years."

"Has it really been that long?"

"It certainly has. When you first started, Jim was still alive and two of my kids were in high school. Now, of course, Jim is in heaven and all five of my children are out of the house. Why, two are married and now have babies of their own."

The reminder of those events made Daisy smile. Eileen had gotten in such a tizzy about those weddings. "Time moves on."

"It always does, doesn't it? Whether we want it to or not." Her tone was filled with resignation and something else. Was it a hint? Or maybe a warning for Daisy to take to heart?

Daisy nodded, thinking of all the life changes Mrs. Cartwright had been going through. She'd lost her husband in a car accident and had been almost inconsolable for months.

Then one day when Daisy walked in her kitchen, she'd found her employer sitting in a light-blue tracksuit and sipping coffee. Her eyes were bright and she was filled with a new purpose. She'd called a travel agent and had booked herself a trip to Australia—and she was going to go by herself.

Daisy was so shocked by her change in behavior, she scrubbed the kitchen floor extra well that day, afraid to say the wrong thing.

Thinking about that day, she said, "What was it that brought you out of your doldrums after Jim died?"

Eileen looked startled. "What do you mean?"

"I was just thinking how one day you looked sad and afraid to leave the house, but the next time I came over, you had on your tracksuit and were talking about Australia."

Her eyes brightened. "Ah. Yes, that was quite a day, wasn't it?" She chuckled softly. "Every time I recall your expression when you walked in the kitchen, I feel like giggling."

"I was mighty surprised."

"You were shocked! Daisy, for a minute there, I thought your eyes were going to bug out of your head."

Embarrassed, but thinking that had probably been the case, Daisy smiled, too. "I was just wondering what brought about that change. One day, you were crying and then next you looked like your regular self again. That is, if you don't mind me asking."

Pulling into the diner, Eileen replied. "I don't mind you asking in the slightest. Goodness, I think that was six years ago now, wasn't it?"

"Thereabouts."

"Well, the short of it was that my children got on the phone and each took a turn telling me that their father would be very upset to see me grieving the way I was."

"And the long of it?"

"It wasn't something so cut and dry. The best way I can explain it, without droning on for hours, is that one morning I forgot to be sad."

"Was it really that simple?"

"No. Not really." Eileen turned off the ignition, unbuckled her seat belt, and opened up her driver's-side door. But instead of getting right out, she turned to Daisy. "It wasn't simple or easy at all. But time does heal. So does allowing other people's love in your heart. I started realizing that I was so consumed by my pain that I was blocking out any chance for happiness. I realized that I'd even been taking my children's love and patience for granted. Kristy told me that she'd felt like she'd lost me, too." Her smile turned wistful. "I couldn't have that."

"So you started allowing happiness back in."

"I did. And hope." After she got out of the car and Daisy did, too, Eileen said softly, "That's when my son Blake reminded me about how much I had always wanted to visit Australia. He asked what I was waiting for." She clicked a button on her key chain and locked the car. "That's when I took a leap of faith and booked that ticket."

Daisy thought there was a pretty big gap between finding hope and traveling to Australia by oneself. "Weren't you afraid?"

She pressed a hand to her chest. "Oh, yes. I can still practically feel how hard my heart was beating when I walked inside that plane and sat down. I hadn't been on a plane in years. I had never been out of the country, and I was going on a two-week journey without a single person that I knew by my side. At that moment, I had never missed my husband more."

"But it went all right."

"It did. And you know why?" When Daisy shook her head, she continued. "Because as I was flying over the ocean, I remembered that my Jim hated to fly. If he was alive, I wouldn't have gone."

Eileen was almost sounding like she was glad that he hadn't been there. "But—"

"I loved Jim, but that didn't mean that everything about us was perfect or that we always wanted the same things." Softly, she added, "I realized that I was still me. God had given me a lovely marriage and a wonderful husband and father of my children. But He was now also giving me the opportunity to do something else and follow other dreams." She smiled again, then started walking toward the diner.

Daisy followed suit.

Just as they opened the door and felt that first blast of air-conditioning on their skin, Daisy said, "So maybe there is a silver lining about my diagnosis?"

"I don't know if anyone would call a lupus diagnosis a blessing. But I do know that life is a whole lot better when you're going forward. Wishing things were different doesn't get you anything good."

Those words stayed with Daisy all through lunch and till later that afternoon, when she was sitting on her back porch watching the bumblebees hover among the lavender like mini blimps.

She vowed then to try to look beyond her pain and worry and uncertainty about the future. She would find her own Australia, even if it was simply starting a new project around the house. Who knew? Maybe she could even take a bus trip to South Dakota. She'd always wanted to do that.

And when her mind flitted on to Stephen Stauffer—for the first time in memory, she didn't push it away. Instead, she tried to think of him in a new light.

And wondered if he, too, had unrealized Australia in his future.

CHAPTER 11

Friday, July 13

The first thing Noah noticed when he got to work was that it was unnaturally quiet. Then he noticed that the fire chief was in his office with Sheriff Brewer and Deputy Beck. When he walked down the hall, he spied Chad and two firefighters sitting in the rec room, nursing cups of coffee and looking grim. There was also another man and a woman in the room. They were looking at their iPad screens and talking.

The whole atmosphere looked so strained that Noah could practically feel the tension through the glass.

Not wanting to be caught staring, Noah rushed on, but drew to a stop again when he spied Chad looking through the window at him. Noah held up a hand in greeting, and Chad waved him on inside.

Mitch and one of the women nodded in his direction when he entered. The chief nodded, too, then leaned over and murmured something to one of the men sitting next to him.

Noah began to feel uneasy. "What's going on?" he asked

Chad when he got to the table. "Did something happen last night that I didn't hear about?" Usually, if there was a big fire or something, he would have gotten a call to come in. But sometimes the men and women on call took care of an emergency that wasn't big enough to ask for more support—only bad enough to stress out everyone who was on duty.

Chad's voice was tense when he replied. "Mitch and Reid got called out last night to another Amish household."

Pulling out an empty chair, Noah sat down. "Oh? What happened?"

"When they arrived, they discovered a man had collapsed. He was barely coherent, in visible pain, and didn't respond to their questions." Chad paused, then said, "What I'm trying to say is that his symptoms were almost a carbon copy to Verba Stauffer's."

Noah felt his body go cold. "What happened to him?"

"He died en route to Caverna."

Belatedly, Noah realized that most everyone else in the room had been watching for his reaction. Fearing even more bad news, he pressed his palm on the top of the table. "What is it that you aren't telling me?"

"That they got the final toxicology reports from the state for Verba."

Chad sighed. "Noah, I hate to tell you this, but it looks like Verba didn't die of natural causes at all. She was poisoned."

"We're pretty positive that he died of the same thing that Verba did."

"Verba Stauffer was in her eighties. Was this man?"

"No. He had just turned fifty."

"But his symptoms were that much like hers?" Noah was trying to imagine a younger man experiencing the same things.

"Yep," Doug, one of the more experienced firefighters, said. "Mitch recorded the same symptoms." He spouted off some more results. "That's when Mitch talked to the chief and the chief called in Brewer and Dr. Kim."

"It looks like both of our victims drank something that had been accidentally tampered with."

Sheriff Brewer's expression was solemn. "As much as it pains me to say it, we also need to consider the possibility that both of these deaths might not be accidental."

Chad's eyebrows rose but he didn't say anything.

Noah sure wished he would have, though. He needed some clarification. At the moment, he was feeling like he was hearing everything but nothing was making sense. Sure, he'd thought there was something strange going on at the Stauffers' house, but there was a big difference between feeling suspicious and suspecting the worst. "I'm no detective, but I don't see how that makes sense. Verba was no different than any other Amish woman in the area. She stayed at home and took care of the house, farm, and her family. There's no reason anyone would want to poison her."

"We don't actually know that, though. Do we?" Mitch asked. When Noah gaped at him, Mitch held out a placating hand. "I'm sorry, but we need to at least consider every possibility, right?"

For a moment, he recalled his mother's words about both Verba and the Stauffer family. While they weren't exactly well liked, Noah didn't believe that they were hated.

And even if the gossip about them selling moonshine was true, it wouldn't have made someone want to kill Verba.

Feeling better about his reasonings, Noah shook his head. "I'm not saying the Amish are perfect people, but we're godly people. Murder isn't a common occurrence."

"I agree with you on both things," Doug said, speaking up. "She did seem like an average grandmother with lots of family surrounding her. And, yes, the Amish are faithful people. But that doesn't change the facts. The toxicology reports don't lie, Noah. There was poison in her bloodstream, and if our hunch is correct, we're going to find the same thing in this latest victim's blood, too."

Noah slumped against his chair, knowing what Doug said was completely true. But if this was now two Amish people who had been poisoned, what in the world was happening? "Who was the man who died?"

Chad flipped through his notes. "His name is John Beachy. Does that ring a bell?"

Noah searched his memory, but he couldn't place him. "Where did he live? Was it in Horse Cave?"

"No, he lived on a pretty substantial farm off Highway 88." He waved his hand. "For what it's worth, the farm took me by surprise. It was like night and day from the Stauffer house. It was large, with at least five bedrooms. It was a showstopper, too. Two story, sprawling, and constructed of both limestone and white siding. Landscaped real nice, too. Lots of tended flower beds, trimmed bushes, and fruit trees."

"It sounds like quite a house."

"It was impressive," Chad said. "Bordering on fancy, too. All of us were surprised when we realized it was Amish owned. I don't know what the family does, but they make a good living."

Doug turned to Noah. "Does anything about that house sound unusual to you?"

Noah shrugged. He knew no one was trying to be rude, but he still felt a little like he was a second-class citizen in their eyes. As much as he worked hard to fit in and simply be thought of as the newest EMT, it was obvious that he was always going to be the *Amish EMT*. Part of the team, yes. But completely fitting in? Maybe not ever.

"It might make sense," he finally replied.

Doug narrowed his eyes. "That's no kind of answer. What does that mean?"

Mitch grunted. "Watch it, Doug."

That soft warning was all Noah needed to feel like he wasn't alone anymore. Feeling more at ease, he looked around the table. "The Amish are just like anyone else. Some are well off, some aren't. Our faith is what connects us, not necessarily our business sense. Now, the fact that his last name is Beachy and that he lived on the outskirts gives me a better idea of what he might be like."

"What do you know?" Mitch said, walking over to him. "Noah, I know we're putting you on the spot, but I'd like an idea of what kind of man this John Beachy was before I go knocking on his family's door and start asking questions."

Noah knew that explanation was fair enough. "All right. Well, there's a new community of Amish that's sprung up in the Cub Run area in the last five years. They're New Order."

While Mitch listened intently, Doug looked around at the rest of them. "I don't know what that means."

"It means that they're more progressive," Noah explained, trying to make it sound as simple as possible. "Different Amish communities have some different rules, if you will. Most of the Amish who have been living here for a while are Old Order, like my family. Basically, we don't allow phones or rubber on the wheels of our buggies. We are private people. Then there's New Order, like the group in Cub Run. Women might have jobs outside the home. Usually, they can have a phone in the house. They can fly on an airplane, and do more mission work outside of the community."

Doug scratched his head, obviously attempting to process it. "Is that all of them?"

"Oh, no. There's even more conservative, like the Swartzen-truber, and even more progressive, like the Electric Amish in the south of our state."

Chad shook his head. "Until I met you and really got to know you, I thought everyone who was Amish was just alike."

Noah couldn't resist smiling. "We get that a lot. Don't worry about it."

Just as Doug was about to say something, they heard footsteps down the hall and saw Sheriff Brewer and Deputy Beck peer in at them.

"This is Noah, Sheriff," Mitch called out.

"Good to meet you, Noah. I'm Pat Brewer," the sheriff said. "This is Eddie Beck. I think we've met in passing once or twice before."

"Yes." As they shook hands, he said, "Hello again."

"Mitch and the fire chief had a lot of good things to say about you. For that matter, Dr. Kim did, too. You're earning a real good reputation."

"Good to hear," Noah said modestly, though inside he had a feeling he was grinning ear to ear. This path he had chosen to take wasn't easy, and there had been many days when he'd gotten on his knees and prayed, asking the Lord why He'd put him on this path in the first place.

After a couple more people shook hands with the deputy, Sheriff Brewer sat down with a sigh at the remaining empty chair surrounding the table. "Noah, since I was hired on here in Hart County, I've had quite a few occasions to work with the Amish on cases."

Noah nodded, thinking of the man stalking Hannah Hilty, the terrible string of attacks against women, and even most recently, the gunfight out at Floyd's Pond. "Things haven't been particularly quiet around here in Hart County, and that's a fact."

Lines crinkled around Sheriff Brewer's pale-gray eyes. "I could say that the string of crime around here has made me feel real useful, but I wouldn't mind having the opportunity to spend a few more nights sleeping instead of worrying about unsolved crimes."

Doug looked around at the group. "I'm still not convinced that these deaths were intentional. I think we need more information."

"I agree," Sheriff Brewer said. After a brief pause, he turned to Noah. "My deputy and me are going to be paying both residences a visit, but you know as well as I do that most Amish don't trust outsiders on a good day."

"Most do try to keep their lives private," Noah agreed.

"If we throw in someone close to one of the victims, well, it's a given that me and Deputy Beck are going to be treated to a lot of stares and silences."

Noah knew he wasn't wrong. Most Amish liked to keep their distance from the police even in the best of circumstances.

But though he was Amish, he was also just an EMT in training. "How does that concern me?"

"Someone told me that they saw you talking with some of the gals living in the Stauffer house. Is that true?"

Noah nodded, thinking people probably saw him standing on the sidewalk with both Esther and Sadie. "Is there something wrong with that?"

"Wrong? Not at all." After exchanging a look with the

other men surrounding them, Sheriff Brewer smiled sheep-ishly. "What I'm trying to ask you is if you'll help me by doing a little talking to folks yourself."

"I'm no detective."

"Of course not! But you are Amish, and you are an EMT. People will trust you. Maybe tell you things that will help us figure out who is poisoning people."

It sounded a lot like he was being asked to lie and snitch on people. That wasn't the type of man he was.

Then there was his new relationship with Sadie. He didn't have to wonder how she would react to him prying out her secrets, then telling them to the sheriff.

She would be hurt and confused and no doubt refuse to speak to him ever again. And he wouldn't blame her, either.

With all that heavy on his mind, he finally spoke. "I'm not sure if I'm the best person for the job." Or, if he even wanted such a job. Actually, he was certain he did not want it.

"No, you're the *only* person for the job," Mitch said, sur-prising him.

Noah grimaced. "Mitch, you don't understand."

"Actually, I don't know if you do," he retorted. "This isn't a game. People's lives are on the line. We need you to help us figure out how people are getting poisoned before another person gets sick."

Though his heart ached to argue the point, his head knew he didn't have a choice. Not only was his task more impor-tant than a burgeoning relationship with a certain girl with violet eyes, it was an order from his boss. He was also in the business of saving lives. And though this wasn't what he'd ever imagined he'd be doing, he couldn't refuse.

If he wanted to keep his job, he couldn't say no.

"I'll do the best I can."

Sheriff Brewer smiled as he stood up. "Thank you. I'm real glad we're all going to be working together. Stop by my office the moment you have some news. No need to call first. I'll stop whatever I'm doing to hear what you've found out."

"I'll do that."

"Today is Friday. Hope to see you by Wednesday, if not before," he added as he strode out the door.

Minutes later, everyone else in the room filed out. Leaving Noah to dwell on his promises and regrets . . . and wondering what he'd just agreed to do.

CHAPTER 12

Saturday, July 14

Sadie was stunned to see Noah drive up the driveway—and in a courting buggy, of all things!

Hearing her gasp, Willis walked to her side and peered through the window. "Why is he here? And what is he doing in that?"

Sadie shook her head. She had no idea what was going through Noah's mind. All she did know was that Willis was gazing at that buggy like it was about to do them all harm.

"Maybe he's coming to deliver more first aid kits," Monroe said with a smirk as he joined them.

"I think he's interested in something besides our welfare," Stephen commented as he approached with Esther.

Inwardly Sadie groaned. Now the whole family was standing in front of the living room window and peering out at Noah. Could anything be more awkward?

"Did you ask Noah to return?" Stephen asked.

"*Nee.* Seeing him is as much a surprise to me as it is to any of you. I was just sitting in the living room sewing when I spied the buggy on the drive."

"Are you sure?" Stephen pressed.

"*Jah*," Sadie replied, once again wishing she understood where all the suspicion and worry was stemming from.

Esther intervened. "Daed, Sadie and I saw him when we went into town on Thursday."

"You didn't tell me that," Stephen replied.

"There was no reason to. Noah ain't here for you. He's here for Sadie. He likes her." Looking smug, Esther said, "I think he's come calling."

Willis turned to Sadie and frowned. "How could he be interested in you?"

"She *is* a pretty thing," Monroe interjected. "I'd be surprised if he *wasn't* interested in you, Sadie."

"But you are pregnant," Willis said.

Feeling like everyone was staring at her stomach, she curved her hands protectively around her middle. "I promise that I didn't ask Noah to come over."

The knock at the door prevented them all from continuing the crazy, disturbing conversation.

"He's here now," Monroe said as he turned to open the door. "Now, I suggest that everyone settle down and try to act normal for once. Let him court Sadie. What can be the harm?"

"He could bring the sheriff here," Stephen muttered.

Sadie was still gaping at her uncle when Monroe opened the door. "Hiya, Noah," he said. "Sorry about the delay."

Noah half smiled at Monroe before he looked over at the rest of the family.

Sadie felt like grabbing his hand and pulling him out into

the bright sunlight. Anything was better than subjecting him to five people's rather rude stares.

But instead of looking perturbed, he met each person's gaze, then at last focused on her. "Hi."

She felt her cheeks heat. "Hello."

Turning to Stephen, he said, "I came over to take Sadie for a ride. May I take her out for a couple of hours?"

Sadie interrupted before her uncle could answer. "*Danke*, Noah."

But Stephen stepped forward, blocking her way. "Why do you need her for so long?"

"I thought I'd take her over to my parents' house. They've been eager to meet Sadie." In spite of Willis and Stephen practically shooting daggers at him, Noah seemed completely at ease.

"I bet," Monroe said. Moving to her side, he said, "Is that what you want to do?"

Sadie hesitated. Though she wanted to spend time with Noah, she couldn't help but think about Willis's warning. He hadn't been wrong. It was almost a certainty that once Noah found out about her condition, he wasn't going to want anything more to do with her.

"Go on," Esther urged. "Remember what I said. All bark, no bite."

"I'd like to go for a ride, Noah. *Danke*. And, *jah*, I'd like to meet your family, too," she said at last. "If you'll give me five minutes, I'll be ready."

Looking pleased, Noah nodded. "Take your time. I'll wait for you outside."

Sadie hurried to Monroe and Stephen's room. Her things were in a bottom dresser drawer. She quickly put on a pair of tennis shoes, then ran down the hall to the bathroom and washed her hands and face. When she walked out, she was relieved to see that Willis and Monroe were gone and Esther was in the kitchen.

"I'll be back soon, Onkle Stephen," she said.

Her uncle looked even more distressed. "Sadie, I don't want to sound uncaring, but I don't think Noah Freeman is here only to introduce you to his family. I think he wants something else."

"What could he want?"

"Information. Don't tell him anything. You hear me?"

That unsettled feeling that she was missing something vital going on returned—tenfold. "Onkle Stephen, I don't know what you are talking about. What could Noah want to know about that is such a secret?"

Pure frustration lit his features. "Just be careful. And whatever you do, don't bring the sheriff back around here."

"Why would the sheriff want to come over?"

Esther rushed out to join them. "Don't mind my *daed*, Sadie," she said with a forced laugh. "He worries too much. Go enjoy yourself, okay?"

Gripping her purse, Sadie rushed out the door. She didn't know what Noah wanted or why her relatives were in such a tizzy, but she hoped to find out and soon.

"MY FAMILY IS real eager to meet you," Noah said as he guided a beautiful, silver-colored gelding down a back road.

Now that they were alone, Sadie kept waiting for him to state why he had really wanted to see her. But so far, nothing seemed out of the ordinary. Actually, his behavior and actions were right along the lines of how Harlan had acted.

Remembering how she'd believed so many things that had been obviously untrue, she steeled herself. "Noah, I'm not sure why you called . . . or why your family would want to meet me."

Holding the reins with one hand, he smiled at her. "I came over because I canna seem to stop thinking about you. And my parents are eager to meet Sadie Detweiler—because I've been talking about you for the last two weeks."

"Really?"

"Really."

"All right, then." Enjoying the feel of the open carriage, she said, "This is the first courting buggy I've ever been in."

"Yeah? Well, what do you think?"

"I like it. My family observes such strict rules, no one was allowed to ride in topless buggies. Every time we passed one on the road, my father would deliver a ten-minute sermon about the dangers of them."

"For your safety?"

"Oh, *nee*. For my soul."

"I'm sorry, Sadie. They sound like they were mighty difficult."

"They were." Even though she felt guilty for even admitting that much, it felt so good to be honest. Realizing then that she'd let her uncle's paranoia sabotage the outing, she said, "I'm sorry about how my uncle acted when you arrived."

"What was going on? Do you know?"

"Nothing. They're just really private people."

"Ah." Glancing her way again, his light-gray eyes seeming to peer into her soul, he seemed to come to a decision. "Sadie, do you feel safe there? I mean, is there something going on in that house that you are worried or upset about?"

"Why would you ask that?"

"No reason," he said quickly. "No offense, but your relatives all seem odd."

She felt like warning lights were going off in her head.

"Everyone has been missing Verba," she said, though she realized with a start that that wasn't the case at all.

"Of course you have."

"It was so sudden. One minute, it seemed like she was her usual cranky self. The next minute, she was on the floor in pain."

"I'm sure that was hard. Uh, why do you think she died? Any idea?"

"I don't know. Noah, why do you ask? I mean, you're the one who has medical training."

"Didn't the doctors say anything to y'all about her death?"

She was feeling flustered now. "If they told Willis or Stephen, neither of them told me. It . . . it was simply the Lord's will."

"So you don't remember her eating or drinking anything unusual?"

"*Nee*. I mean, I don't think so."

"Are you sure?"

It seemed Stephen was right after all. Noah hadn't come over because he liked her. He had come for answers, and he was using her to get them.

Maybe he wasn't any better than Harlan. He was obviously only planning to pretend to like her until he got what he wanted.

Feeling like her world had just caved in, she said quietly, "I think I'd like to go home now."

"But we're almost at my *haus*."

"I don't want to meet your parents or your family anymore. Please take me home."

He pulled the buggy over to the side of the road and pulled up the brake. "Sadie, don't get upset. I'm sorry if I overstepped myself."

"You certainly did. You've been interrogating me like you were with the police."

Something flashed in his eyes before he attempted to hide it. "If I did sound like that, I had good reason. I care about you."

She didn't know a lot of things, but Sadie knew that he wasn't asking her those questions because he was concerned about her. "Noah, you should know something about me. Before I moved here, I was involved in a serious relationship with a man. I thought I loved him."

"You only thought?"

"I discovered that he didn't love me back after I . . ." She took a deep breath, intending to tell him about the baby. But as much as she wanted to blurt her news, she simply couldn't. His questioning had been hard enough to deal with. She didn't want to see his disgust, too.

"After what?"

"After I . . . after I gave him my trust."

Noah frowned. "He really hurt you, didn't he?"

She nodded. "Because of that, I guess I'm a little skittish where relationships are concerned. I'm not sure what your intentions are, but I'm . . . well, I'm not sure if I am ready for a relationship right now."

He stared at her, looking upset. "I understand."

"I'm glad you do." She wondered if it was because he felt guilty about questioning her about Verba's death, or if there was another reason.

Still acting pensive, he coaxed the horse to turn around on the road, then headed back to the Stauffers' home.

Feeling like she'd just lost something important while also gaining something back of herself, Sadie clasped her hands tightly on her lap and looked straight ahead.

She tried to ignore the tension wafting from Noah.

Tried to not notice how much fun riding in a courting buggy was, or how good the breeze felt on her face and body.

Fifteen minutes after they had first left the Stauffers, Noah at last pulled onto the drive as he said, "This sure didn't go how I thought it would. I am sorry."

"I am, too."

Reaching out for her hand, he said, "I know I handled everything wrong, but I really do like you. I'll do better next time."

Sadie liked him, too. But she'd made mistakes before. She knew it would hurt even more if she let down her guard and got her heart stomped on because of that. She needed to end things now.

"My relatives don't want you here, Noah. And because I owe them so much, I don't think it's a good idea for us to go out on any more drives together." She took another deep breath, then forced herself to finish her little speech. "As a matter of fact, I think you should stay away."

"Stay away?" His eyes lit up. "I'm sorry but I don't think that's possible. You've bewitched me, you see."

"Oh, Noah." Her heart softened . . . until she realized that he now wasn't even looking at her.

Noah was staring at Monroe climbing out of the storm cellar with a cardboard box in his hands.

CHAPTER 13

Monday, July 16

The weeds were unruly and stubborn, and Noah had two sizable blisters on his palms to show for it. His shirt was also soaked with sweat. It clung to him like a wet rag. He would give a lot of money to be able to take it off and finish the job bare-chested.

Since that wasn't possible, he pushed the brim of his hat farther down on his face and picked up the spade again. If he kept up the pace, he'd have a good section of his mother's garden tamed within the hour.

Maybe.

Or, maybe not, he decided as he heard the back door open.

"Noah, I couldn't believe it when I looked outside and saw you standing there," his little brother, Harry, called out. "What are you doing?"

Noah leaned back on his heels. "I'm thinking it's pretty obvious. Ain't so?"

Harry, who at nineteen wasn't all that little, tilted his head to one side. "Not really. Looks to me like you are trying to kill Mamm's zucchinis."

"*Nee*, I'm trying to pull out these weeds that are choking them."

"*Jah*, you're doing that, for sure," Harry said in a superior tone of voice as he joined Noah in the garden. "Except for the fact that you're taking out a good amount of the zucchini roots, too." As if Noah was a child, Harry bent down and picked up one of the roots. "See? You're killing them."

Taking a better look at his work, Noah feared his brother might be right. He'd been slaving away in the hot afternoon sun, trying to do something of worth . . . but all he'd done was butcher innocent plants.

He sighed.

Harry grinned, revealing the best teeth in the family.

Actually, Harry had gotten all the best looks in the family, too. Oh, it wasn't that the rest of them were ugly. It was that Harry was mighty good looking. Their sister Melody had once described him as heart-stoppingly handsome. It seemed all the girls thought so.

Harry would have probably gotten a big head about that, too, *if* Melody had said that phrase in a less-sarcastic tone.

So, Harry was handsome. Dark-blue eyes. Dark-brown hair, athletic build, and blinding white, perfectly straight teeth. However, all that had ever mattered to Noah was that his little brother had also been blessed with an aptitude for farming, which meant their father never chided Noah for wanting to pursue a different occupation.

Climbing to his feet, Noah said, "I thought you were going to be working in the barn with Daed today."

"I did. He and I went out to look at the cornfields, too, but

Daed had to go. He wanted to take Mamm over to the Dollar Store and out to lunch today."

"Oh, yeah? Where'd they go?"

"They went to El Mazatlan in Munfordville."

"Sounds good. You didn't want to go?"

"I wasn't invited." He grinned. "It was just as well. They've got marriage on their minds."

"Marriage and who?"

"You."

"Me? I'm not courting anyone."

"That's not what I heard," Harry said in a singsong voice. "I heard you pulled out the courting buggy."

"If you heard that, then you probably heard that my efforts didn't go too well."

After taking another look at the garden, Noah sighed and headed up the back porch. A few years back, Silas and some of his construction employees built a real nice wooden porch with an overhang. It was cool and comfortable, thanks to the wicker furniture that all the kids had gone in on for their parents' thirtieth anniversary.

Harry picked up the spade and hoe that Noah had left near the zucchini. After setting them against the house, he went inside to get them both some water.

Noah sipped it gratefully . . . and realized that nothing about Harry's visit was unplanned. His brother didn't carry pitchers of water outside for family members unless there was a reason behind it. "Who asked you to stay? Mamm or Daed?"

"Mamm." Looking a little guilty, he added, "And Joanna."

"Joanna, too? Why?"

"Joanna thinks you should stay away from that girl."

"Sadie is a perfectly nice woman."

Harry shrugged. "Maybe she is. I saw her from a distance the other day. She's real pretty, I'll give her that. But there are lots of pretty, nice women in the area who aren't connected to the Stauffer family."

"I didn't think you were the type of man to pay so much attention to gossip."

"I'm not."

"But?"

"Well, we're all real proud of you, Noah. None of us wants you to get involved with a girl who might bring you trouble. Joanna says all the time that she didn't just marry Andrew; she married his family, too. Would you really want to get stuck with them?"

"What I want isn't going to matter anyway. Sadie asked me to stay away from her."

"Oh. *Gut.*"

"I didn't say I would do it though." He coughed. "But I might."

"Because of all of us warning you off?"

"*Nee.* Because I saw something when I dropped Sadie off. That's why I've been in Mamm's garden, killing vegetables. I've been trying to figure out if I should go speak to the sheriff."

Harry's dark-blue eyes widened. "What did you see? Was it that bad?"

Not wanting to go into the whole story about how he'd been asked to question and spy on Sadie's relatives, Noah shrugged. "I'm still trying to decide what to do."

Harry stretched out his legs. "This might not mean anything to you, but . . . do you remember when all of us broke the door?"

Noah grinned. "*Jah.*"

When all of them were still in school, their parents had left to attend a funeral. They'd been given strict instructions to behave and look after Melody. Of course, within two hours, he, Joanna, Silas, and Harry got in a fight. Two of them— maybe it was Jo and Harry?—ran into their parents' room and slammed the door.

That, of course, led to a lot of yelling, shoving, and pounding on it. And, ultimately, a broken door.

All five of them were staring at it in horror when their parents came home.

They were mad. *Real* mad.

However, the five of them, even Mel, stood together and refused to point fingers.

Their father, after yelling until he was good and hoarse, finally looked at their mother in dismay.

She, to everyone's surprise, started laughing. "At least no one is bleeding, John," their mother murmured.

As they realized the yelling was over, they all relaxed. That's when Melody blurted, "They took real *gut* care of me, Daed."

Which made everyone in the room start laughing.

"You all sure don't make our lives easy," Daed said at last. "But I wouldn't have you any other way."

Thinking back to that evening, Noah smiled. "We had to do hours and hours of chores to make up for that night."

"It was a real *gut* night."

"It was. But I have no idea why you brought it up."

"Well, I was thinking that if you didn't feel good about telling on the rest of us when you were fourteen or so . . ."

Noah nodded as he finally understood. "Then I shouldn't feel much different about tattling on Sadie's family."

Harry nodded slowly. "I came out here to warn you off . . . but maybe you gave me a good reminder about things, too."

"What is that? Not to tattle?"

"Yeah. But also that sometimes good people make foolish choices."

Harry was right. Right about everything. Noah wasn't going to start reporting back to the sheriff. He wasn't going to let all his fears about what "might" be happening interfere with his pursuit of Sadie.

"I got paid two days ago. Want to go to get some lunch?"

Harry grinned. "Sure."

Noah pulled at his damp shirt. "Give me ten minutes to shower and then we'll go."

"Thanks, Noah."

Noah didn't respond, but he knew he didn't need to. Something had happened between him and Harry today—and it was pretty special.

It might have even changed his life.

CHAPTER 14

Monday night, July 16

It was late. Easily past eleven. Sadie's body was tired and she yearned to fall into a deep sleep, but no matter how much she tried to relax, she couldn't stop thinking about their stressful day.

It hadn't started out that way. She, Esther, and Monroe had tended the garden in the morning while Stephen and Willis worked in the cellar. Monroe was a great help, and his penchant for joking made the chore much easier.

But when Sheriff Brewer stopped by that afternoon, all the ease of the morning vanished in an instant. He said he'd come to see how they were doing after Verba's death, but everyone in the house knew he'd had a different agenda in mind when he sat at the kitchen table.

No sheriff called without a reason.

Not sure where she fit into the conversation, Sadie lurked in the doorway. Because she hadn't known Verba all that well, she didn't feel as if she had anything to add to the conversation. But she also couldn't seem to stay completely out of sight. The sheriff's questions about Willis's and Stephen's business were too compelling.

Sadie was embarrassed to admit it, but until that moment, she hadn't dared to question what, exactly, her male relatives did to make money. Oh, she wasn't a fool. She knew they were doing something in the cellar, and sensed that it was probably something no one should know about. But she also had a lifetime of being told to not question anything her father did. Though she now realized that her parents' rules had been excessive, it still felt almost impossible to not honor an older relative's wishes.

Then, of course, there was the fact that these relatives had also taken her in when she had no one else, and were both caring and supportive of her. How could she question or betray how they chose to live their lives when they'd accepted her so easily?

But even though she was loyal to them, the sheriff's presence in the house brought forth a new sense of foreboding. What if something was actually very wrong in this house? What would she do then?

Though Sheriff Brewer's visit had only lasted thirty minutes, its effects were felt for hours. Esther seemed more worried than usual. Monroe's good mood vanished, and he started snapping at everyone. Willis paced in the living room, and Stephen acted like a fierce wind might knock him down.

Sadie was never so glad when the time came to pull out her pallet in the kitchen and lie down. Things had to look better in the morning. They had to.

Just as she was finally about to fall asleep, she heard all three men start arguing, then walk out the front door. It slammed behind them.

Esther jerked awake. When she looked at Sadie and realized her eyes were open, she sat up. "What's going on?"

"The men are arguing," she whispered.

Esther rubbed her eyes. "About what?"

"The sheriff's visit, I think."

Before Esther could ask Sadie another sleepy question, the men's voices got louder.

"You shouldn't have said a thing to the sheriff!" Willis yelled.

"I didn't have much of a choice. He asked me about the moonshine," Monroe fired back. "It ain't like he couldn't go down to the cellar and find it."

"Watch your mouth, boy," Stephen interjected.

"Oh, Daed, please. Don't act as if I'm a child."

"You might as well be."

"It's too late for that. If we get charged with trafficking, I'll get in as much trouble as both of you." Monroe's voice rose and became even more frustrated. "And that really burns me, since I didn't want to do this in the first place."

"That might make you feel better, but you are still involved, Monroe," his grandfather said, now whispering. "You better start watching what you're doing."

"You're one to talk. You're the one who's making all the mistakes."

"Halt!" Willis barked.

"Daed, you know I'm right," Monroe said softly.

From her pallet on the floor, Sadie closed her eyes and tried to ignore the angry voices drifting through the walls from the yard, but it was a hopeless task. The men were whispering and screaming at each other, mostly loudly enough for her to hear every word.

"I think Monroe might have a point," Stephen said to

Willis, his voice an oasis of calm now. "I think the sheriff is worried about something more than just us making liquor. Something must have happened."

"We have too many orders to fill to stop," Willis retorted. "If we stop, we lose everything."

"If we don't, we may lose it just the same," Stephen said.

"Oh, boy," Esther murmured in the darkness. "My grandfather hates it when my *daed* talks down to him like that." After a second, she looked at Sadie. "I guess you're pretty shocked about what you're hearing, huh?"

That her relatives were brewing moonshine and distributing it? Sadie couldn't lie. "I am."

As Willis began some long story about his ancestors, his voice faded into mere staccato beats punctuating the air.

After a few seconds passed, Esther spoke again. "Do you hate us now? I know what they do is bad."

Esther sounded shaken up. Peering over at her, Sadie's eyes adjusted to the darkness. Faint bands of moonlight shone through the window. The bands cast the room into various shades of gray—and enabled Sadie to catch a good look at her cousin. Esther was sitting upright on her pallet, clenching her sheets against her chest as if she was attempting to shield herself from what she might hear.

"I don't hate you."

"Just my brother, father, and grandfather?"

"*Nee.* Not even them," she replied, meaning every word. "You all took me in when I had no one. I could never hate any of you."

"I hope you still mean that in the morning. I really like you, Sadie. I would hate it if you started ignoring me."

"I wouldn't do that. I won't do that."

As the men started yelling again, Sadie noticed Esther

looked even more alone. "Has this happened before? I mean, these late-night arguments?" Sadie knew some families were loud by nature. Maybe this was the case, and she just hadn't experienced it here until now.

"It has," Esther replied, "but not for a while." With a sigh, she continued. "I guess it's to be expected, what with three generations of men all living under one roof. They are bound to have disagreements."

Thinking back to the sprawling farmhouse where she grew up in Millersburg, Sadie nodded. When she was a little girl, she used to imagine that the whole world lived somewhere in that big house. It had been added on to so many times that it resembled a rabbit warren, zigging and zagging along the property, narrow hallways connecting multiple living areas. At one time, they'd had four generations living together.

And, yes, there had been disagreements from time to time. But it had been about chores or money or how a child was behaving. They'd taken place in the kitchen or in front of many people. Never in the dark in the middle of the night.

And never—not even when they'd kicked her out—had anyone yelled like the way the men were.

All at once the emotions she'd tried so hard to forget and stifle flooded back. For a single, fanciful moment, Sadie allowed herself to imagine what it would have felt like to stand up for herself and yell at her parents and grandfather.

To tell them that although she had made a mistake, she wasn't a liar and that the unwanted baby she was carrying was a member of the family, too. To lift her chin, look at them all in the eye, and tell them that they should be ashamed of themselves for casting her aside like something used and tainted.

But she hadn't.

She and Esther were silent for a while. Sadie closed her eyes and tried to block out the noise. More minutes passed. She curved her arms around her stomach, maybe unconsciously trying to muffle the sound of the angry words so her baby wouldn't hear.

Then they heard a fist slam against a wall.

Beside her, Esther cringed. "This is a really bad fight. I don't know if I've ever heard them get so out of control."

All Sadie knew to do was try to calm her cousin. "This is the first time they've argued since your grandmother went to heaven. Ain't so?"

Esther nodded. "*Jah*."

"Maybe that is part of what they are feeling. They're uncomfortable because she's not here to calm everyone down."

Esther grunted. "Um, I don't know about that. No one would have ever called her presence in the *haus* especially comforting."

Sadie kept her silence but privately agreed with that. Verba had been efficient and collected, not warm or comforting. Thinking back to her first few days in the house, Verba had found her a cot and bedding to sleep on but had never gone out of her way to hug her, ask about how she was doing, or make her feel welcome.

Sadie hadn't minded too much, though. After all, being given a place to sleep was better than being told to leave.

Esther sighed again. "Mommi wasn't real nice, but she wouldn't have allowed the men to come to blows. Right now I would give a lot for her to be here."

"What would she be doing to help this situation?"

"She would have marched outside and snapped at all of them for waking her up. Oh, but she would have yelled at them good. Even Dawdi would have told her he was sorry."

Sadie couldn't help but smile at the image. At the moment, all three of the men outside were yelling really hateful things at each other. "You really think they would have listened to her?" she whispered when at last the voices fell silent again.

"Oh, to be sure. They knew better than not to listen. She would have made them pay."

"Goodness. She really was tough, wasn't she?" said Sadie.

"Oh, *jah*. She wasn't that nice to any of us, and the worst to my *daed*."

"That's awful."

"*Jah*. I think the men are secretly happy she's gone."

"Even Monroe?" asked Sadie. "Monroe is so kind. Out of all of them, he seems to be the most easygoing and warm member of the family."

"Oh, *jah*. Of course even Monroe. He's nice, but he doesn't like it when people don't act the way they should. He's tougher than he looks, Sadie."

Esther's words sounded ominous. Feeling a chill run down her spine, Sadie said, "Though she wasn't very nice, right now I'm kind of wishing she was here so they would listen. At least they respected her enough to do that!"

"They didn't mind her because they respected her, Sadie."

"Why did they, then?" she asked hesitantly, half afraid to hear the answer.

"It was because they were afraid of her." The air between them went still, almost as if the Lord needed Sadie to hear Esther's words—and take them to heart. "Fear can make a person do most anything, you know."

Was that true? Sadie wasn't sure. She didn't want it to be.

"Esther, I don't know if that's right. I mean—"

"Hush!" Esther hissed under her breath. "I just heard the door open," she whispered, her voice panicked. "Whatever you do, pretend you are asleep. You don't want the men to know you overheard them."

Sadie immediately closed her eyes and pulled the sheet and quilt up around her shoulders.

And tried to remain motionless when a pair of footsteps walked into the kitchen and paused for a full minute before stepping away again.

Heart pounding, she closed her eyes tight, curved her arms more firmly around herself.

And tried very, very hard to think about what she could do to calm her fearful heart.

Only later, when the rest of the house fell silent and Esther was sleeping soundly next to her, did Sadie realize that during her discussion with Esther, she'd forgotten a very important question.

She'd neglected to ask what it was about Verba Stauffer that had made the men in the house so afraid.

CHAPTER 15

Wednesday, July 18

The letter came as a surprise. If she was honest with herself, though, Sadie knew she should have expected to hear something from her mother. Mamm had a kind heart; and even though she would never go against her husband's wishes, she wouldn't have agreed to *never* communicate with Sadie again.

But that didn't mean that her mother's letter was going to be pleasant to read.

"What do you think she wrote?" Monroe asked.

"I couldn't begin to imagine." Sadie smiled hesitantly at her cousin.

Monroe had brought in the letter only a few minutes before. He'd done it without fanfare, too. After calling out her name, he set it next to her latest sewing project before reaching in a cabinet to get a glass for water. Now he was sitting next to her, sipping his water and not even making fun of her for staring at the envelope like it could blow up at any second.

His presence gave her the peace of mind to divulge a little more. "I was close to her. I'm thinking she might be missing me as much as I miss her."

"Ah."

She couldn't resist smiling at him. "I know what you're thinking. She didn't treat me too good, did she?"

"Kicking you out with little more than a hope that some long-lost relatives would take you in? No, she didn't treat you good at all, Sadie. It was shameful."

Shameful. She wasn't sure if their actions were shameful or not. She did know that Monroe's support felt good. "*Danke* for saying that."

"It's the truth." He nudged the envelope a little closer. "Go ahead and open it, Sadie. You'll never know what she's written if you don't go ahead and read the letter. If she is making amends, you'll feel better."

"And if she isn't?" Because that, she realized, was what she was really concerned about. What was she going to do if the letter was another blow to her fragile frame of mind? She would be crushed.

"That's easy. All you have to do is throw it away."

Even the thought of doing something like that made her feel like looking over her shoulder in case she was in trouble. "Do ya think that is allowed?"

He grinned. "Who do you think is gonna get mad? None of us here is going to say a word. And if your mother was so worried about you, she wouldn't have sent you away."

"I guess you are right."

"I know I am."

Monroe's words were a bit brash, but she knew he was right. In spite of their faults, Monroe and his family didn't ever try to force her to bend to their will. Actually, they usually treated her with a kind of absent-minded regard.

And though they argued and fought, and there was a layer of suspicion surrounding them, life with them was almost easy. She no longer worried about getting yelled at for imagined infractions or caned because she'd sinned. She wondered if she could ever allow herself to be treated so unjustly ever again. She kind of doubted it.

Monroe eyed the letter like it contained a hundred secrets. "Do you want me to stay nearby or leave you in peace? I'll do whatever you want."

She'd thought she wanted his support, but now was worried that he was about to see her falling apart, and she didn't want a witness for that.

"I think I should read this by myself."

Monroe's eyes lit with approval. "All right. Why don't you go to my room? No one is in there, and my *daed* is going to come in soon."

Having a whole room to herself would be such a gift right at this moment. "*Danke*, Monroe."

"No reason to thank me," he said, looking chagrined. "I don't know what the right thing for a woman in your situation is, but I do know it ain't being sent here to live with us."

If Sadie hadn't been so disturbed by the letter, she probably would have questioned him about that. Instead, she knew it was time to seize the opportunity to be alone and enjoy some privacy. There was no telling when the opportunity would come along again.

Though she'd been in his room many times, the sight of it still caught her off guard. Growing up, her brothers' rooms looked like empty shells. Practically all that was in their rooms were single twin beds, desks, wooden chairs, and small dressers. Hooks and knobs on the walls had been the only ornamentation. She supposed the order and simplicity were meant to encourage her brothers to live simple, Plain lives.

She'd often thought that it made them yearn for so much more, however. It was so hard to accept very little when temptation always loomed in the distance.

Monroe's room, on the other hand, had a double bed that was unmade, a bedside table with two flashlights on it, a pile of books on the floor, a dresser, and a desk piled high with papers, notebooks, and drawing paper. Maybe he, too, understood something about dreams and keeping secrets.

Gingerly, she sat on the chair at Monroe's desk. All right, then, she thought . . . and tore open the envelope, pulling out one rather small piece of stationery.

To her surprise, two twenty-dollar bills floated out. Sadie stared at the money settling on the floor before carefully unfolding the note. It was written in flowing cursive. Her mother truly did have beautiful handwriting.

Then, just because the temptation was so great and there was no one around her to see, she held the paper up to her face. It smelled like magnolias. Her mother carefully nurtured her magnolia tree and pressed several of the blooms each season. She'd soak them in oil, and would use a touch of it every time she washed and rinsed her hair. All of them had grown up being comforted by this faint scent that always lingered around her.

And sure enough, that same scent clung to the paper as well.

Finally, knowing that she couldn't put it off any longer, Sadie read—

Dear Sadie,

I've wanted to write to you from the moment you left but I didn't know what to say. I was upset with you and upset with myself for not raising you well enough to behave like a good Christian girl should.

With a gasp, Sadie threw down the letter and jumped to her feet. *That* was why her mother had been so upset? That Sadie had rushed things with the man she thought she was going to marry?

Fuming, she began to pace. In her head, she thought of all the retorts she could have made if her mother was standing in the same room. She might have described how scared she'd been on that bus. How hungry she'd been with no food and next to no money to pay for any.

How scary some of the men at the bus station had looked when they'd stopped for breaks. How afraid she'd been to talk to anyone who'd tried to talk to her.

And finally, she'd tell both her mother and father about how awful it had been to wait three hours at the bus station because she'd had to depend on the deputy who stopped by to drive her to the Stauffers' home.

It all hadn't just been difficult, it had been almost unbearable. And so very frightening. Every time she thought of treating her unborn baby that way, Sadie wanted to cry out.

She couldn't imagine treating him or her so callously.

Sadie had just turned the corner, about to continue her pacing when she drew to an abrupt stop.

She was different than she used to be.

Never when she lived at home would she even have considered looking her parents in the eyes when they were angry with her. It certainly wouldn't have crossed her mind to yell at them! But here she was, planning a lecture.

She had changed, and it was for the better.

Feeling more at ease, she picked up the letter, smoothed it out, and continued to read.

> *We received some news on Sunday that made your father and I wonder if we had been too hasty in sending you away. Sadie, it seems that Harlan did lie to us and to his parents. Another woman has come forth and told a tale of him promising things that he never intended to do. When your father and his father spoke to him about it, Harlan admitted that he had done that very same thing to you.*

"That snake," Sadie said out loud. "What a slimy, terrible man to treat women so terribly."

There was only one paragraph left. Sadie focused back on the writing, a half-smile on her face. Surely, now her mother was going to apologize profusely and ask for her forgiveness.

> *After much thought and prayer, we have decided to provide you with some money for a bus ticket home. That is what the enclosed money is for. Purchase a ticket and come back as soon as possible. Don't forget to bring us the change. After you return, we'll get you married to Harlan immediately.*
>
> *I'm sure the Lord will one day forgive your transgressions, especially if He sees that you are now doing your best to behave in a modest and becoming way.*

I hope and pray your journey home will be un-
eventful. Conduct yourself in a way that will do both
your family and your future husband proud.

Mamm

Sadie's hands were shaking as each word registered. She was supposed to take the money, pack up herself, and sit back on a bus for hours and hours. All so she could return to parents who punished and shunned her—and eventually marry a man who used her. Who had not only lied to her but told lies about her, too.

And, to make matters worse, they wanted her to marry Harlan so it would save their reputation. They didn't even care what kind of man she would be tied to for the rest of her life!

It seemed they had no shame where she was concerned.

With care, she folded her mother's letter and placed it back in the envelope. Picked up the money—and neatly placed the bills in the pocket of her blue apron.

Then took a deep breath and opened Monroe's bedroom door.

Esther was sitting at the table, a sandwich on the plate in front of her. "Hiya, Sadie!" she said with a smile. "I didn't know you were home. What were you doing in Monroe's room?"

"I received a letter from my mother. Monroe offered his room so I could read it in private."

"Oh. I hope the letter was okay?" She frowned. "I mean as okay as could be expected?"

"It was fine."

Looking concerned, she got to her feet. "What did she

want? Or do you not want to say? You don't have to tell me if you don't want to."

Walking to the kitchen, she tore the envelope into shreds and tossed it in the trash. "My mother didn't want anything, only to tell me some news about home."

"Oh? Did something happen?"

"*Nee*. Everything there is exactly the same." She shrugged. "It turns out that I'm not missing much of anything being here."

Esther grinned. "That's good because I've got some news for you."

"I could use some good news. What is it?"

"I bought us some turkey and ham! Swiss cheese, too. Make yourself a sandwich and sit with me for a couple of minutes."

Sadie laughed. "Hold your horses. I'll be right there. And thanks for buying the lunch meat. I'm starving," she said as she quickly made herself a sandwich.

"Eat up, cousin," Esther urged as she sat down with her plate. After all, you're eating for two."

Sadie proceeded to do just that, and without the slightest bit of doubt or regret.

She had already changed.

Now she was going to do everything she could to survive on her own terms. Going back home was no longer an option.

CHAPTER 16

Thursday, July 19

Noah had long decided that his mother could debate the pros and cons of rosebushes for hours. She loved them, loved to nurture them and give them special food—and was constantly asking people for advice on how to make hers look even more spectacular.

That was why they had been standing in the middle of Blooms and Berries for over an hour. Well, he was standing next to Mark Fisher; Mamm was kneeling next to Henry Lehmann and examining two rather pricey rosebushes the way he imagined some Englisher women might gaze at expensive diamonds.

It was kind of cute. Well, it would have been—if she wasn't so determined to buy the best one, and wasn't holding up his whole day.

"Mamm, you about ready?" he called out.

"Almost," she said back. Which was the same thing she'd said twenty minutes before. Then, before he could point that out, she turned back to Mr. Lehmann and gestured to the roses on the left bush.

They looked the same to him. Noah was ready to buy them both.

"Does this happen much?" he murmured to Mark.

Mark Fisher was Mr. Lehmann's right-hand man, and for the most part managed the store. Noah had always liked him, though they didn't have much occasion to talk to each other. Mark lived in Horse Cave, which was a good buggy ride away from his house. Then, too, Mark was married now, so he had even less time for single men.

"Have a customer sidle up to Henry and make him feel like he was the best authority on plants in the whole state?"

"Yeah."

Mark grinned. "Not as much as you are thinking . . . or as he might wish."

Realizing that his mother's indecision was making Mr. Lehmann's day, Noah forced himself to relax. "*Danke*. I needed a reminder about what was important."

Mark shook his head. "No need for thanks." He was leaning against one of the back walls and watching Henry and Noah's mother with a smile on his face. "I'm not going to lie. There have been times when Henry gets so carried away that his enthusiasm can try the patience of a saint."

"That might be true of all of us."

Mark laughed out loud. "Amen to that."

Glancing at his friend again, he said, "How are you feeling? I heard about your surgery." Mark had been diagnosed with a form of kidney cancer and had to have one of his kidneys removed.

Mark smiled. "Almost as good as new. The doctors are having me visit them every three months; but if the cancer stays away for a whole year, they say I won't even have to get chemotherapy."

"That's terrific!"

"*Jah*. The best." Gesturing toward Noah's mother, he said, "After everything we've been through, I've got a new appreciation for the simple things that make us happy. That's why I don't want you to worry about your *mamm*. There aren't a great many people who are as passionate about flowers as your mother. It's sweet, and makes Henry feel important."

Looking at his mother's eyes shine, he had to agree. "She's having a good time."

"And you're a *gut* man. Not every son would take his mother here and then wait for her so patiently."

Noah was about to shrug off the compliment, then decided to be a little more honest. "I've been working a lot of overtime lately. *Mei daed* reminded me that I've been neglecting some more important things. I'm trying to make up for it." Hearing his confession out loud, he said, "I don't know if a trip to the nursery makes up for it or not."

"How is your work going? Do you like riding in that ambulance?"

"*Jah*. I like everything about it. But now that I have three days off, I can't deny I like standing around here as if it's the only thing I have to do today."

"Rest is *gut*."

"It is." He paused, wavering between being quiet and sharing his worries. Finally, he decided, maybe God had brought them to Blooms and Berries so his mother could help Henry, but also so he could have a man like Mark Fisher to talk to. "To be honest, things at work have been kind of tough lately."

"Riding around the county, helping people who are sick or hurt . . . you must see a lot of disturbing things."

"We do. But though this might sound bad, I'm usually not disturbed by that."

"No?"

"Not at all. I mean, we see people sick. And we have pulled up to some motor vehicle accidents that are terrible. My bosses start shouting orders to me, and I'm concentrating so hard that I'm sweating in the middle of the winter. But it makes me feel good."

"Because you are helping them."

"*Jah*. Exactly because of that. Instead of feeling disturbed, I feel almost like the Lord put me there for a reason. And like I'm doing a job that means something."

"A job to be proud of," Mark murmured.

Noah nodded, glad Mark understood his fumbling explanation. "Exactly."

"What changed? Has something different happened, then?"

After making sure his mother was still happily occupied, Noah answered. "Yeah. We've had a couple of deaths lately."

Mark frowned. "I'm sorry to hear that. I'm sure it has been difficult."

"The other EMTs say I'll get used to it. I don't know if I want that to happen or not."

Mark stewed on that for a moment. Then he looked at Noah closely. "This might just be me, but I ain't sure that I would want to get used to death."

Reminded again of Mark's recent battle, Noah stilled. "You know what? You're right."

"Maybe you should be concentrating on each day. Do you like the job?"

"I do," he replied after a pause. "Even when I have a bad day, I wouldn't want to do anything else."

"There's your answer, then."

"I guess so." Glancing at Mark again, he noticed that he

seemed beyond content. "Do you feel that way about working here?"

"At Blooms and Berries? Well, I don't know about that. I like working with Henry, and with my wife, Waneta, from time to time."

"I heard you met Waneta here."

"We met years ago in school, but we fell in love while working here." Before he hardly took a breath, he fired off his question. "Are *you* courting anyone?"

"Me? *Nee.*"

"Why not? You're, what, twenty-five?"

"Twenty-six."

"What's wrong, then? You haven't found the right woman yet?"

Because Noah was fairly sure that he actually had, and also fairly sure that she was the absolute last person he should be interested in, he coughed. Though a dull ache throbbed in his insides, he tried to brush it off. "I'm too busy."

"Ah."

Mark Fisher must have been a genius because, with just that one word, he conveyed everything both he and Noah were feeling. The fact was, he wanted to court Sadie.

Noah was about to see what he could do to move his mother along when the door chimed and in came Sadie herself . . . and her cousins, Esther and Monroe.

Mark went right up to them. "Y'all be needing any help?"

"*Danke*, but not yet," Monroe said.

Mark linked his fingers behind his back. "Fair enough. Well, let me know when you are ready and I'll help if I'm able."

"Will do," Monroe replied.

Esther had already wandered down the aisle, but Sadie

stayed where she was. Practically waiting for Noah to make his move.

Unable to help himself, he stepped forward. "Hey," he said—rather stupidly.

Sadie met his gaze, and smiled hesitantly.

And what a smile that was. Sweet and genuine. Feeling like maybe he hadn't been making a mistake after all, he smiled right back.

But then, just as he was about to approach her, Monroe looked at him, scowled, and gestured for her to join his sister down the aisle and over on the other side of the store.

Noah felt as if he'd just been given the cold shoulder, which was ridiculous. After all, what had even happened? They'd smiled. That was it.

He had to get out of there.

Turning to Mark, he said, "You know what? I'm going to go see if I can give Henry a hand with my mother. If we're not careful, she's going to take up all his attention for the next hour and you're going to have to deal with everyone else."

"He won't care. But what I want to know is what just happened."

"What do you mean?"

"Come on. With that girl." He narrowed his eyes. "Who was she, anyway?"

"Her name is Sadie Detweiler. She's a recent transplant from Ohio." Because he was sure Mark was going to ask it, too, he added, "She is with her cousins, Monroe and Esther Stauffer."

"He was acting like he was guarding her from you."

"He might have been."

"Because?"

"No real reason. I mean, nothing beyond the fact that I

don't think the Stauffers particularly like me." And he'd badgered her with questions when he picked her up in a courting buggy.

"Why is that?" Before Noah could answer, he said, "Wait a minute, one of their relatives recently passed away, didn't she? Were you called out there?"

"*Jah*." He wouldn't have advertised the fact that he'd been with Verba right before she died, but he wasn't going to lie about it, either.

"I'm guessing you know about my past? How I was once *falsely* accused of assaulting a woman?"

"I do."

"Well, if it helps, I've learned that some people can't get past it. They won't ever be able to get past the mistaken identity. But if that's the case, it's their problem not mine."

"I agree," Noah said quietly. "There's nothing I can do about the past anyway."

When they both spied Sadie glance at Noah, blush, then hurriedly dart down another aisle, Mark nudged him with his shoulder. "Maybe every person in the household doesn't dislike you."

"Maybe . . . maybe not. I'm not sure anymore."

"She's sure a pretty thing."

"She is. Sweet, too."

"You like her?"

Yes, he did. "I don't know her all that well."

"Okay. How about this. Do you want to know her better?"

He did. "Maybe," he allowed.

Mark's eyes gleamed.

Noah now felt even more foolish. He was a grown man, an EMT! He helped save lives for a living. He didn't need this.

What was he doing, getting dating advice in the middle of a garden store?

"*Jah*, I do."

"Then go over there and say hello."

It wasn't that easy. Not at all. "I don't mean to be rude, but you don't understand."

"Noah, if you knew what I went through to have my Waneta, you wouldn't say that." He nodded his head. "Go on, now. I'll speak to your mother and help Henry get her settled. You make plans to go calling."

"All right. Fine."

Mark grinned and started walking over to Noah's *mamm*. This meant it was now or never.

Gathering his courage, he walked toward Sadie, who was standing next to a pair of ornamental watering cans. However, it was obvious that she wasn't really seeing anything.

"Hi."

"Hello, Noah." With a bemused expression, she gestured around the store. "I never expected to find you here."

He chuckled. "You're right. Blooms and Berries isn't my usual hangout. But I'm with my mother today. She loves to hang out here and talk plants with Henry."

"And you?"

"I love to make her happy. So here I am."

She smiled at him. "That's mighty sweet of you."

He shrugged. "Standing at a nursery ain't a hardship." Realizing that her cousins were returning, he hurried. "I came over here to talk to you about something."

She leaned forward. "Yes?"

"I'd like to call on you tonight."

"Call on me?"

Lord, but it seemed as if every single thing that was said had multiple meanings. "Yes. May I?"

Warily, she glanced at Monroe. "I don't think that would be a good idea."

That wasn't the same thing as her saying that she didn't want anything to do with him. "Sadie, I promise I won't pester you with questions this time."

"Oh? Then what will we talk about?"

"I don't know. Maybe the weather," he said with a smile. "Maybe our families. Maybe I'll tell you embarrassing stories about myself to make you laugh."

"That does sound intriguing."

"Then say yes. Please?"

She glanced at Monroe again. "Well . . ."

"Come on, Sadie. I'm trying to do this the right way. I'm asking for permission. I'm even asking in front of your cousins." When she continued to hesitate, he added, "Look, if you don't have any interest in me, then I'll leave you alone. But if you do, then I hope you will allow me to stop by. We could sit out by your barn."

Longing filled her eyes. "Noah, this ain't the time or the place, but I have a real good reason for thinking that we wouldn't suit."

He was pretty sure that he knew what that reason was. She was sweet and shy. Innocent and careful. "I don't need to know your reasons. I like the way you are."

But instead of looking relieved, his words seemed to only make her more nervous. Glancing at her cousins, she clenched her hands by her sides. "I'm sorry, but I must say no."

She was refusing him. "Because you don't like me."

"It's not that. It's—"

"It's because she's pregnant, Noah," Monroe said. His voice was quiet and not unkind.

"*What?*"

"You heard right. She's going to have a baby."

Monroe might as well have thrown a couple of sharp knives Noah's way. The news hurt that bad.

Suddenly, well aware that they were having this conversation, this very private conversation, in the middle of Blooms and Berries Nursery, Noah attempted to compose himself. He doubted he succeeded. Actually, his voice was hoarse when he turned to Sadie. "You're pregnant?"

Looking miserable, she nodded.

How? When? Who?

A dozen questions ran through his head. Some of which were rather obvious, others which were absolutely none of his business. And because he couldn't think of anything worthwhile to say, he ended up standing there like a fool. Gaping. Trying to come to grips that the girl, the woman he'd been so taken with, was absolutely nothing like he'd thought.

How could he have been so wrong about so much?

As the silence pulled taut between them, Monroe put his arm around Sadie's shoulders. "Let's go home," he murmured as he ushered her out of the store.

Head tucked, she walked out the door by his side. Esther followed, but not before glaring at Noah. Just like he was the one who had done something wrong.

He stared at the door after it closed, rethinking all that had just happened.

"Are you ready, Noah?" Mamm called out. "Come help me carry everything out."

Feeling like a robot, he automatically walked to the counter, picked up the cardboard box, and hefted it into his arms. "I'll carry this out to the buggy."

Noah turned away before his mother responded.

His ears were ringing, his brain felt thick, and he wasn't sure about anything anymore.

CHAPTER 17

July 19

Esther held Sadie's hand in the buggy the whole way home. Monroe, who was driving and sitting on Esther's left, didn't say anything, but Sadie could tell that he was just as upset by what had taken place.

What she didn't know was why he'd decided to reveal her news to Noah in the middle of the nursery.

"Are you all right?" Esther asked for what had to be the third or fourth time. "I tell you, I thought you were going to pass out in there. I'm so glad you didn't. We have to keep you safe and sound for your baby," she said, her words coming out in a tremendous rush, each one practically tumbling over the next.

Sadie had kept her silence until her cousins' home was in sight. But when it was obvious that Esther was about to blather on about nothing again, all to fill the strained silence, she spoke. "I'm fine."

Monroe jerked his head her way and spoke for the first time since he'd gathered them into the buggy. "Are you sure about that?"

What could she say? It wasn't like she knew what to expect during a pregnancy or had anyone to talk to about it. So far, all she'd been focused on was having a place to live.

But since she didn't know how to admit any of that, she asked a question of her own. "Monroe, why did you tell Noah about my pregnancy?"

"Because it was real obvious that you weren't about to tell him."

"It is my body, and he was wanting to court me. It was my choice to tell him about my baby."

He frowned. "You didn't actually want Noah Freeman to come calling on you, did you?"

"I don't know. Maybe."

"Why would you even consider it? He works on an ambulance."

"What's wrong with that?"

Monroe wrinkled his nose. "There's nothing good about it. He's straddling two worlds."

Hating that Monroe was being so judgmental, Sadie said, "What two worlds? His being Amish helped when he was tending to Verba."

Esther inhaled sharply. "But she died."

"That wasn't his fault." When neither of her cousins agreed, she gaped at them. "Wait, you both don't think that EMTs were at fault, do you?"

"She was alive when the ambulance took her away," Monroe said. "And they wouldn't let any of us in there. Maybe they made a mistake."

Sadie knew that she had been standing off to the side, but she definitely remembered that Verba had been in distress. She'd been in a lot of pain. She'd been crying out before they'd given her drugs in her IV line.

"I don't know if I agree with you two. Those men seemed honest and like they were trying their best."

"My father talked to the doctors at the hospital and they couldn't tell him exactly what was wrong." Monroe waved a hand. "Actually, they said they were going to do a lot of tests of her blood. But her blood was fine."

"We don't know that for sure. What did the blood tests say?"

"They haven't told Daed yet." His lips pursed, then he said darkly, "One of the doctors even suggested that they do an autopsy."

"I don't know what that is," Sadie responded.

"They wanted to cut her open after she was dead," Esther said, illustrating that she, too, had been discussing things whenever Sadie wasn't around.

"Oh, my word. What did your father say?"

"He refused to let them, of course," Monroe said. "We Amish don't believe in autopsies."

"Oh. Of course."

Monroe's voice hardened. "Noah should've told those doctors that so they wouldn't have asked my father."

"To be fair," said Sadie, "Noah might not have known what the doctors wanted to do."

"Maybe. Or maybe not. He rides around in an ambulance, hangs out with Englishers all the time. He might be forgetting our ways."

Sadie didn't know a lot of things, but she knew Monroe was mistaken—and not one to cast stones, given the way he and his father and grandfather were making money.

Just because Noah knew more about medicine didn't mean he was too worldly, or knew what all the doctors in the hospital were thinking.

"Noah has been a *gut* friend to me," she said quietly. "You may not trust him, but I do. And now he thinks I'm a liar. Probably everyone in that store thinks that."

Monroe flushed. "You're right. It wasn't the best place, but at least it's out in the open now. Sadie, if you really do like Noah so much, then you had to tell him sooner or later. He had to learn the truth. You know that."

As much as Sadie wanted to hold on to her anger, she knew Monroe wasn't the one at fault. "I know. I just wish he had taken the news better." Remembering how blank his expression became, and the way he turned from her like she was a stranger? Well, that had hurt.

"I bet he'll come to call on you tomorrow," Esther said. "Anyone would have been shocked by the news. After he thinks about it, he'll come back."

"I don't think so. He probably thinks I have a boyfriend or something."

"This is all such a mess."

"*Jah*. It is," Monroe said as he carefully guided the horse and buggy to the barn and pulled on the buggy's brake when they came to a stop. "But don't forget something, okay?"

"What is that?"

"No matter what, you're *our* mess. You don't need that guy anyway. You can stay here."

"See, Sadie?" Esther said as she opened the door to the buggy and hopped out. "Everything ain't all bad."

"True." She smiled weakly—because suddenly her whole world was stifling. She felt dizzy and off balance. Was it the heat that was making her feel dizzy or her dismay and anger at the whole situation . . . at the knowledge that Noah Freeman was now going to be avoiding her like the plague?

Esther noticed. Reaching for her hand, she said, "Oh, my. Scoot out, Sadie. You don't look too *gut*."

She felt so limp. Saliva pooled in her mouth as she fought to get her bearings.

Just as she attempted to move, Monroe said, "*Nee*, Sadie. Stay there. I'm going to come around and help you down."

She didn't argue. Actually, she didn't know if she could have argued with him even if she'd wanted to. She was so dizzy that all she seemed to be able to do was—

Monroe gripped her waist with his hands and helped her to the ground.

"Easy now," he said quietly. "It's hot out here. We should have thought about that."

Her dizziness increased, making her feel light-headed and her breath hitch.

"I think . . ." She faltered, feeling short of breath.

Esther leaned closer . . .

She was swimming in front of Sadie's eyes.

"Sadie!"

But she didn't reply.

Because she gave up trying to hold on.

Instead, she allowed her world to fade to black.

CHAPTER 18

July 19

Even though she knew it was vain, Daisy found herself walking into the bathroom and studying her face. She didn't know why. Her new medication would take a few days to kick in, at the earliest. The rash across the bridge of her nose wasn't going to fade away immediately.

Besides, an unsightly rash on her skin hadn't been what was keeping her up at night. It was the fact that she now knew that she had a disease. She had lupus. *Systemic lupus.* A disease of her immune system.

Soon, the doctors said, she would look "normal"—

But she wouldn't really be ever again.

As she walked into her kitchen, the doctor's warnings and diagnosis burned her ears. All of his words jumbled and scrambled in her head, making her wonder if she was ever going to make sense of it. Remission. A normal life. Treatment plans. Plaquenil. Kidney damage. Exhaustion. Fevers. Seizures.

She was thirty-eight years old and had a long-term disease.

Try as she might, she couldn't figure out how she might have contracted it, though the doctor said women of all types got lupus. She supposed it didn't matter. Whatever reason, God had decided to give it to her.

Taking a peek at the pamphlets the nurse had handed her before she left the office, Daisy knew she should put on her reading glasses and read them again. Once she understood everything, she would start to feel better.

But she would still be tainted, a sneaky voice whispered in her ear.

She was growing to hate that voice. The whiny one riddled with selfish wishes and huge insecurities. The one that pointed out that she was almost forty and was still an old maid. While all of her friends had gotten married, had children, or even grandchildren, she'd been on her own.

Sometimes, in the middle of the night, that voice even tried to persuade her that she wasn't worthy of love and marriage.

After allowing herself one more minute of doldrums, she added ice to a Mason jar and poured in some water, then she slipped a straw hat on over her *kapp* and went outside to the front porch, picking up her latest crochet project on the way. She'd begun crocheting baby blankets to give to a local charity organization that delivered them to new mothers in Appalachia.

As her mother had often told her, it was far better to focus on others' needs than her own.

It seemed her mother hadn't been wrong. An hour later she felt better. Maybe not like her normal self, but far more positive. She also had a lovely soft pink blanket to show for it.

"I guess this was perfect timing," a voice called out.

Missing a stitch, Daisy's hands stilled as she watched

Stephen Stauffer stride up her walkway with a brown paper shopping bag in his right hand.

"Hi, Stephen." Just as she was about to stand up, she noticed his gaze search her face. His easy smile turned into concern.

"You're upset."

She shrugged, and set her yarn aside. "A little. I've still got this rash."

Without a concern for her personal space, he dropped the bag, leaned closer, and cradled her chin in his hand. In his large, rough, surprisingly gentle hand. For a moment she closed her eyes, allowed his touch to seep into her soul. Then, as reality returned, she pulled away—just as she should have done in the first place.

"I'm fine."

"Are you?"

"I will be."

After looking at her closely again, Stephen pushed her yarn away and sat down on the cushioned bench next to her.

Right next to her.

She would have scooted away if there was any place to scoot. "I don't know if there is room for two of us on this bench."

He laughed. "*Nee*, I think this bench was made for two people."

Knowing that he was talking about courting and kissing and such, she blushed. Even though she was truly far too old for such nonsense. "Want to tell me why you came by?"

"I brought you something."

She eyed the brown sack. "What is it?" And more importantly, why was he bringing her anything at all?

"You're gonna have to wait to find out." Kicking his feet

out, he grinned. "Actually, I'm thinking now that maybe I should hold that sack hostage until you tell me about your doctor visits. What did you discover?"

He was making her uncomfortable. Not because he was sharing a small bench, curving a hand around her jaw, or bringing her presents. No, it was because of who he was.

Her best friend's husband for twenty years.

And also the man she had secretly liked for most of her life. Ever since they had all attended a frolic back when they were fourteen, and she spied him across the way, looking so worldly and bored with the silly games that the adults had planned for them.

Right away, she'd found herself stealing glances at him. Hoping to catch his attention, too.

And she did, when they'd stood in line to get ice cream.

He'd started whispering to her, wondering if scoops of vanilla and chocolate ice cream could make up for things some of the other teenagers were doing—the ones who'd started their *rumspringa* and were no doubt imbibing far more dangerous items.

She'd gotten brave then, and admitted she'd been invited by some kids to go to the movies, that she'd almost gone but her natural wariness had taken over and she did the safe thing instead.

He'd looked at her then with appreciation. Had even suggested that they go together one day.

And just when she was about to agree, Jean had come running up to them. She was everything beautiful and innocent; and would have no more thought about going to the movies than she would have considered disobeying her parents.

Jean had glanced up at Stephen, smiled shyly, and asked if

he minded terribly if she cut in line so she could stand next to Daisy.

And right before her eyes, Stephen Stauffer was dumbstruck. And Daisy disappeared from his sight.

"Daisy? I don't mind spending the afternoon sitting by your side in silence . . . but I'd rather we talk about what's obviously on your mind."

"You mean that, don't you?"

"Yep. So, will you just tell me? Or are you going to make me guess?"

"I have lupus."

He blinked slowly. "Say again?"

She tilted her head down, took a deep breath, and told him about everything she'd learned. She told him about all the blood the doctors took and how they looked at her ankles and other joints. She told him about the rash and her new medicine, and how she could be just fine for years and years.

Or how she might not.

In typical Stephen fashion, he got straight to the point. "How are you feeling now?"

"Better." And she did feel better. It seemed that what she needed more than anything was a friend to confide in.

At last he smiled. "I'm glad."

Summoning a smile, too, she folded her hands over the edge of the bench. "Now maybe you will tell me why you are here?"

"Okay." He stood up, reclaimed the sack, and then presented it to her. "I was at the store and I saw this. I thought you might like it."

Feeling foolish, she took the sack from him and parted the handles carefully. There, waiting for her, were three skeins of pink and ivory yarn.

Forgetting he was standing there watching her, she pulled them out—and almost cried at the texture. They were *very* fine. Maybe they had alpaca? Maybe silk. No matter what, they were soft and luxurious to the touch. And the colors! Calling them mere pink and ivory was something of a travesty. They were much more beautiful than that. The pink was neighboring on blush and the ivory was the shade of her mother's antique china teacups. Or the baby lamb's wool. Not quite white—pure, without a tinge of yellow.

Suddenly, she realized that she was hugging the skeins of yarn to her just like a baby. Feeling her skin heat, she loosened her grip.

"Danke."

"You're welcome. So, you like them?"

"I more than like them. They . . . well, they are lovely. Some of the prettiest skeins of yarn I've seen in some time." Belatedly realizing that yarns like this didn't come cheap—and that they really weren't anything to each other—she said, "May I help you pay for them?"

Stephen flinched. "Of course not. They're a gift."

He looked hurt and she immediately felt embarrassed. No woman of her age should be so socially awkward. "Of course. I'm sorry. I didn't mean to offend you. It's just that they caught me by surprise."

It was true. The gift of the beautiful yarns had caught her by surprise. But she didn't love yarn that much. No, the problem was his visit being the surprise.

And she didn't know how to handle Stephen being here.

Sitting back down on the bench, he nodded, just as if everything she said was expected. "Daisy, I know you don't know what to make of me. But, well, when we saw each other at the store the other day, you said something that stayed with me."

"What was that?"

"How I didn't really know you." He rubbed his cheeks, which were covered, but only with a very short beard. "You were right. I think I've been taking you for granted these twenty years."

That sounded rather harsh, even coming from her mouth. "I didn't say that."

He didn't take his eyes off her. "It was close enough."

"Well, now . . ."

"It was also true."

"I've developed the unfortunate habit that old women sometimes have. We say what's on our minds. It comes off as unfiltered and unnecessary."

"One might say that is true, but I never have thought of you as particularly blunt." His expression warmed. "Or old."

If she didn't know him better, she would have said that he was gazing at her with appreciation. But that couldn't be right. "Stephen, I'm sorry if I am being obtuse, but I truly do not know what to make of this conversation. Jean and I were close all our lives, but you never acted as if you more than tolerated me."

"That wasn't the case. I more than tolerated you. But I was also married to Jean."

"So now the time is right?"

"I don't know. Maybe now is right. Maybe I decided that I needed someone new in my life."

"Are things that bad at home?"

He froze. "What is that supposed to mean?"

Daisy knew she could excuse her comment on a number of things. She could even blame it on Verba's recent death.

But she thought that they would both see through that. "I'm talking about the moonshine, Stephen."

He ran a hand over his face. "I guess it was too much to wish that you had no idea about it."

"Are you really that naïve? Everyone knows about it."

"Jean never did."

"Of course she did, Stephen," she said gently. "And before you start reinventing the past, I'll just say what I know to be true. Jean didn't like what y'all were doing, but she would've never stopped you."

"And why was that?"

"Because in some ways, she thought you felt that was all you had."

"I had Jean. And my children. I loved them."

"I know. She knew. But what I'm asking is if you ever took the time to count your blessings?"

Stung, he edged away. "I've always known you to be blunt, but this is a new low for you."

"I'm not trying to shock you, Stephen. But with my future being the way it is, I don't want to pretend anymore."

Stephen took off his straw hat and ran a hand through his hair. "Sorry. You are right. I'm glad we're being honest with each other."

Feeling like she'd already lost him but not wanting to give up on their relationship, she said, "I hope I didn't ruin everything. I . . . well, I have really enjoyed our friendship."

"I have, too." He sighed. "Let's talk about something else."

"Like what?" She couldn't think of anything to erase what she'd just said.

"How about you tell me what all we can do to help you. What advice did the doctors give ya?"

"They said to do as much as possible, that it was important to go out and do things instead of sit home and worry."

"That sounds like good advice. Especially since I have something in mind for you to do."

"And what is that?"

"I think we should go to Mammoth Cave."

"The national park?" She couldn't keep the surprise out of her voice. It was a busy place. Really busy. Thousands of people went there each day, some on buses.

Stephen was nodding like it was the best idea in the world. "*Jah.* It's real close. Have you ever been?"

She shook her head. "*Gut.* I haven't, either. Will you accompany me? I'm going to hire a driver."

"Why are you asking?" Not wanting to misconstrue anything, she said, "Is it just because you feel sorry for me?"

"*Nee.* It's not that. It's because I want to be with you. It's because even though we might want to pretend that we *merely* tolerated each other, I think there's something more."

"Do you really think so?"

"Jean was too smart to have kept us both so close if she thought we had nothing in common but her."

He did have a point. "All right, then. Yes."

"Yes? Already?" He chuckled. "And here I thought it was going to take me another hour to convince you."

She shrugged. "Maybe I've gotten tired of treating you like a stranger, Stephen. And you know . . . I've always had a soft spot for really good yarn."

"*Danke,* Daisy."

"You're welcome. Thank you for the invitation." Though she still wasn't sure if it was a good idea or not, she was pleased.

Now she had to hope she hadn't just made a big mistake.

CHAPTER 19

July 20

"Noah, yesterday I saw that girl you were so taken with," Reid said. The two EMTs, along with Chad, were walking out of the hospital after dropping off a teenager who'd been in a car accident.

"Who might that be?" Noah asked lightly. No doubt Reid was matchmaking again. Ever since he got engaged, he seemed to think that everyone needed to be paired up into twos.

"That Amish girl with the violet eyes. You know, the one y'all were telling me lived near Cub Run."

Noah drew to a stop. "Sadie?"

Reid snapped his fingers. "Yeah. Her. Sorry, her name slipped my mind."

Chad stopped walking, too, focusing on Reid.

"How did you see her? Was someone in her family ill?" asked Noah.

"Not ill, but she had a scare. Her cousins brought her into the clinic to make sure she was doing all right." Reid was a paramedic but also volunteered at a free clinic once a month.

"*Was* she all right?"

Reid, careful about keeping patients' ailments confidential, looked taken aback.

"I know she's pregnant," Noah added. "She told me herself."

"Oh. Well, then I can tell you that she passed out."

"Is she okay?"

"Yes. I mean, I think so." Reid shook his head. "I'm used to the Amish not running to the doctor much, but she hadn't even seen a midwife. She needs some looking after."

Noah thought about how her family seemed to value secrets more than her health. "I bet she does."

"Anyway, I gave her some prenatal vitamins and told her to take it easy, especially in the afternoons. This heat can be a killer."

"Don't even joke about *that*," Chad warned. "We're bringing in at least one person a shift who's suffering from heat exhaustion."

"Sorry." Smiling again at Noah, Reid said, "Anyway, I'm only mentioning Sadie because she asked about you."

"Really?"

"Yup. She was real interested in your schedule."

"She was?"

Reid nodded. "I think she was a little disappointed that you weren't at the clinic. Hey, maybe you should stop by and see her soon. Just to make sure she's taking care of herself."

"I'll do that," he replied, though he wasn't real sure how he was going to feel about doing that. "Thanks again for letting me know."

Turning to Chad, Noah said, "Ready?"

"Yep," and they started walking.

"Hang in there, Reid," they both called out as they went their ways.

"You, too. Be safe," he replied before disappearing through the doors leading to the emergency wing.

Chad turned to Noah as they walked to the ambulance. "I'm beginning to think that there is something more going on with that girl that you aren't saying."

"You would be right," Noah said as they got in. Mitch was in the driver's seat, talking on the phone.

After letting Mitch know all was taken care of, they headed back to the firehouse. While Mitch was driving, Chad turned back to Noah. "So . . . want to talk about it? You know she's pregnant . . . I bet you were surprised. It's really too bad y'all don't wear wedding rings. Then you would have known that she was taken."

"She ain't married."

"Oh. Wow."

"Yeah. I don't know what her story is, but I don't think it's good. Now, at least, I understand why she was sent away from her community. If she got pregnant out of wedlock and the man wasn't stepping up to the plate, her family was no doubt upset with her."

Chad frowned. "A girl doesn't get pregnant on her own, Noah."

"I realize that. But an unmarried woman getting pregnant is still something of a crisis for a lot of people, whether they're Amish or not."

"I hear what you're saying. But still . . . that's too bad, her being all alone. She seems like a sweet thing."

"It is too bad." Noah also thought that Sadie seemed sweet, but decided to keep that thought to himself.

Chad took a deep breath, looking like he was ready to discuss it some more, but Noah wasn't ready to talk about Amish customs, Sadie's pregnancy, or why she was occupying his thoughts. "Do you still want me to check tanks when we get back, Mitch?"

"Hmm? Yeah. But that phone call I took while you were in the hospital was Chief Garcia. He wants us to meet with Deputy Beck. The police are still working on those two deaths."

"Why do they want to speak to us?" Chad asked.

"I don't know," Mitch murmured as he maneuvered the vehicle around a horse and buggy. "Probably because we found the first case in the area."

"There have only been two, though. Right?" Chad asked.

"That's what I thought, but the chief sounded pretty concerned," Mitch replied. "So, who knows? Maybe there's been another victim."

Noah swallowed, a bitter taste entering his mouth as he put everything back into perspective. Yes, an unplanned pregnancy was a crisis, but it wasn't a tragedy. Not like either of those deaths or the majority of the cases they found themselves involved in during each shift. Though he wasn't looking forward to meeting with the sheriff and not providing the answers they'd wanted, he didn't regret his choice. Sadie came first.

As if he was reading Noah's mind, Chad glanced his way. "Never a dull moment, huh?"

"Never."

"And . . . that's why we like it," Mitch said as he pulled into their slot in the firehouse. "It keeps us on our toes."

Noah wasn't sure if he liked it or not. But maybe it didn't matter. People got in accidents, got sick, and even died. If those things didn't happen, he wouldn't have a job.

After climbing out of the back, he began wiping down and restocking the ambulance, only half listening while Mitch and Chad veered the conversation toward Mitch's in-laws and a home repair project they were working on.

The two men continued to chat while filling out paperwork and helping with the cleaning.

Noah allowed his mind to drift.

Allowed himself to come to terms with the fact that almost every conversation of late centered on Sadie. He didn't know what to make of it, but he decided not to dwell on it. He needed to come to terms with how he felt about her not being the innocent woman he imagined.

He just wasn't sure why it mattered.

ONE HOUR LATER, Noah, Chad, and Mitch were summoned to the meeting in the chief's office just moments after the new crew clocked in. They all took seats and Chief Garcia stood up. "There isn't any good way to say this, so I'm going to be blunt. Another two people died of similar symptoms to Verba and John Beachy, but over in Bowling Green."

"In Bowling Green? Were they Amish?"

Deputy Beck shook his head. "Nope. Both were young males in their twenties who, as far as we can determine, have no ties to the Amish at all." Flipping through the file he'd brought with him, he added, "One of the men was in college at Western Kentucky and here from Arkansas. The city, too. I'd be pretty surprised if he even knew who the Amish were."

Chief Garcia nodded. "And the other?"

"That one is from Bowling Green. But he was a partier. I guess he's the one who brought the moonshine to the party."

"Where did he get it from?"

Beck smiled grimly. "That's why we're involved. From what the authorities there can discern, his parents drove up to Mammoth Cave, decided to spend the day touring the country, and brought home a Mason jar of moonshine from an Amish fella on the side of the road." He closed the folder again. "I've been doing this long enough to know that people don't always tell the whole story, but this sounds like it might actually be the truth."

Noah frowned. "Which means it came from an Amish fella in the area."

"Yep. Any ideas, Noah?" Beck asked.

Though he could have mentioned the Stauffers here, he elected to keep silent. "Nope. I'm not the authority on the whole Amish population."

Beck held up his hands. "Easy, now. You know I mean no disrespect. My wife grew up Amish in Horse Cave."

"Sorry. I'd forgotten that."

"All I'm trying to say is, I know better than to make general assumptions."

"You're right." Noah cleared his head and tried to think about everything objectively. "Here's my guess. Some Amish teens in their *rumspringa* do some pretty stupid stuff. They might take risks that they wouldn't if they were older."

"So they act like any other teenagers."

"Yep. But depending on the kid, he might be really gullible. Some parents try so hard to keep the outside world away from their children that they have absolutely no idea how to behave around Englishers. And some of those folks count on that."

Beck nodded. "I see where you're going with this. So it could be that a couple of naïve kids got hold of some moonshine."

"But that doesn't explain how a woman like Verba Stauffer died," said Noah.

"What about this?" the chief asked. "How about some Amish kids who are real gullible are also real eager to make money. Maybe they buy some tainted moonshine and sell it—"

"But Verba—" Noah cut in.

"Some Amish men and women might have a little bit of alcohol in the house for medicinal purposes," the chief quickly continued his thought.

"Would that be allowed?" asked Beck.

"I don't think any bishop is going to start recommending it or anything," said Noah. "But I can't imagine someone getting into trouble if they take a couple of sips from some wine—or moonshine, say—if they're real sick and need help sleeping."

Deputy Eddie Beck nodded. "I think you're right. This scenario makes the most sense, too. Let's all keep our eyes and ears open for word about some Amish boys selling jars of moonshine."

"Will do," Chad said.

Mitch frowned. "This still seems awfully neat to me. Are we sure only two men over in Bowling Green tried it? Maybe it comes from someone around those parts."

Deputy Beck shook his head. "A couple other folks said they tried it, but just small sips."

"You think they're telling the truth?"

"Probably, they don't have any reason to lie."

"What do you need us to do?"

"I'm going to go talk to some folks in the hospital, too, but I think we need to put the word out to the public to not drink anything because it might be tainted—and, of course, catch whoever is selling it."

Everyone else nodded, but Noah got the feeling the other men were thinking the same thing that he was. It was going to be like trying to find a needle in the haystack.

If someone was sneaking something into food or drink they shouldn't, and now they knew people were looking for that person . . . ?

Well, there was every possibility in the world that no one would hear about it ever again.

Or at least until another person died.

CHAPTER 20

Saturday afternoon, July 28

The day was glorious. The sky was a robin's-egg blue and there was hardly any humidity in the air, two things that Sadie was learning hardly ever happened in the middle of summer in central Kentucky.

Unfortunately, they'd spent most of the morning canning several quarts of tomatoes in the hot kitchen. But that was okay; she and Esther had a lot to smile and chat about.

To everyone's surprise, Stephen had taken the day off to visit Mammoth Cave with a woman.

He announced that bit of information right in the middle of breakfast, like it was a common occurrence. Monroe, who hardly ever lost his composure, gaped at his father in wonder. Esther giggled. Willis, on the other hand, looked so irritated that Sadie worried he was going to throw the saltshaker in his hand at the wall.

As for Sadie? She was shocked. Stephen was so contained and solemn. She couldn't imagine that he could either take the day off or go courting. She was also surprised that her cousins weren't more bothered by it.

Hours later, as she sat next to Esther on the steps right outside the kitchen door, Sadie wondered how the outing might be going. "Do you know this Daisy?"

Esther nodded. "Oh, *jah*. Daisy was my mother's best friend. She was at our house a lot when me and Monroe were small."

"I don't want to be mean, but I'm kind of surprised that you and Monroe are not more disturbed than you seemed at breakfast."

"Oh, I do think both of us are in shock," Esther confided with a laugh, "but mainly because Daed has never acted like he considered Daisy to be one of his friends. Sometimes, I was certain that they didn't even like each other. Why, whenever we saw Daisy at church, she and my father never said more than two words to each other."

"Do you mind that your father is courting her?"

Surprise lit Esther's features before she replied. "I don't know if Daed is or isn't courting Daisy. Maybe he's just taking her out and getting a break from all of us. If that's the case, I don't blame him."

"Your grandfather seemed to think he was going courting."

"He did, didn't he?" she mused. "If Daed is, then I'm happy for him. We have a hard life here, you know. And Daed has to bear the brunt of a lot of it because my grandfather can be real hard and difficult."

"That makes sense."

"It's just a day off. I think Monroe is the happiest about the news—now he won't feel so bad when *he* takes the day off to see his friends."

Sadie smiled. "I'm glad he takes off from time to time. He should."

"I think so, too."

They worked on the projects they'd brought outside for a few moments. Sadie was crocheting a baby blanket and Esther was sorting out some yarn and fabric she'd bought at a rummage sale two days previously.

"Are you ever going to open the letter that arrived this morning?" Esther asked.

And just like that, her light mood evaporated. Monroe had passed on another letter when they were canning. Sadie stuffed it in her pocket and promptly forgot about it.

Well, pretended it wasn't there.

But now, with Esther eyeing her carefully, Sadie pulled it back out. "I've been putting it off," she said.

"Why?"

"The last one my mother sent . . . well, it was an order to come home." Feeling her cheeks heat, she shared the embarrassing truth. "Actually, I did something pretty bad. They sent me forty dollars for the bus fare home. I pocketed the money and tore up the letter."

Esther's eyes widened. "Sadie!"

"I know. It's sinful. Ain't so?"

Esther gazed at her longer, but then shook her head. "I don't know if it was that terrible or not. Actually, I think I would have probably done the same thing. They really were awful to you."

Looking at the neat handwriting on the front, Sadie said, "I guess I need to read this one. Stay with me while I do?"

"Of course."

Feeling like she was about to enter an angry horse's stall

and get kicked for the effort, she carefully tore open the envelope and unfolded the letter.

When it was spread open across her lap, Esther leaned close.

"Dear Sadie," she began. *"After waiting for your return, then finally contacting Stephen, we now realize that you ignored our wishes and are staying in Kentucky."*

Esther looked up. "Did my *daed* talk to you about that?"

"Nee."

Esther looked down at the page and started reading again.

"We are disappointed in you and now realize that you have become even more willful. If you don't return by the twenty-eighth, we'll be forced to take matters into our own hands."

"Today is the twenty-eighth, isn't it?"

"Jah." Looking at the letter again, Esther said, "Your mother doesn't say much else. Only that she hopes you have come to your senses."

"I guess I didn't." Sadie felt her hands tremble. She pushed them under her thighs so Esther wouldn't see. But even her trembling couldn't hold back her anger. "My parents knew this letter wouldn't arrive before the twenty-eighth. They love to manipulate me."

"What do you think they're going to do?"

"Come retrieve me and force me to go back with them."

"But that's not fair."

"You're right. It ain't. But it's what they've always done. They've probably been telling my brothers and sisters how terrible I am. They'll no doubt tell them that I'm most likely hungry and sick and alone, all so they'll be afraid to defy them." Grabbing the letter, she crumpled it in her hands. "The sad thing is that they don't even need to make stuff up.

What they've done is bad enough. My parents not only called me a liar, they kicked me out of the house. I had five dollars. That's it."

Esther looked down at her hands. "Ever since I realized that everyone didn't live the way we do, I've wished that things here were better. I wished I had my own room, that each of us had our own room. That we had enough food and money. But now I'm starting to realize that I should've been counting my blessings. Your parents sound very mean."

Sadie shivered . . . remembering how scared and alone she'd felt the times she was locked in her room. "They were harsh with me, that is true." She shook her head. "Now that I've gotten away from them, I think they should feel ashamed. I hope that I never treat a stranger with such unkindness, let alone my own flesh and blood."

"You won't. I'm sure you'll be a caring and sweet mother to your baby."

"I hope so." She swallowed. "I hope your father and Willis won't make me go if they show up."

"I don't think they will. I don't think Daed likes your parents all that much. We'll tell Monroe and Dawdi about your note."

Sadie gulped but nodded. "I hope you're right. I know my being here is hard on y'all, but I don't want to go back to my parents."

"Or to Harlan?" Esther asked.

"Definitely not him."

"Are you sure about that?"

"I'm positive. I told you, he lied about me."

"I know. But . . . he's the father of your babe. And when it's born, well, what are you going to do then?"

The words floated around her, sank in, and then drilled deep into her heart. Making her realize two things. One was that she'd been acting like a child herself. She'd been holding her grief and hurt and fear so close to herself that she hadn't given more than a passing thought to what her life would be like after the baby came.

With a start, she realized she'd just assumed that she'd continue to live with the Stauffers.

But where? On a cot in the kitchen? Is that really how she intended to take care of this baby? And how *had* she planned to take care of it and all its needs?

Had she really expected Esther and her family to provide for her for the next year?

With some dismay, Sadie supposed that she had. Her mouth suddenly felt like cotton. "I'm not sure what I'm going to do," she said at last. "I'm embarrassed to admit this, but I think I've been so focused on how my family hurt and disappointed me, as well as Harlan, that I haven't given a lot of thought to the future. But I will."

Esther's posture didn't change. No, she seemed just as tense as she had been before broaching the question of what Sadie was going to do.

"Esther, what is really the matter? Are you worried about my future . . . or yours?"

Esther paled, then abruptly got to her feet. "Haven't you realized anything yet? Each person's decisions and activities affect everyone else's in this house. Whether we want to be or not, our lives are delicately intertwined. We need to get you out of this house, Sadie, before your parents come. And before the baby arrives."

She rushed back inside.

Sadie stayed where she was. Esther obviously needed some

time to herself. And she needed a few minutes to think about what had just been said.

Because though they'd been talking about her and her baby, she was now more certain than ever that they'd been talking about something so much more.

Esther was afraid.

CHAPTER 21

July 28

Stephen felt vaguely like he was playing hooky from his life. Maybe he was. After pulling out some money from a box he kept hidden underneath a drawer, he'd called for a driver to pick him up at nine in the morning at Daisy's house.

Only then did he walk into the kitchen and tell his father, Sadie, Monroe, and Esther that he was going to be gone for the day. That he was taking Daisy Lapp to Mammoth Cave.

The four of them had stared at him in shock. He didn't blame them, he was still surprised at himself. But then he simply walked out the door.

He probably should've talked to his children about it. They were grown, it was true. But they had loved their mother dearly. He owed it to them to at least try to explain his relationship with Daisy.

If he could ever figure out *how* to explain it.

Maybe that was the problem. Maybe he didn't want to analyze what was happening between them. If he did, the day would seem less special. Less . . . well, less magical, he guessed, though he'd never been one to believe in magic. All he did know was that this day felt so good, like such a relief, that he didn't want anything to ruin it, not even his children's curiosity.

It was barely a thirty-minute walk, but it might as well have been thirty miles away, her home was so different than his own.

Daisy's house had been her parents' and grandparents'. After her eldest brother died suddenly, she'd inherited it. Her younger brother had jumped the fence and was no longer Amish.

Though she lived alone and the house was rather big, she didn't seem to have any problem keeping up with it. The garden was well tended and the flower beds were neatly cared for, with not a weed in sight.

She had a lovely wide front porch that spanned both the side and the front of the house.

When Stephen walked up, she invited him in for a glass of lemonade while they waited for the driver.

Once again, he felt the care she'd brought to the house gleamed in every room. Furniture was well dusted, and lemon oil and Pine-Sol scented the air. It smelled fresh and clean and pure.

Three things he never associated with his own home.

"Are you looking forward to going to Mammoth Cave as much as I am?" she asked as she led the way into the kitchen.

"Yes." He smiled at her, liking how she'd put on a marigold-colored dress for the occasion. The bright color made her brown eyes shine. Or maybe it was her happiness . . . and how her kitchen shimmered.

"I'm also fairly amazed at your house."

"Oh?"

"It's sparkling clean. Outside and in."

"Oh!" She laughed. "I cleaned all morning for you."

"There was no need for that. You should have been resting."

"I keep a clean house, so there wasn't much to do. I also asked a neighbor girl to come over and help me."

"I'm glad about that." Unbidden, a memory, long forgotten, hit him hard. He remembered Jean looking exhausted when Monroe was a toddler and she was expecting Esther. He hadn't been around and his mother had expected Jean to cook and clean for all of them. One evening, after his wife had practically collapsed in their bed, she'd whispered that she needed help.

He'd known it.

But he'd been too afraid of how his parents would react to make any changes. Instead, he'd given her a gruff response and rolled over, pretended to go to sleep. What he really did, however, was listen to her try not to cry.

He'd lain in bed wide awake for hours that night, trying to figure out a way to change their life. Change their living situation. Their financial situation. Their marriage. But try as he might, he couldn't think of a single thing. So he let her continue doing too much while he pretended not to notice.

And he was still ashamed about that.

"Stephen?"

He started. Daisy was staring at him, concern etched in her eyes. "Sorry. My mind was drifting. I guess I didn't get enough sleep last night."

"Oh?" She shifted, unease showing in her actions. "You know, if you'd like to postpone our trip we can."

"I don't." He smiled, hoping to reassure her. "I'm sorry. Don't mind me. Now, I think the driver is coming in ten minutes. Do you need any help getting ready?"

Picking up her purse, she shook her head. "*Nee*. I'm good. I don't think I need anything more at all."

IT TURNED OUT that Daisy loved Mammoth Cave. Her eyes lit up at the crowds of tourists, at the fancy hotel nearby, at the number of choices of tours they could take.

She'd walked right up onto the converted school bus they had to take to reach their tour's entrance. And she smiled at the park ranger and listened when he explained the park's history.

None of those things were Stephen's usual type of activities. He was a simple man, used to working in silence in a cellar and making deliveries under a cloud of secrecy. Because of all that, he had a natural aversion to both crowds and any men or women in uniform.

But every time he felt that unease return, he focused on Daisy and her smile. Focused on how she never shied away from people's curious stares when they took in her *kapp* or clothes.

Actually, she seemed to embrace their curiosity. She spoke to people about being Amish and even laughed when a little girl wanted to touch her apron.

Watching her smiles and easy nature made everything seem brighter. Both their surroundings and his future.

Now he was trailing behind her as she wandered around the gift shop. His former self would have pointed out that neither of them had use for T-shirts or sweatshirts emblazoned with Mammoth Cave on them. He would have complained about the crowds.

Instead, he kept his peace—and even found himself watching with amusement as she bought a coffee mug with *See Mammoth Cave* printed on the side, two postcards, and an expensive hardcover book listing fifty other National Parks to visit.

In fact, the only time he intruded on her shopping was when he noticed the time.

"We need to finish up, Daisy. Our driver will be arriving soon."

She held up her sack. "I'm all done. We can walk outside now."

Gallantly, he took the sack from her. "Are you feeling all right? Do you need a bottle of water before we leave?"

"I'm fine, but it's probably a *gut* idea to be prepared."

"Let's go to the snack bar, then."

After finding her a chair, he got water bottles and granola bars in case they got hungry. They'd eaten sandwiches and ice cream when they arrived, but that had been hours ago.

"Here ya go."

Her eyes sparkled. "You worried that I'll get hungry during our drive back?"

"Maybe." That was part of the reason. The other was that he didn't want anything to mar one of the best days he'd ever had in his life.

After taking a sip of water, she walked by his side to the agreed-upon waiting area. Five minutes later their driver arrived.

And then they were on their way.

"How was it?" the driver asked. "I've always wanted to go but never have."

"It was wonderful," Daisy said. "Dark and beautiful and blissfully cool."

"It's hot as July out here," the driver joked. "I should have gone in, too."

Stephen's former self would have complained about the

prices, or how they had plenty of caves closer to their town. Instead, he smiled at Daisy as he replied to the driver, "You should put it on your to-do list, then. It was a good day."

"I'll do that."

As the driver entered the highway and focused on the road, Daisy looked at him. "You are serious, aren't you?"

"About today? *Jah*. I'm glad we did this. I'm even more glad you came with me."

Lowering her voice, she gazed at him longer. "Please don't take this the wrong way, but you seem different."

"That's probably because I feel different," he answered. He felt clean and untainted by both his life and the choices he'd made.

He was also feeling something when they were deep in the cavern—and that was hope. He'd gotten a glimpse of what his life could be like if he completely pulled away from his family and what they were doing.

He began to see, there in the dark, that he had options. Even at his age he could make a new path. It might involve some darkness and maybe even some scary moments, but if he pressed on and didn't give up, he had the chance of uncovering something beautiful and previously unimagined.

It was a reaffirmation that everything was better with hope and faith.

Daisy stared at him, obviously waiting for him to continue. But when he didn't, she simply nodded and looked out the window.

Allowing him to slowly relax . . .

And to wonder if he'd ever have the words to describe the transformation that was taking place inside him.

CHAPTER 22

Monday, July 30

W hy are you here, Noah? I canna think we have anything to say to each other," Sadie announced after Esther practically shoved her toward the front door when he arrived.

She braced herself, half expecting some throwaway joke about him being in the neighborhood. Instead, he shoved his hands in his pockets and shifted awkwardly.

"I don't blame you for thinking that," Noah said at last. "The other time we saw each other, I didn't behave very well."

He'd stared at her like she was a stranger, which made her feel more awkward than she already did. So, no, he hadn't behaved well, at least not toward her.

But had she really expected him to react much differently? Not really. There was a reason why she had kept her pregnancy a secret, and it was because she feared a reaction like his.

Now she just wanted to keep her distance from him. "That doesn't answer my question."

He blinked. Flushed. "No, I suppose it doesn't. Does it?"

"You're letting flies in, girl!" Willis called out. "Bring the man in or take him outside."

Knowing there was really only one choice, Sadie stepped forward and shut the door behind her.

Noah smiled.

She inwardly groaned. Now they were standing far too close, and everything she'd been trying to ignore about him was much too apparent. Noah smelled like soap and shampoo and fresh laundry. Even though it was over ninety degrees out, he looked cool and comfortable.

He was also patiently watching her examine him.

This was awful!

Noah gestured toward a winding path near the barn. "Do you want to go for a walk or something?"

It was so very warm and the humidity so thick, for once the saying about cutting it with a butter knife didn't seem like an exaggeration.

So, no, she didn't want to go for a walk. But she wanted him standing on the front porch with Willis watching from the window even less.

"We can go for a walk, if you want."

His eyes lit up, like he was tempted to say something but kept that to himself. "*Danke,*" he said simply. Then held out a hand so she could take his help when she walked down the stairs.

She didn't need his help; didn't especially want to take his hand. But her body *had* suddenly decided to shift and change this week. She now had a small rounded tummy. Her hips felt a little wider, too. Though she was barefoot, and steady on her feet, going down stairs was a little less easy.

When she put her hand in his, he clasped it like it was

made of spun glass and helped her down the three narrow steps.

He seemed content to hold her hand when they got to solid ground, too.

But she took care of that and pulled away. Folded her hands in front of her stomach just to make sure he didn't get any ideas about reaching for them again.

He pointed to a well-worn dirt path just beyond the barn. "That trail looks like a good one, and well used. Do you walk on it a lot? Where does it lead to?"

"I've only been on it a time or two. It leads to an Amish schoolhouse and a couple of other farms that are nearby."

"Should we walk toward the schoolhouse, then?"

"It doesn't matter to me." Tired of whatever game he was playing, she blurted, "Noah, we can take a short walk, but I want to know why you are here. You still haven't told me."

"I guess it's fairly obvious that I'm procrastinating."

"About what?"

"I feel like I've got about a dozen questions and comments floating around my head. I'm scared to death I'm going to open my mouth and the wrong thing is going to slip out."

"Why don't you give it a try?"

"All right." He exhaled. "Try as I might, I canna figure out how you are here, without your family, without your man, and hiding a pregnancy." He winced. "See what I mean? It's too much. I'm sorry . . ."

He looked so appalled, she almost laughed. Almost! That took her by surprise. "You know, I had made up my mind to not tell you anything."

"Because I hurt your feelings?"

"Because my body and my situation ain't any of your concern."

"You can still keep me away. I'll be disappointed, but I'll understand."

Keep him away. For some reason that turn of phrase made her want to listen to what he had to say. "Why will you be disappointed? Are you really that interested in some new pregnant girl in town?"

"*Nee.*"

Well, that was what she got for pushing him, wasn't it? She'd asked him for honesty and now she got it. In spades. "All right, then."

His lips curved up. "I have something more to say if you want to hear it." She nodded. "What I'm trying to tell you is that I'm not interested in just any pregnant woman. I'm interested in you, Sadie."

"Oh."

"Yeah. Oh." He pointed to the trail that was really no more than a narrow passage of tamped-down prairie grass. "Do you still want to go for a walk?"

She felt so flustered and embarrassed, she didn't trust her voice. So instead of answering, she started walking. A handful of bugs set up a little alarm, and a couple even sprung out and flew in front of her face. She waved them off.

As they walked on, every few feet brought more growth and shade. The added coolness and comfort seemed to temper her emotions. Finally, after another five minutes, she was ready to tell him her story. "I had a boyfriend back in Millersburg. His name is Harlan."

"Had?"

"*Jah.*" Though she'd told this story before, it didn't get any easier. Mainly because she now felt like she had to prepare herself to be ignored or called a liar. Feeling like every word was being pulled out of her, she continued. "Harlan was a favorite of my father's. He is handsome, well-spoken, very dutiful, and devout."

She could practically feel Noah's eyebrows raise and thick skepticism float off of him. However, he stayed quiet.

But because she had often felt the same way, especially when she remembered how eager he'd been for the marriage bed without marriage, she felt herself breathe easier. "He might tell the story differently, but I was sure we were going to be married soon. My mother and siblings thought so, too."

"If he was courting you openly for any length of time, I'm sure everyone thought that."

She nodded. "I didn't know if I loved him, but I knew I wanted to."

"Because your parents wanted you together."

"*Jah*. And his did, too." They walked on. There were some trees overhead now. Those trees and the cloudy conditions made the ground underfoot cooler, almost soft. The flattened grass and patches of mud felt cool against her bare skin.

Remembering the night, she murmured, "One night we went to his barn . . . and I got pregnant."

"If you're waiting for me to be shocked, I ain't. I know how babies are made."

She realized she'd been holding her breath. She exhaled. "What do you want to know, then?"

"I want to know why you are alone here, Sadie."

"Oh. Well, when I told my family and Harlan about the baby, Harlan lied. He said it must be someone else's."

"Like who?" he asked darkly. "Like you had some secret man on the side."

"I guess so. Anyway, next thing I knew, I was getting in

trouble for being pregnant and lying and, well, everything. So they sent me here."

"What are you going to do when the baby comes?"

"Actually, Esther and I were just talking about that the other day." Feeling pleased that she had something to share that sounded grown-up and responsible, she said, "I'm going to get a job and start looking for someplace else to live."

His steps slowed. "So you don't plan to go back to Millersburg."

"I can't. I'm afraid if I do, it will kill me."

His eyes widened, but he didn't comment on that.

She was glad, because part of her wondered if she hadn't been exaggerating. She was really that afraid to go back.

After another ten minutes, they came upon a clearing. A creek ran nearby, and someone at some time had taken the time to carve a bench out of an abandoned log.

"Want to sit down?" Noah asked.

"That sounds *gut*." She sat down, then tensed as he scooted beside her. Really, there wasn't much extra room at all. But as usual, Noah didn't act bothered by the fact that their bodies were touching. Maybe he didn't even notice. Instead, he kicked out his legs.

She kicked out her feet, too, enjoying the cool earth under her bare feet.

"How are you feeling?"

"I'm fine. It's warm, but not terrible here with the trees around."

"I meant with your pregnancy, silly." He turned his head to smile at her. "Have you forgotten that I'm an EMT? I've had medical training."

"You know what? I think I had forgotten about your job."

She'd been too busy thinking about him as a man. A man she was hoping found her attractive, or at least one who did not think she was a terrible person.

"So? Are you nauseous? Tired?"

"I was both of those things for the first couple of weeks, but now I feel like me." Well, herself with a baby nestled inside of her.

"It's exciting, *jah*?"

A lump formed in her throat as she realized he was the first person to ask her such personal questions about the changes in her body. More than that, he was reminding her that a small miracle was taking place inside of her.

A small, tiny blessing, no matter what the cause.

Though she knew she sounded hoarse, she replied honestly. "Now that I'm not afraid of people knowing, it is exciting." It still made her scared for the future and sad about the life she was living, since it was the complete opposite of what she'd hoped it would be. "I feel calmer now."

"Would you like me to try to help you find a job?"

"I think I'm going to sew for people. I'm a *gut* seamstress."

"I'll pass that on."

"Thanks. Now, do you mind if we don't talk about me anymore?"

Looking amused, he shook his head. "I don't mind. What should we talk about instead?"

"You."

He laughed. "All right. What do you want to know?"

She liked how he didn't try to push off her request. "Tell me about your family?"

"I'm one of five *kinner*. I live with my brother Silas. We live next door to my parents and close to my sister and her husband. Harry and Melody are still at home."

"Is Silas married?"

"*Nee*. He had a girlfriend for a while. We all thought they would get married, but they didn't."

"I bet that was hard on him."

"I think it was, but he's far more quiet than me. He's not one to go on and on about his feelings."

She thought about that and figured Silas was a lot like her. She did feel things, but had long been taught to either hide her emotions or pretend she didn't feel anything.

That was maybe why she didn't feel completely uncomfortable with Esther, Monroe, and their *daed* and grandfather. Yes, their anger and words did frighten her at times. It definitely caught her off guard.

But now that she was getting more used to them, she was beginning to realize that there was a certain comfort in bluntness. She liked knowing what other people were thinking, even if it was bad. Even if it scared her.

"I'm glad we're talking," she said. "This is nice. It's probably the most relaxed I've been since I got here."

"I like it, too." He looked like he was about to say more, but his attention sharpened on something just behind her.

Before she could turn around to see, he was on his feet and reaching for her hand. "Someone's coming. Stay near me."

She almost laughed as she turned around. "Oh! It's just Monroe and Onkle Stephen." She smiled at them and waved a hand. Then realized they were holding wooden crates, and looked exhausted. She now knew what they were carrying, however. Moonshine.

When they saw her and Noah, they froze.

"What are you doing out here, Sadie?" Stephen barked. "And why is he here?"

"We were out for a walk. That's all."

Monroe glared. "Coming back here was a mistake."

"I don't know if I'm the only one here who has made one," Noah said, staring at the crates.

And that's when Sadie knew. All of the family's secrets really weren't that secret anymore. Or, maybe they never had been, and they'd all been fooling themselves.

CHAPTER 23

Monday, July 30

Though Noah was eager to step in front of Sadie and take charge of the situation, he knew that was the wrong way to go.

No, it would be better to stand back and let Sadie handle her family. At least for the first couple of minutes. He didn't know them, and knew enough about family dynamics to realize that getting in the middle of a disagreement would make him unwelcome with both Sadie and her relatives.

But hearing Monroe speak to her like she was nothing to him, without an ounce of concern in his tone? That grated on him something awful.

After a few moments, he walked to her side and placed a hand on her back. He wanted her to remember that she wasn't alone.

She was also an expectant mother. She did not need to be breathing like she was, practically hyperventilating. She started in surprise at his touch, but then gradually relaxed next to him.

Feeling better about her health, he lifted his chin at Monroe. "That is no way to speak to Sadie. You need to calm down."

"This ain't your business," Monroe replied. "I'd advise you to stay out of it."

"That's too late. Sadie means something to me."

"I seriously doubt that. Why, for all we know, you have relationships with women all over the county."

Sadie gasped. And Noah saw red. Stepping forward, he said quietly, "You need to apologize."

Monroe carefully set down the wooden crate by his feet. "I don't know you, and you don't know what you're talking about. I'd advise you to stop interfering in our family."

"I didn't come here to interfere. But maybe I should." Gesturing to the crates, he said, "What's in those?"

"What's in there isn't any of your business."

"If it's moonshine . . . I think it is," he blurted, finally bringing all their suspicions and worries out into the open.

Monroe's hands fisted. "You've overstepped yourself. I'd advise you to leave now."

"I'm not leaving until I get some answers."

Stephen looked taken aback before he visibly regained his composure. "What are you going to do, Noah? Report us to the sheriff?"

"I should. What you're doing is illegal and dangerous."

Monroe smirked. "Why don't you let us worry about the danger?"

"I can't. Not with Sadie here." Not with the other people who had died because of it. Though he wanted to mention them, he was afraid to. He didn't know what the sheriff was telling people.

"You're overreacting, Noah," Stephen said in a calm tone. "My niece isn't going to be affected by moonshine."

"The still could blow up. And she's innocent in this. You know that."

Monroe shook his head. "Innocent in what? Selling alcohol to people who want it?"

"It might be tainted."

"Our family has been selling moonshine for years," Stephen said. "For generations! It ain't tainted."

"How do you know? Do you try every batch?"

Monroe grinned. "We'd be drunk as skunks if we did that. And don't start talking to me about quality control, or some such. I bet even ol' Jim Beam doesn't try every batch of his bourbon."

"I don't think a pregnant woman should be around a still. It's dangerous."

"Don't worry about me," Sadie said. "I'm fine."

She might have been saying she was fine, but it was obviously she was shaken up. Her voice sounded strained.

Noah wondered what was bothering her so much. Was it the fact that her relatives' occupation was being discussed so openly? Or was it because he was bringing up his concerns about her pregnancy?

Stephen stared at Noah. "I actually agree with you. I've been thinking maybe we should do something."

Sadie stepped forward. "Do what?"

"We'll discuss it at home."

Monroe picked up his crate and started down the path. Seconds later, he was out of sight, covered up by the thick foliage.

"I can't believe this just happened," Sadie whispered.

Thinking she looked a little pale, Noah guided her back to the log they were sitting on. "Let's sit down for a moment."

It was a testament to how poorly she felt that Sadie sat down immediately.

Instead of following his son, Stephen walked with them, watching her with a worried expression. "Are you all right?" he asked.

"I'm right as rain," Sadie answered. "I only feel a little light-headed."

Ignoring her, Stephen set down his crate and continued to stare at Noah. "She fainted the other day."

Noah nodded. "I heard. She needs to rest more. She needs a calmer, safer environment."

"Women have babies all the time."

"This is true. But it doesn't matter how other women might feel. She needs to rest more."

"I'm fine," Sadie protested again.

Looking more worried, Stephen crouched down in front of her. "Sadie, when I was with Daisy, I talked to her about something. You see, she just discovered she has lupus. She's not feeling real badly or anything, but I think it would be good if she wasn't alone in that house all the time. And she has a real nice house, too." After looking down at the ground, he raised his chin. "It ain't like ours. It's big. Roomy. You would have a real bed to sleep in. Some privacy."

"You want to send me away, Onkle?"

"I want you to feel safe and to be able to rest." Rising back to his feet, he added, "It would be good for the both of you."

"I am going to start taking in sewing. I'll be able to help with the baby's expenses."

"No one in the family is expecting you to support yourself."

"But still, my being here is causing a lot of tension."

Stephen smiled, though the warmth didn't reach his eyes. "I'm sorry to say that the tension in my family was alive and well before you got here. It will be here when you leave as well. Please say you'll go over to Daisy's."

She glanced at Noah. "What do you think?"

"I think if you are sleeping in your own room in a real bed, it would better for you and your baby."

"Would I still see you?"

"I hope so." Looking over at Stephen, he said, "I not only came over here to see Sadie, I wanted to tell you I aim to start courting her. I hope you don't have any objections?"

Sadie made an embarrassed moan, but Noah ignored it, concentrating on her uncle's answer.

After meeting Noah's gaze, Stephen turned to Sadie. "I might be wrong, but as far as I'm concerned, I think that Sadie is the one who should be answering this." His voice gentling, he said, "Sadie, do you know what you want to do about Noah here?" Before she could answer, he added, "And if you don't know, that is all right. You can take things one step at a time."

Noah liked that. Liked how he phrased it, and liked how he was putting Sadie's future in her own hands. He had a feeling far too few people had allowed her to do that.

As Sadie visibly mulled it over, he felt suddenly awkward. He'd intended to grovel a bit more before the men had showed up.

"*Danke*, Onkle Stephen. I will move to Daisy's *haus*," she said softly before turning back to Noah. "You may come calling, but I'm not going to make any promises."

She'd forgiven him.

Feeling like he'd just won a fierce battle, Noah smiled. "That's enough for me, Sadie. More than enough."

CHAPTER 24

Wednesday, August 1

Just two days after that walk in the woods, Stephen pulled out a canvas tote bag and told Sadie to put her belongings in it. "I'll take you over to Daisy's after lunch," he announced before walking back outside.

Esther stared at the tote dubiously. "When Daed told me you were leaving, I didn't think he was serious. I guess you're pretty happy to be getting out of here."

"I'm more nervous than anything. I don't know this woman. What if she doesn't really want me at her house? Maybe Stephen is just saying she does."

"He wouldn't do that to you or Daisy. She must be fine with the arrangement. You're going to like it over there."

Sadie had been meaning to tell Esther about Monroe, the crates, and how Noah had said that the moonshine might be tainted. Now that she was leaving, she felt like she had no choice. "Noah feels that it would be better for the baby if I wasn't near your family's still."

Esther blinked slowly. "So it's out in the open now."

"I think so. Noah mentioned it."

She smiled tightly. "I'm not surprised. A lot of people buy our liquor. They've been buying it for years. They just all pretend they don't."

"Does it bother you?"

"Sure it does, but there's nothing I can do about it, right? I eat food. The moonshine allows me to do that." After a moment, she added, "It allowed you to eat, too."

"I know. I would have never said anything against it. Your family has been very good to me."

"Why am I getting the feeling that you have something more to say?"

Sadie didn't want to hurt Esther's feelings any more than she already was. But she couldn't leave and not warn her. "Noah said that people are getting real sick from some tainted moonshine. A couple of people have even died."

Worry flared in her eyes before she tamped it down. "Are you saying that my family is poisoning people?"

"*Nee*! But . . . what if Noah is right?"

"This may come as a big surprise to you, but we aren't the only family in the state of Kentucky brewing liquor," Esther fired back. "Just because you don't approve of something doesn't mean that you get to start accusing us of awful things."

"I'm not. I just don't want anyone to get in trouble."

Esther picked up a rag and began to slowly wipe the already clean counter. "Sadie, after you move into your new home, I think you should really start thinking about who has been having problems and who hasn't. No one here has gotten pregnant out of wedlock or is having to depend on the kindness of strangers for a roof over their heads. I think it's time for you to start worrying about yourself instead of all of us."

Sadie closed her eyes, feeling both the pinch of Esther's words and the knowledge that she had just broken the fragile bond they'd forged while she'd been living there. Her body reacted, too. She felt her abdomen cramp, then cramp again. Stunned, she grabbed the edge of a chair to steady herself.

Esther noticed. "Sadie? Are you all right?"

There was no way she was going to mention anything that had to do with the babe. "*Jah.*" She smiled tightly. "Of course. I . . . well, before I leave . . . please know I'm real sorry. I didn't mean to make you upset."

Esther turned to the window and braced both of her hands on the edge of the sink.

As the silence between them lengthened, Sadie realized that Esther was done talking to her. Feeling terrible, she picked up the tote and started walking to Monroe's room.

"Wait."

Hopeful, Sadie paused. "Yes?"

"I . . . I hope you will get some rest at Daisy's *haus*, Sadie. You and your baby deserve that."

"Please don't hate me." Her stomach cramped again. Rubbing her back, she hoped the pains would lessen soon.

"I don't hate you. Just, well, be careful, *jah*?"

"I'll try. Please be careful, too."

Esther didn't say another word. Just turned on the sink. And as the water ran, Sadie watched Esther hold both of her hands under the cold liquid. Simply held them out while the clean water cascaded in rivulets along her skin.

AN HOUR LATER, Uncle Stephen was as good as his word. After hitching up the buggy, he took her over to Daisy's house.

He hadn't lied. The house was lovely. Pure white with a gleaming black door and a broad front porch that was filled with flower pots. It looked like something out of a magazine.

Inside was just as pristine and pretty.

And Daisy? Well, Daisy seemed to match the home. She was graceful and slim, and her eyes shone when Stephen introduced them.

"Welcome, Sadie. I hope you will feel comfortable here."

"*Danke*. It's kind of you to take me in."

"I think we're both going to help each other out. I'll be glad for the company."

When Sadie noticed that her uncle was looking longingly at Daisy, she gestured to the stairs. "I don't want to be rude, but is my room upstairs? I'm feeling awfully tired all of the sudden."

"Oh! Of course! Come this way."

After hugging her uncle, Sadie picked up her tote and followed Daisy up the stairs. Passing two other bedrooms and a large bath, Daisy led Sadie to a large room with a queen-sized bed covered in a bright-aqua quilt. A large padded rocking chair was in the corner next to a brass lamp and a small bookshelf filled with books. Next to the window was a beautifully fashioned hope chest.

Sheer muslin curtains covered the twin windows and the faint scent of lavender filled the air. It was truly the prettiest room Sadie had ever seen.

"This is beautiful."

Daisy smiled. "I'm glad you like it. I hope you will be happy here."

After Daisy showed her where extra blankets and towels were, she went downstairs to Stephen.

Sadie took off her shoes and lay down on the bed, closed her eyes. She was exhausted and her belly was still cramping. However, she also felt completely relaxed for the first time in weeks.

She was thankful for that.

She counted her blessings as she let sleep claim her.

CHAPTER 25

August 3

The shrill shriek of the alarm pulled Noah from his sleep and reverberated through his bones. Scrambling to his feet, he glanced at the clock. It was one in the morning.

Time to work again. He pulled on his shirt, grabbed his ball cap, then stuffed his feet into his boots. "You ready, Mitch?"

"Yep, though I wish it was three instead of one. I could have used two more hours of sleep," Mitch grumbled as he raced down the hall.

In spite of the seriousness of the moment, Noah found himself grinning as he followed Mitch into the garage. He'd been thinking almost the same thing.

Though Noah was only seconds behind, Mitch was already on the phone and talking to both whoever was on the other line and Reid when he walked into the garage bay.

"Need anything?" he asked when he entered the ambulance.

"Not yet," Reid said, his expression grim. The moment Noah pulled the door shut, Reid pulled out of the garage, sirens blaring and lights flashing.

Mitch cursed under his breath as he punched in another number. The second it was connected, he said, "Y'all gonna be ready? Uh-huh. Pretty sure. Yep. Bye."

It was nothing new for the guys to be speaking in staccato shorthand, but Noah was feeling an underlying tension that was new. As he noticed that Reid wasn't heading toward town but out into the country, he called out, "What happened? Motor vehicle accident?"

"Nope," Mitch said. "We got a call about someone collapsing at home."

"Any word what the problem is?" Noah asked, eyeing both the defibrillator and the collar. "Heart attack?"

"No . . ." Mitch cleared his throat. "Noah, I don't know how to tell you this, but it's at the Stauffer residence again."

In spite of the fact that they were barreling down the highway at seventy miles an hour, Noah felt as if his world had just stopped. "Something happened at Sadie's house?"

"Yeah."

He could barely form words. "Did they say who it was?"

"Female."

"Sadie's pregnant. Maybe there's a problem with the baby."

"Maybe, but the dispatcher usually would still be on the line with the caller if that was the case."

Looking at the digital watch he wore for work, Noah realized they were still at least seven minutes out. "We gotta get there. Reid, can't you go any faster?"

"In the middle of the night without a single light for miles? No."

Mitch turned around again. "Noah, you have to pull yourself together."

"I am."

Mitch's gaze hardened. "I'm gonna be real honest with ya. I didn't want you on this run. If it wasn't for the fact that the family is Amish and you might be needed to speak Pennsylvania Dutch, I would've requested you stay back."

"I know what I'm doing."

"I don't doubt your knowledge. I doubt your ability to distance yourself." Looking at him in the eye, he said, "I know you care for this girl, but the moment we arrive, you are there as an EMT, not as a concerned boyfriend."

"I can be both."

"Are you hearing me? Because I'm not *asking* if you think you can handle it. I'm *telling* you to handle it."

"I will handle it."

Looking relieved, Mitch sighed. "Good. But prepare yourself, okay? It's gonna be hard. No matter what you see or her family says, your first priority is the patient's health and my directions."

"I hear you."

Reid started to slow the vehicle. With some surprise, Noah realized that they were less than three or four minutes from the Stauffers' home.

It felt like both seconds speeding by and an eternity, then Reid slowed into a turn and pulled into the driveway.

To Noah's surprise, Willis was standing on the front porch and waving them in with a panicked expression on his face. Noah was too worried to comment on the fact that Willis was outside instead of inside by Sadie's side.

The moment he stopped, Mitch got out. "Grab the bag, Noah," he said as he strode toward the door.

Noah did as he asked and rushed to Mitch's side.

"She's in here," Willis said in Deutsch.

Noah noticed the elderly man didn't spare him a second's glance. Reminding himself to keep his emotions in check, Noah followed Mitch inside and hoped the Lord would be with them all. He had a feeling they were going to need every bit of His help as possible.

CHAPTER 26

August 4

Noah was so surprised, he stopped in his tracks and gaped at the woman lying on the ground. He blinked, then blinked again as his heart reset itself.

It wasn't Sadie.

Within seconds, his training kicked in and he rushed to Esther's side. Noticing she was pale and having difficulty breathing, he knelt by her. Picking up her wrist, he felt for a pulse. It was faint but steady. She was still alive. They hadn't lost her yet.

Right then and there, he vowed that he would do whatever it took to save Esther. They were not going to lose another person in this household.

"Mitch?" he murmured, ready to do whatever his team leader told him to do.

The directives came fast and furious. "Give me her vitals. Then we need to flush out her system, Noah. Ipecac first, then we're going to administer an IV in the bus. Understand?"

"I understand."

Noah pulled out the Ipecac from their kit and helped Esther drink it. Simply having her vomit the poison would be the easiest and most beneficial course of action . . . if it wasn't too late.

Getting the medicine down her throat was a difficult endeavor. She was breathing erratically and appeared disoriented.

But that only lasted the barest of seconds before she started vomiting into the container that Mitch held. They knew the container would need to be sealed and taken to the lab to be analyzed to see if the poison that had been killing other people was present in her system.

"Is she going to be all right?" Willis asked.

"I don't know," Noah answered. "I hope and pray we got to her in time."

As Noah continued to hold Esther and monitor her heart and breathing while Mitch ran an IV, he heard more sirens, car doors slam, and then the front door opened.

Seconds later Sheriff Brewer was standing over them. "Is she still alive?"

"She is for now," Mitch said.

Monroe, who'd been standing stoically the whole time, made a noise like he'd just been kicked in the stomach. "For now? That's the best you can do?"

Mitch glanced up at Esther's brother. "We are doing our best to get your sister stable so she can be moved. I can't make any promises, though. We don't know how long it's been in her system."

His heart going out to the family, Noah looked at Monroe encouragingly. "We're doing the best we can," he said in Pennsylvania Dutch. "No one wants to lose her, you know that."

Stephen sighed. *"Danke."*

When Mitch gestured for Reid to join them with the stretcher, Sheriff Brewer walked over to talk to Stephen, Willis, and Monroe.

Noah watched them talk, realized that Sadie wasn't lurking in the back of the room. She had to have gone. Sadie would've been right by their side if she had been there.

He was just about to ask where she was when Reid brought in the stretcher. Returning to his job, he studied their patient.

Esther's color returned and she was breathing more normally. Her eyes opened for a brief moment before closing again.

The knot that had formed in Noah's insides loosened. Maybe they wouldn't lose her, too. He helped get Esther settled and secure while the sheriff fired off questions.

"When did she ingest the moonshine? What time?"

"My granddaughter doesn't drink liquor," Willis puffed.

"We don't have time for your lies. The hospital needs to know what to expect. How much did she ingest and how long ago did she have it?"

Willis's voice rose. "And I'm telling you, *English*, we don't know what you are talking about."

"About thirty minutes ago," Monroe interrupted. "Maybe forty. The minute I realized something was wrong, I called 911 from my cell phone."

Noah lifted his head long enough to watch Monroe's grandfather stare at him for a long moment. Then, Willis very deliberately slapped him hard.

Just as Sheriff Brewer was about to grab Willis, Stephen stepped in between his father and his son. *"Nee.* No longer, Daed. This is my daughter and that is my son."

"Nee. This is our business. Family business."

Obviously ignoring his grandfather's bluster, Monroe strode

to Noah's and Reid's side as they guided the gurney out the door. "I don't know the exact amount of moonshine, but I don't think it was more than a tablespoon or so."

"Why would she be doing that?" Sheriff Brewer asked slowly.

"She said she was upset and wasn't feeling too good. Moonshine has been in our family a long time, Sheriff. It ain't uncommon for one of us to take a sip of it every now and then." He shrugged. "I guess it was a really strong batch and made her sick."

Noah felt his stomach tighten as the reality of the situation hit him. Stephen, Monroe, and Willis still didn't want to believe that the liquor they'd been brewing could be tainted.

"I just got off with the emergency room. They're waiting on us. Let's go," Mitch ordered, leading the way.

"Wait!" Stephen called out. "That's my daughter. Can I come along?"

Before Mitch could reply, Sheriff Brewer said, "The three of you will need to go down to the station. It looks like we've got a lot to talk about."

As they guided the gurney down the steps, Noah made them pause. "Where is Sadie?"

To his surprise, it wasn't Monroe who answered but Stephen. "She already moved in with Daisy."

"So soon? I thought y'all were going to wait a few more days."

"There was no reason to wait."

But before Noah could ask another question Mitch spoke. "Do your job, Noah."

"Sorry." He rushed to the ambulance, ashamed that he'd let his personal feelings interfere with his job. With another person's life and well-being.

Getting into the ambulance, he immediately knelt by Esther's side and began checking her vitals. Seconds later, Reid pulled out and they were rushing to the hospital. Beside him, Mitch was talking on his phone to one of the doctors in the emergency room.

As they rode over a bump, Esther opened her eyes again. "What is going on?"

"We're in an ambulance, Esther. You're going to the hospital," Noah replied.

When she still looked confused and frightened, he reached for her hand. "You're safe," he said quietly. "You're with me."

Little by little, some of the uneasiness in her face eased. Seconds later she closed her eyes again. Noah hoped that it had been his reassurance that helped, but he was fairly sure that it was the drug that Reid had injected into her line.

He hoped she was going to be all right.

After racing down Highway 88 and turning right onto South Dixie, Mitch pulled into the emergency port of the hospital.

The minute they came to a complete stop, orderlies, a nurse, and a doctor rushed out to meet them. For the next few minutes, Noah was aware of nothing but Reid's and Mitch's directives, the orderlies' help, and Esther's still form.

Lord, please be with her, he silently prayed.

"We got her now," the doctor told Reid after instructing two nurses and the orderlies to take Esther into the emergency room.

"Can I stay and assist?" Reid asked.

"It's all right with me," the doctor replied. "Mitch, you need him?"

"Nah, Chad's waiting on us at the firehouse."

"Thanks, Mitch," Reid said over his shoulder before he followed the doc through the automatic metal doors.

"We better get back to the station," Mitch said.

Feeling exhausted, Noah followed and got into the passenger side.

He noticed Mitch seemed especially tense and he knew why. He'd made a mistake. A big one. "Listen, I'm sorry for what I did back at the Stauffers'."

"What part are you sorry for?" Mitch asked, tension thick in his voice. "For bringing your personal issues to a call? Or for making us wait on you?"

"Both." He swallowed uncomfortably. "All of it."

"You aren't a new trainee, Noah. You've been with me almost a year. I was ready to sign the paperwork to put you on full-time. But now? I just don't know."

Each word felt like a punch to his throat. From the moment he first walked into the firehouse, it had been his goal to one day be a real part of the team. To be taken seriously by men who were well respected.

More and more, he'd felt like getting that respect had been in sight. Now, in the space of an hour, he'd ruined all of his efforts.

The worst part was that he knew Mitch was right, and hadn't been overstating the situation. Mistakes like the one he'd just made could have dire consequences.

And perhaps it already had, he thought with a sinking feeling. His selfishness might have killed her.

Still fuming as he drove, Mitch continued. "You're a grown man and I know you don't need me talking to you like this, but I have to tell you, I don't know where your mind was. You knowing Penn Dutch is a help. It always has been. But it doesn't give you license to do or say what you want."

"I understand."

"Do you?" Before Noah could answer, Mitch sighed. "Sorry. I know these people mean something to you. If I knew them well, I probably would've been *tempted* to get personal, too."

"No, you are right. I have no excuse," Noah said as Mitch parked. After Mitch cut the engine, Noah waited, half expecting to be told to take off his uniform and not come back.

"You're off the clock. But instead of going home, you're going to clean this bus up, top to bottom. And then you're going to restock," he ordered as they got out. "Do it right and be quick about it, too. If anyone on the next shift has to go hunting for supplies, that's going to be on your back."

"You won't be searching. I'll make sure everything is ready."

Mitch nodded as he walked away.

One of the firemen who was working on the engine looked his way and raised his eyebrows. Noah knew Bruce. He was a good man, and easy to talk to. But Noah didn't think he could carry on a conversation even if he'd had the time to have one. His mouth felt like it was made of cardboard and his mind was spinning. Worrying about Esther. Worrying about his job.

And, he realized, thinking about Sadie and realizing that there was a mighty good reason why he hadn't been able to not ask about her.

She'd become important to him. He cared about her. So much so, he realized, that he might even be willing to put everything in jeopardy for her.

Even his future.

CHAPTER 27

August 4

She'd been cramping something awful for hours. She was also hesitant to tell Daisy. Therefore, Sadie did what she always did when something uncomfortable happened. She tried to pretend things were all right.

Unfortunately her body—or maybe it was simply the baby—didn't seem content with that plan. Instead of feeling better, she found herself tossing and turning restlessly, trying to find a more comfortable position. Every ten or fifteen minutes, her belly would cramp. The pains affected her mind as much as her body. She didn't know what could be happening.

Was she about to lose the baby? Had all her negative thoughts and stress finally gotten the best of her? Or, was it something else? Remembering the way Verba had been fine, then all at once wracked by pain, Sadie wondered if that was her fate.

Feeling frustrated, scared, and more alone than ever before,

Sadie closed her eyes and tried not to cry. She'd learned that crying did no good.

She'd almost convinced herself that her pains were subsiding when her door swung open.

"Sadie, you must get up right now," Daisy said as she hurried in. "Esther is in the hospital."

Sadie sat up abruptly. The movement spurred another cramp and she clenched the edge of the mattress in order to hide her discomfort. "What has happened?"

"I ain't sure, but it's bad." Daisy looked unusually flustered. "Can you be ready to go in ten minutes? We must hurry."

"*Jah*. Of course."

"*Gut*. I'll meet you downstairs. Please don't tarry."

Sadie nodded as she gingerly walked to her dresser and replaced the kerchief with a *kapp*. Then she hurried into the bathroom and washed her face . . . and even took a moment to make sure that she wasn't bleeding.

She didn't know much about miscarriages, but she did remember one of her aunts whispering about a woman bleeding when she was close to losing her babe.

Fortunately, she didn't spy any blood, so she figured she must be all right. Or at least as well as she could be at the moment.

"Sadie!" Daisy called out, her voice even more agitated. "We must leave."

Hurrying downstairs, the niggling worry that had teased her doubled in size. From the time she'd first met Daisy, she'd been nothing but calm and welcoming. Onkle Stephen had even claimed that nothing could ever disturb her.

But obviously that wasn't the case.

Sadie kept her worries to herself, though, as she obediently followed Daisy out the front door and into the driver's car. The driver was a woman who looked to be in her mid-thirties. She smiled at them distractedly before putting the vehicle in drive and starting on their way.

As her stomach muscles began to cramp yet again, Sadie pressed her hands to her abdomen. She really, really needed her body to relax.

"What is wrong with you?" Daisy asked in Pennsylvania Dutch.

"My belly is cramping."

Daisy stared at her in alarm. "Why?"

"I don't know. I've been having cramps for several hours. They've been pretty bad."

"And you didn't think to tell me?"

Her voice was harsh and angry-sounding. Sadie felt herself flinch in response. "At first I wasn't sure what was wrong. Then I wasn't sure what we could do," she said quietly. Of course there had been other issues, too: her uncle's house was in disarray; she'd been too embarrassed to talk to him about such personal things . . . And Daisy? Well, Daisy was practically a complete stranger.

Daisy frowned at her. "We could've taken you to the mid-wife."

"I was hoping they would go away."

"That was foolhardy. Ain't so?"

Sadie couldn't figure out if Daisy was upset with the whole situation or more irritated about her cramping.

Feeling even more at a loss of what to do, Sadie said, "Why are you so upset? Did something terrible happen to Esther and you don't want to tell me?"

After glancing at the driver, Daisy finally answered. "Es-ther might have drunk some tainted moonshine." While Sadie attempted to grasp that statement, Daisy continued. "They think your grandmother died of the same thing."

Remembering Verba's pain, she flinched. "Is Esther in pain? Is she dying?" The tears that she'd been attempting to hold at bay pierced her eyes.

When Daisy hesitated, Sadie's heart felt like it was breaking. "Is . . . is she already dead?"

"*Nee*. She's alive. But I don't know what's going on. He didn't make it sound like she was about to die, though. At least, that's not what Noah said."

"Noah? You spoke to him?"

"He's the only one I could talk to. Stephen, Willis, and your cousin Monroe got taken to the sheriff's office."

"Why?" she asked, though there was only one answer. It seemed her male relatives had something to do with Verba's death and Esther's collapse. "Did they really do this? Why?"

"I don't know what they did, but Sheriff Brewer seems to think they are at fault." Gripping the folds of her dress tightly, Daisy said, "This is really bad, Sadie. To be honest, I'm not sure if I've ever experienced anything so scary and disconcerting before."

The choice of words took her off guard. "Disconcerting?"

"*Jah*. I don't know what I'm supposed to do, Sadie."

"Maybe when we get to the hospital, we'll learn some answers."

"Maybe so," Daisy agreed as the driver pulled into the visitors' entrance.

"We're here," she said unnecessarily.

"Indeed we are." After Daisy paid the driver, Sadie followed her in.

They walked directly to the receptionist desk. When Daisy merely stood there, Sadie realized that the other woman was now purposely pulling back from the situation. Maybe she really hadn't cared about Stephen all that much and now that he was in trouble, she didn't want anything to do with him.

If that was the case, where did that leave her? Was she going to have to go back to sleeping next to Esther in the kitchen?

"May I help you?" the receptionist asked again.

"*Jah*. My cousin Esther was taken here by ambulance."

"Last name?"

"Stauffer."

"Let me look." She started punching buttons on the computer in front of her, scanning the information.

Then she paused.

"Did you find her name?" Anxious, Sadie leaned forward.

"I did." When she looked back up at Sadie, her expression was softer, filled with regret. Pointing to another set of silver doors, she said, "She's in intensive care. You need to go down to that waiting room."

They started walking down the hall. Sadie supposed they passed all numbers of people and official-looking carts and other items, but it was too much to take in. If she let herself, she would start to worry about Monroe and the other men in the family and what they could have possibly done.

Instead, she forced herself to focus on her need to get to Esther. "Maybe since I'm family, they'll let me see her."

"They might at that. Especially since you're going to be the only family that's here."

"I feel like everything is out of control, Daisy. Esther is in danger and the men—well, I think the men are in trouble, too."

"I'm afraid so."

The waiting room for the intensive care patients was little

more than a small room with dark-green carpet on the floor, six chairs, a small table with some magazines, and a good reading light. Other than that, it was the opposite of the bustling entrance area that they had just been in. There wasn't even a television on the wall. Sadie wasn't used to watching TV, of course, but she certainly was used to always seeing one where Englishers were waiting.

It seemed oddly quiet. After another few seconds, she realized that the room was silent. No television or canned music muffled the sounds of the hospital workers.

All she could hear was beeping from nearby rooms, nurses' and doctors' voices, and the soft swoosh of people walking by in a purposeful way. It was nerve-wracking.

"May I help you?" a volunteer asked in a kind voice.

"*Jah*. I'm here to see Esther Stauffer."

The woman looked at her closely. "You're family?"

"Yes. Her cousin." She smiled again. "May I see her?"

"I'll tell the nurses on duty that you're here. I can't promise anything, though."

"I understand." As she went to sit down, she noticed that Daisy was still standing by the room's entrance. She looked tense. "Are you going to come in here, too?"

"No." She sighed. "Sadie, I am sorry. I'm going to have to leave you here."

"You're dropping me off?"

Daisy nodded. "I can't stay here when I know that Stephen might have had something to do with this. It wouldn't be right."

Sadie felt that it would have been right for her, if she were in this predicament. She would have wanted to be there for Esther, no matter what.

Then there was the thought that she had no idea how

she was going to be able to get back home. Though she had twenty dollars in her pocket, she feared that might not be enough for some of the drivers.

"Are you sure, Daisy?" Of course, what she was really thinking was . . . did Daisy really have to leave her alone in the waiting room?

"I know this is leaving you in the lurch, but I really can't handle being here any longer."

"I understand. Thank you for taking me."

"I'm sorry, Sadie."

"We all need to do what we need to do. That is enough." She smiled, hoping her smile would offer a dose of encouragement. But Daisy had already gone.

As she shifted, her cramping started again. She held herself stiff, hoping and praying that her body would settle down soon.

"Are you here for Esther?" an older-looking nurse asked from the doorway.

She stood back up. "I am."

"The doctor pulled her through. She's going to survive. I can't let you into her room, but would you like to see her through the window?"

"Yes, please," she said as she stood up quickly. Right away, a wave of dizziness hit her hard. She gripped the edge of the chair tightly as she tried to regain her balance.

"What's wrong? Are you all right?"

"I'm fine. I'm only a bit dizzy. I'm pregnant, you see."

The nurse stepped forward, her hands up. "Take your time, now. We don't need you falling."

After she blinked a few times, the world righted itself again. Then, ever so slowly, she made her way across the room, following the nurse down a narrow hall until they came to a room that had a small window on the side of one of its walls.

"Here you go," the nurse said. "You can see Esther here."

Sadie peeked in, then realized it was a bad mistake. Even the simple act of leaning made her feel off balance. She held out her hands, wanting to press them on the window but was afraid that wasn't allowed.

She swayed, trying to get her bearings. But the sight of poor Esther, all pale skin, tubes, and wires, was terrifying.

It was the flash of pain, followed by the sudden trickle of warmth on her thighs, that brought her up short.

She was bleeding. Bleeding something awful.

"Miss?"

Feeling as if she were standing outside her body, she turned to the nurse. "Help, my baby . . ."

And that was her last coherent thought before she collapsed on the floor.

CHAPTER 28

August 4, 1:00 P.M.

They'd decided to hold them in separate interrogation rooms at the sheriff's office. During that time, Stephen was questioned by Sheriff Brewer, Deputy Beck, and even a pair of men in suits from some kind of federal department. Each of the conversations was difficult and frustrating.

And, yes, scary, too. Stephen didn't know what to say except for the truth—and the truth didn't seem to be what any of them wanted to hear.

But though the questioning was difficult, it wasn't the worst part of the experience. It was sitting helplessly by himself in a small windowless room, having no idea what was going on with his daughter. No one who stopped by periodically would tell him anything, either. All he could do was sit on a metal chair, watch the hands of the clock on the wall slowly turn on the dial, and worry about Esther.

What was he going to do if she didn't make it?

You mean died, a small, abrasive voice whispered in his

head. He flinched, hating even the idea of losing his daughter. But, he supposed it was a mighty strong possibility.

When the door opened again and Sheriff Brewer strode through, it was all Stephen could do to remain sitting and not rush forward demanding answers.

Instead, he kept his hands tightly clasped together and waited impatiently for the man to start this latest round of questioning. Surely, sooner or later, he would be done and let him go.

But instead of firing off a new question, Sheriff Brewer sat down across from him and acted as if he was trying to find the right words to say.

And that, Stephen realized, was even more excruciating than being accused of murdering his own mother. Something must have happened to Esther.

Please God, he silently prayed. *I know Your will must be done, but give me the strength to bear it.* Boy, did he need to be able to handle what was sure to come.

"Stephen, I just got a call from the hospital. There's been a development."

Every muscle in his body tightened. "What has happened?"

"Your daughter, Esther, woke up. They've admitted her and all, but it's just as a precaution. The docs think she's gonna be just fine."

Tears he hadn't realized were in danger of falling slid down his cheeks. He let them, not even caring that the sheriff was watching him cry. "Praise God," he murmured.

Sheriff Brewer cleared his throat. "I'm afraid there is more."

His stomach turned over. "What?"

"Your niece Sadie collapsed in the middle of the ICU while she was visiting." Looking just beyond Stephen, he said,

"When the nurses went to revive her, they noticed that she was bleeding. It seems she is pregnant?"

He could barely reply. "*Jah*." Despair raced through him.

Sheriff Brewer quietly continued. "They admitted her. I'm sorry, but there's a good chance she will lose the baby."

"Ah." His throat felt as if it was closing. How much was his family going to have to bear?

The sheriff was still eyeing him carefully. "I'm sorry, but I think I need to know a little more about your niece. Have you known about her pregnancy for some time?"

"I did. It was the reason she moved here."

"Where did she move here from?"

"Ohio."

"Long way for a girl in her situation, unless y'all are close. Are you close?"

During another time, Stephen might have tried to evade the personal questions. But he felt so raw, so vulnerable, he decided to answer as openly and honestly as possible. "*Nee*. I had never met her before."

Sheriff Brewer frowned. "Never?"

"Me and my brother don't view the world in the same way."

"But she still came to Munfordville."

"Sadie didn't have a lot of choice. Her news wasn't exactly welcomed in my brother's house. He kicked her out." He shrugged. "I mean, he sent her my way. I guess he figured our standards weren't as high."

Sheriff Brewer's eyebrows lifted, but he only nodded his head. "And the father of the baby? Does he know about the baby? Do you know?"

Stephen was desperate enough to get out of the room to answer any question the sheriff fired off. But he didn't understand why the man was so interested in his niece's situation.

Surely, he didn't think Sadie's appearance had anything to do with moonshine. "I'm uncertain why it matters to you."

"It doesn't, not beyond that I feel sorry for the girl. I was going to call him for her. You know, let him know about the baby."

"Oh. That's kind of you, but you should probably call my brother's phone number instead. They'll hear your message when they check their phone shanty." He sighed. "The man does know about Sadie's condition, but there's no reason for you to contact him. He lied about his relationship with my niece."

Looking aggrieved, Sheriff Brewer leaned back in his chair. "Poor thing. She's really been having a time of it, hasn't she?"

"She has." Just saying it made Stephen remember that he wasn't the only person who had been experiencing a fair share of hurt and difficulties. Here Sadie had been ignored by her boyfriend, called a liar by her parents, sent away from home, and now might even be losing her baby.

In comparison, his problems, which had just moments ago seemed too heavy to bear, now seemed almost light.

"I need to go to the hospital, Sheriff."

"I know you do. I'm going to take you myself."

"What about my son? Will you be taking Monroe, too?"

"No. We released him an hour ago. Deputy Beck already took him to the hospital."

"And my father?"

Sheriff Brewer's expression turned carefully blank. "I'm sorry, but Willis is going to need to stay here awhile longer."

A dozen questions rose to mind, but he carefully tamped them down. There would be other times to try to figure out what was going on with his father. For now, he had to concentrate on those two girls he was in charge of.

"May we go now?" he asked, getting to his feet.

"Yeah. Absolutely." Sheriff Brewer stood up, opened the door, and held it for him.

Stephen walked out, ignoring the curious stares that were directed at him. All his life, he'd resented the interest that his way of life spurred among outsiders. He'd hoped and prayed to one day be only seen as another man, not as only an Amish man.

But now, as he forced himself to continue walking and not meet anyone else's eyes, he realized that his wish had just been granted.

No one was looking at him because he was an Amish man. No, they were staring at him because they feared he was a murderer.

"Let's go over this way," Sheriff Brewer said, pointing down a back hallway that was narrow and winding. "This building is so old and convoluted, only the staff takes that way out."

Stephen gestured for the sheriff to lead the way. He was beyond caring where they went, as long as they left the building and headed toward the hospital.

Just as they were about to turn, they heard a prattle of footsteps behind them.

"Stephen?" a pretty, high-pitched voice called out.

Recognizing the voice, Stephen turned. "Daisy?"

"May I help you?" Sheriff Brewer asked politely.

Daisy's eyes widened. Then, clutching her handbag firmly, like she was worried that he might reach out and snatch it, she said, "I'm sorry for interrupting, but it is very important that I speak to Stephen. Right now."

"Ma'am—"

"What are you doing here?" Stephen blurted on the sheriff's heels.

"After I dropped off Sadie at the hospital, I decided to wait here for you," she explained, her voice sounding brittle and strained.

Though it was obvious that Daisy was upset, Stephen found himself focusing on the fact that she had left Sadie there.

"You left her in a waiting room all alone?" he asked, feeling even worse about the whole situation. That poor girl.

Daisy looked puzzled. "Well, *jah*. I figured someone else could take her home after she was done visiting Esther. What is the problem?"

"She was admitted to the hospital," Sheriff Brewer said.

She covered her mouth with a hand. "Oh, my word. What happened to her?"

"She collapsed in the hallway," Sheriff Brewer said.

"There might be a problem with the baby," Stephen added.

Daisy looked stricken. "I'm sorry, Stephen. She said she had experienced some cramps. I had no idea. I guess she was afraid to tell me that she needed help."

There were so many regrets and questions floating through his head, Stephen hardly knew where to start.

"No need for apologies, Daisy. I think it's more than obvious that all of us are experiencing a lot of things that we didn't expect."

"You ready?" Brewer asked.

"I'm heading to the hospital," he said to Daisy. "I'm afraid we'll have to talk about everything later."

"All right. I'll talk to you when you bring her back to my house."

Though he was anxious to get to the hospital, he knew he couldn't simply leave Daisy like this. "I need a minute," he said to the sheriff.

Taking her hand, he walked her a few feet away. "*Danke* for taking her to the hospital. Thank you for caring, too."

Daisy, always so forthright, looked hesitant. "Stephen, I don't understand what is going on with you, but I'm trusting that you'll help me understand when the time is right."

Reaching for her other hand, Stephen felt so much relief and gratitude in his heart, he could barely catch his breath. "You don't know how much your words mean to me. I promise, I will explain everything as best I can. Don't give up on us."

"I don't want to. I want to believe that what we have is real."

"It is. One day you'll never have any doubts."

When her eyes softened and her hands gripped his tightly, Stephen knew the Lord had indeed heard his prayers. He'd given Stephen Daisy to help him shoulder his burdens.

After gazing into her face for a long moment, he released her hands and walked back to the sheriff's side.

Minutes later, as Sheriff Brewer was driving them down the highway, he looked over at Stephen. "Is she your girlfriend?"

"I don't know. I hope one day she might be."

"Ah."

He was very glad that Sheriff Brewer had learned when to speak and when to keep quiet. Stephen didn't think he could handle another conversation. He simply had no more words.

CHAPTER 29

August 4

The first thing Sadie noticed after she woke up was that she wasn't in the Intensive Care Unit. Instead, she was lying in a comfortable bed, her sheets were a comforting pale pink and felt crisp and cool. A matching pink blanket was neatly folded at her feet. There were also not one but two pillows behind her head.

Sadie didn't know if she'd ever enjoyed so much space, care, or luxury.

"Ah, there you are," a bright, cheery voice said. "I was beginning to wonder when you were going to join us again."

Warily, Sadie turned her head and came face to face with a rosy-cheeked nurse. "I just woke up. Was I asleep very long?"

The nurse, whose nameplate said Karen, stepped forward and picked up her wrist. Pressing two fingers on Sadie's wrist, she checked her pulse. After she wrote something down on a chart, she glanced at the clock. "Several hours. Since it seemed like you were exhausted, we decided to let you rest instead of waking you up every thirty minutes."

"I'm not sure what happened."

"You collapsed outside your cousin's window in the Intensive Care Unit. Do you remember that, honey?"

"Oh! Yes! Esther. How is she?"

"I'm afraid I can't give you too many details, but I can share that she's going to survive."

Esther was going to survive. That was both the best news and something far from it, too. Survival was good, but she knew that there was a long way between survival and being all right.

When she felt the muscles in her belly pull, she rested her palm on it . . . and remembered once again how afraid she'd been. "My baby?" she asked hesitantly, not able to even go so far as to utter her worst fear aloud.

The nurse's smile widened. "Now, that, I can tell you about. Your baby is going to be just fine. Look at that heartbeat."

Sadie realized then that a cord was attached to her stomach and her baby had its own monitor.

Its very own monitor.

Just like it was its own unique person. "It's okay?" she murmured, watching a line blip across the screen. "That's its heartbeat?"

"It is. It looks good, don't you think?"

"*Jah.* It sounds *gut*, too." She was fairly certain that she could sit and watch the monitor for hours.

The door swung open. "Are you teasing the patients again, Karen?" a gray-haired doctor with kind-looking eyes behind metal wire rims murmured.

Karen winked at Sadie. "Only the ones I like."

He grinned. "Sounds like you've been in good hands, Miss Detweiler. How are you feeling? Any cramps?"

Sadie took a minute to take stock of her symptoms. "*Nee*. I think I'm only a little sore. Right now I feel all right."

"You had some bleeding, but it seems to have stopped." He looked at both the chart that Karen handed him and the computer screen. "I'd like to keep you here for another couple of hours, just to make sure you are rested and feeling better."

"All right. *Danke*."

"You're welcome. Now, are you up for a visitor? There are quite a few outside waiting to see you."

"For me? Um, yes, of course."

"I'll go get your guy," Karen said with a smile as she walked out behind the doctor.

Sadie barely had a moment to wonder who was there when Noah walked in. She felt herself turn three shades of red as he stood at the side of her bed and examined her closely.

"Hiya," he said at last.

"Hi."

Reaching out, he tenderly brushed a lock of hair from her brow. "I heard you've been giving everyone a scare."

"I scared myself some, too."

"Are you feeling better?"

"I think so. The baby seems to be all right, so that is good."

His gaze warmed. "I think so, too."

She opened her mouth, thinking that she should say something, anything, but her mind had gone blank.

He sat down on the chair where the nurse had been sitting. "I checked on Esther before I came here. Your cousin Monroe is holding vigil outside her room."

"The nurse told me that she had survived."

His brows pulled together. "More than that, Sadie. The doctors seem to think she will be right as rain soon."

"That's wonderful." She smiled wanly. "I don't know what happened to her, or even what is going on with my family. Did you hear that the sheriff took them in for questioning?"

"I did. But it must not be too bad if Monroe is already back."

"That's true."

"Sadie, one of the reasons I stopped by was to see if you were comfortable at Daisy's. Do you think you'll be all right there? Has she been nice to you?"

"To be honest, we haven't had much occasion to talk. I went to sleep almost the minute I got to her house. Then she woke me up early this morning to see Esther."

"Do you think you'll be happy living with her there?"

"I don't know." She hesitated, not wanting to divulge too much information, then realized that probably nothing in her life was a secret anymore. "Noah, to be honest, I'm not sure that she'll still want me to be staying there with her."

"Why?"

"I think she might be afraid of what trouble my relatives might be in. She liked my uncle Stephen, you see."

He stared at her quietly, then said, "I have another idea for you. How about you move in with my parents?"

"I couldn't do that." The last thing she wanted to do was be yet another family's unwanted, unexpected guest.

"Of course you could. They have a big house. My mother would enjoy your company, too. My little sister, Melody, would, too. And you would love her."

"I'm sure I would. But, Noah, I think you are forgetting something."

"What is that?"

"Whoever takes me in will be taking in another person, too." She pointed to the monitor. "That's my baby's monitor. I'm a package deal, you see."

Instead of being taken aback by her honesty, he laughed. "I know that. And my parents know that, too."

"Your mother won't mind that I'm not married?"

He grinned, just like she'd said the most entertaining joke. "Not at all."

"I've been getting tired. The doctor says I can't do a whole lot right now," she warned. "Your mother might not like that."

"My *mamm* had five *kinner*. I think she's familiar with pregnant women, Sadie. She won't mind looking after you." Reaching for one of her hands, he continued. "I also live right next to my parents. So even though you'll be living with them, I'll only be a few steps away."

But that wasn't the point, was it? It wasn't that she feared his mother not being able to handle her, it was that she would want to be around her at all.

It was hard to wrap her mind around the fact that one family could be so accepting of her while her own never wanted to see her again.

Then she realized that she was going to be released in an hour or two and she had nowhere to go—no place where she was sure she was going to be welcomed. "Would it be all right if I spend the night at your parents' house tonight?"

"Of course. I'm going to let my parents know and then come back to get you. I promise I'll be back within two hours. Don't leave without me."

"I won't." She smiled slightly. "Don't forget, Noah, I don't have anywhere else to go. At least not for tonight, anyway."

"You aren't going to have to worry about that tomorrow, either."

She didn't want to depend on that. Not on anyone, not anymore. "How about we talk about that tomorrow?"

Getting to his feet, he said, "Look at me. I'm not going to

abandon you today. I'm not going to cast you off tomorrow or even the next day. You now have someone you can depend on."

She wished she could believe that. But even though his words sounded too good to be true, she pretended she believed him. "All right. *Danke*."

"You don't have to thank me. See you soon." Shaking a finger at her, he teased, "Now, don't you leave without me."

She giggled. "I won't."

He flew out the door, obviously on a mission. Alone again, she turned her face to the monitor and took comfort in the lines that jumped at reassuring points, telling her that her baby's heart was strong and healthy.

Just as she was closing her eyes, the door opened again.

It was Karen, and she was smiling brightly. "You popular girl, you have another visitor."

"Another? Already?"

"Yep, and he's been real anxious to see you, too. May I let him in?"

Thinking that it was Monroe, she nodded and pushed the button on the bed to get into a sitting position.

"Sadie," her father said with a frown. "It looks like I came here just in time."

CHAPTER 30

August 4, early afternoon

Instead of going right to Esther's room or checking on Sadie, Stephen found himself wandering around the parking lot in front of the hospital. He felt like his head was about to explode. And it was no wonder. Sheriff Brewer had asked him a lot of questions that he hadn't had the answers to.

And that, in itself, had created a sense of foreboding deep inside. Why hadn't he asked more questions about the moonshine? Why had he never questioned his father's motivation?

More importantly, why hadn't he ever asked himself those questions?

He'd told the sheriff that he'd first been too distraught about Jean's death to do more than attempt to get through each day.

And that had been true. He was stunned by his wife's sudden death—and had felt helpless for quite some time. Nothing, not even his two precious children, had seemed to matter.

But that hadn't been the extent of his feelings.

He'd also been worried about his future and was disappointed in himself. He'd just turned forty and felt like a failure. He'd always thought he would be more successful than his father, that he'd make more money, that he'd be better.

But he wasn't. He'd taken a good look at himself and felt as if he hadn't done anything of worth besides marry Jean and have two children. With her gone, he felt the need to prove himself in some way.

Over that next year, he'd floundered—and wished and prayed for a way out of poverty. An easy way out. But of course, there was no road to success that didn't involve hard work and dedication.

When Stephen discovered his father had built himself a still in the root cellar and was making moonshine, he decided to capitalize on Willis's weakness for alcohol.

And other men's and women's weaknesses, too.

Practically overnight, other men heard about Willis's product. When they started offering a good amount if Stephen would be willing to deliver it on the sly, he didn't even consider refusing. Money was money.

Next thing they knew, money was coming in and he could afford to pay off Jean's bills. Then they bought an oven that actually worked well. His goals of being able to pay for his family's needs soon shifted. Now, instead of only focusing on what he needed, he began to think of items that he desired.

He'd started putting cash both in the bank and in hiding places around the house. Then, when business boomed even more, he did the unthinkable and got Monroe involved.

Even when he knew that Monroe did not want to have anything to do with it.

The only thing Stephen did right was keep everything from the women, but in the end, that was wrong, too.

As it turned out, their business became a dirty secret for the women as well. It also became something dangerous.

Both his mother and Esther had taken sips of the deadly brew.

His mother had died. His daughter almost had. And his son was taken in along with him for questioning.

Had he put his family's lives on the line for his own financial security? He'd like to believe he hadn't.

Whatever had happened with the moonshine was a mistake—a tainted batch. One tainted batch in a line of dozens of batches that were fine.

He hadn't done anything wrong on purpose . . .

Had he?

Surely, the Lord wouldn't blame him for brewing it. He'd brewed and sold alcohol to adult men, not sold it to children or ever coerced anyone to take something they didn't want.

Sure, it was against the Amish way of life; it wasn't anything to be proud of. And it *was* a crime. But creating poison? That . . . well, that was the terrible thing indeed.

No, it was murder.

But wasn't it an accident? Had they used some tainted products or mistakenly allowed wood shavings from treated lumber to fly into the still? He knew that it didn't take much to ruin a batch.

Then a darker idea took hold.

Had his father created a deadly potion on purpose? Had he only pretended to sample the liquor?

For what purpose that could be, Stephen couldn't begin to guess. But maybe his father didn't need a reason. He'd been acting so cantankerous and unstable of late. Maybe he was losing his mind.

Either way, he needed to be stopped. Perhaps it was for the best that Sheriff Brewer was keeping him close. No doubt Daed was so angry and upset, he was willing to take it out on almost anything.

Exhaling, Stephen closed his eyes and prayed for both peace and forgiveness. Peace for his future, and forgiveness for what he was about to do.

Accusing his father of murder was a terrible thing. But he was certain now that he could no longer stand aside and hope everything would continue as always. That was no way to live at all.

But would his father ever forgive him? Would Monroe or Esther? And what about his conscience? More doubts set in.

Did any of that even matter if doing nothing would only hurt more people and cause more pain?

He knew the answer, of course. Nothing mattered beyond saving lives. He was going to have to share every truth and every suspicion with the sheriff.

"Excuse me, sir," a uniformed security guard said as he approached. "Are you lost?"

"Hmm?"

"You've been walking around the parking lot for half an hour." The young man seemed, now that he was standing in front of Stephen, really young, and he eyed him closely. "A lady called security. She was worried about you."

Stephen pushed the brim of his straw hat farther back on his head so he could see the man's eyes. "Well, there was no reason for that. I was only getting some fresh air."

Suspicion entered his expression. "Yeah, I can see why

you'd be wanting to enjoy the fresh air, given that it's almost a hundred degrees out here."

"It didn't seem that hot to me." It hadn't, but the young man did have a point. His excuse did seem rather foolish at best.

"Let me walk you inside."

"I don't need any help walking."

"I guess I should tell ya that the other concern was that you were trying to break into someone's car."

"I'm Amish. I won't be stealing anybody's car."

"Yeah, but you could be stealing something from inside one as easy as anyone," he said belligerently. "And don't you start telling me how no one who is Amish would ever do anything like that. Because I know some would. You all are just like the rest of us."

"I wasn't stealing, but I hear you. *Jah*. I'll walk inside right now."

Looking pleased that he got his way, the security guard lifted his chin and escorted Stephen to the front door. "Here you go."

"Thanks."

Right before he turned away, the young man eyed him again. "You got family here?"

Stephen nodded. "My daughter. She's in the ICU, and I just learned that my niece is having problems with her pregnancy. She's been admitted, too."

"I'm sorry about that. Hope they feel better soon."

"Thanks," he said before going inside the automatic sliding doors.

He was instantly greeted by a blast of cold air. It lit into his skin like icy fingers and caused him to shiver. Only then did he look around the large lobby and notice a variety of signs, chairs, and counters. To his surprise, there didn't seem to be many people in the waiting room. Maybe that was why he'd been noticed? Everything looked a little worn down but functional. Feeling a bit of whimsy, Stephen thought it all looked a bit like himself.

A woman about his age was standing in front of a computer under a big sign that said Reception. She looked at him with a tentative smile when he approached.

"May I help you?"

"*Jah*. I'm here to see my daughter and my niece. One is in intensive care and the other had some problems with her pregnancy," he said, feeling his cheeks heat. It seemed even with everything going on, he was still uncomfortable talking about women's issues, especially with strangers.

She sat up a little straighter. "Which one do you want to visit first?"

"My daughter. Her name is Esther. Esther Stauffer."

"Of course." After taking down his name, Esther's name, and looking at the computer, she handed him a tag. "Put that on and then I'll buzz you into the main building. Go through the doors and keep walking until you see the signs for the Intensive Care Unit, the ICU."

"ICU. Got it."

He clipped on his visitor pass, went through the doors when they buzzed, then did as he was instructed. It was all easy enough. A nurse met him when he got to the ICU and kindly walked him to Esther's room.

"You came in the nick of time," she said with a smile.

His hands began to shake. "Why is that?"

"We were just about to move your daughter into a more private room."

"She is doing that well?" he asked hesitantly. He was so afraid to hope.

She smiled. "She is. She was even asking for something to eat, which is a good sign."

Though he'd heard Esther was better, this still caught him by surprise. A little bit of his fear edged away as his spirits lifted at that news. "My daughter was born hungry," he said, feeling his lips turn into an unexpected smile. "We used to call her the bottomless pit when she was just a tiny thing."

"I bet she loved that."

"We stopped about the time she cared," he replied, the sweet, long-forgotten memory catching him by surprise. He'd also pushed so many sweet memories of his Jean away. It hurt too badly. He'd always assumed this would make things easier to bear. But it didn't. The habit only served to make him feel empty. "So, were you able to feed her?"

"We gave her some gelatin, and I believe a couple of crackers. We'll move on from there if she doesn't have any problems."

"I'm glad she's doing so well. I owe all of you a great deal of thanks."

The nurse waved off his comment. "We're all glad she's doing better. That's enough for us." Softening her voice, she said, "Your daughter is right in there, Mr. Stauffer. Go on in when you are ready."

Glad that she was giving him a moment to collect his thoughts, Stephen peered through the large window. He had expected to see Monroe there but, to his surprise, Esther was sitting by herself. She was awake and was staring off into the distance.

They'd dressed her in some kind of hospital smock. She also had a kerchief over her hair. It had been so long since he'd seen it that way, he stared at her for a moment, remembering how she used to beg her momma for colorful kerchiefs to wear around the house.

Though she looked a little pale, she definitely did not look like she'd just been transported in an ambulance. Actually, he thought she'd never looked prettier.

She also looked so very alone.

A rush of emotion filled him as he opened the door. She was his little girl and he'd almost lost her.

The moment she heard the door open, she turned her head. Happiness lit her expression and melted his heart. "Daed, you came."

"Of course I did." Crossing the room, he gingerly enfolded her in his arms. He had to be careful about all the wires and cords attached to her. But underneath all of that, she felt the same.

Tears pricked his eyes. "Esther, Praise God. I was afraid we were going to lose you."

When he pulled back, she treated him to a watery smile. "For a while there, I thought I was going to see Mamm and Mommi today. I'm so glad Jesus decided to let me stay here on Earth a little while longer."

Tears choked his throat. "Me, too."

"I was so scared."

"Me, too." After squeezing her hand again, he released it and sat down on the chair next to her bedside. "Now ain't the time to talk about it, but I don't think I'll ever be able to forgive your grandfather for encouraging you to try that moonshine. I don't know what he was thinking."

Her eyes widened. "Oh, it wasn't *Dawdi* who gave me the moonshine, Daed."

"Say again?"

"It wasn't Dawdi. It was Monroe."

Everything inside of him tensed up. "Your *bruder*?" he whispered. "Are you sure?"

"*Jah*. He was daring me to sip it."

"Daring you?"

"*Jah*. Like we used to do back when we were small. Remember? I used to dare him to try to jump across the creek and he used to dare me to eat Mommi's Brussels sprouts."

"You two are old now. And moonshine . . . well, that ain't something a girl like you should be trying."

Looking mystified, she shrugged her shoulders. "I thought the same thing. I mean, it wasn't like anyone I knew was going to care one way or the other if I tried liquor." She lowered her voice. "You probably aren't going to want to hear this, but I've tried it before, anyway. Back when I was fifteen, I wanted to see what all the fuss was about."

As the implications of what she was saying registered, the room began to spin. "Are you sure Monroe encouraged you to try it?"

She looked at him curiously. "Of course."

"Where is he?"

She flinched at his tone. "I don't know."

He looked around frantically. "Where did you see him last?"

"I don't know."

"Esther, I need to know where he is." His head was pounding. So was his heart. Every bit of him felt like it was on fire.

Esther was looking alarmed. "Daed, please, don't get upset."

"How can I not? You almost died."

"But we know Monroe didn't think I was going to get so sick from just one sip. After all, that doesn't happen ever. Does it?"

He shook his head slowly, but his mind was spinning. He was thinking about his mother and the way she'd collapsed.

Thinking about the rumors of the two men out in Cub Run who had died. He'd been thinking it was all some terrible consequence, but maybe it wasn't.

"When Monroe was here, did he say anything to you?"

"I promise, I don't remember." She squeezed her eyes tight. "Maybe? They gave me a lot of medicine. Everything was fuzzy."

Getting to his feet, he started toward the door. "He's probably around here somewhere. I need to go find him."

"I'm sure he's just sitting in the cafeteria or something. I mean, where else would he be?"

"Sadie had a problem with her baby. She's in another room." Keeping his voice even, he said, "You know, I bet he's sitting with her."

"Sadie is here, too?"

"Don't worry, child. She'll be all right." He didn't know if he was lying or not, but he couldn't risk Esther getting upset.

"Oh. Well, all right." Looking pained, she leaned her head back against the pillows. "Boy, when it rains, it pours, doesn't it?"

Stephen knew he wasn't going to be able to keep a hold on his temper for another minute. "I better get out of here, dear. I, uh, talked to the nurse before I came in here. She said that they are about to switch your rooms."

"I heard that, too. But that was an hour ago."

"I have a feeling everything around here takes time, but she did sound certain. I'm going to go check on your cousin so they can move you."

After pressing his lips to her brow, he walked toward the door. "I'll see you in your new room, child."

"You're not leaving the hospital, are you?"

"*Nee*, child. I won't leave here anytime soon. Not yet."

Pleased when he saw the wrinkle in Esther's brow ease, he walked out into the hall. He was certainly going to see Sadie. But first he intended to look for his son.

It seemed they had a great many things to talk about.

CHAPTER 31

August 4

Stephen found his son around the rear of the hospital, sitting on an iron bench near a playground. Monroe was alone. Stephen wondered whether it was the heat or the location that was the reason no one else was there. He couldn't imagine many folks visiting loved ones would want to take their children so far from the main entrance.

Stephen's feet crunched on the pebbles underfoot. Monroe didn't so much as glance his way, however. Instead, he was staring at the empty swing set.

He didn't even budge when Stephen sat down beside him.

"I've been looking for you everywhere," Stephen said, taking care to keep his voice light. "I'd just about given up when I spied you from one of the upstairs windows. What are you doing out here?"

Monroe shrugged. After another minute passed, he finally answered. "Thinking about things, I guess."

"I just got here myself. Well, I mean, I've already gone inside to check on Esther." When Monroe didn't comment on that, Stephen continued on like a magpie. "Sheriff Brewer drove me here. I thought it was nice of him. I sure didn't expect it, you know?"

When his son still stayed silent, Stephen touched his forearm. "Sheriff Brewer said Deputy Beck drove you. Is that right?"

"*Jah.*"

"What did he question you about?"

At last Monroe turned. "About the same things that they questioned you about, I suspect," he said, his eyes looking carefully blank. "They wanted to know about the still, what we did, why we sold moonshine." He swallowed. "Is Esther . . ."

Stephen felt like his heart was lodged in his chest. "She's going to be fine. The doctors said she'll be suffering no lasting effects."

"Not like Mommi, huh?"

Pain, sudden and unexpected, rushed through him. He hadn't really mourned his mother's loss. There'd been too much stress, too much worry. Then, too, there had always been the looming knowledge inside of him that his mother had been willful and difficult. She'd also loved to talk out of both sides of her mouth, constantly leaving Stephen unsure of how to please her.

Their moonshine business had been an example of that. She'd enjoyed both sampling their product and the money it brought them . . . just as she had also loved to profess that what they were doing was sinful and wrong.

He'd long since given up trying to make her either happy or proud.

Stephen had no idea how to explain all this to his son. Perhaps it would be better if he never did. The boy needed some good memories of his grandmother . . . or at least some that weren't too tainted. So, instead of saying all that, he reverted back to old habits. He tried to excuse himself.

To make excuses for all of them. "We didn't know that one of our batches was tainted. I mean, how could we? And it wasn't our fault your grandmother tried some of that bad batch. She took a jigger of moonshine at least once a week ever since we started."

Monroe shook his head. "It was at least once a day, Daed. Mommi enjoyed a few sips of that moonshine on a daily basis. It wasn't a secret. If we're going to start admitting our sins, let's be honest about it."

"I didn't know it was that often." *Had he?*

"Did you really not know?" Monroe asked, the bitterness in his tone making each word feel sharp. "Or did you choose not to be aware of it?"

"Both, I guess."

Monroe studied him some more, those hazel eyes he'd inherited from his mother filling with resignation. "Daed, you knew that I never wanted to do it."

"Make and sell moonshine? I knew." Guilt beckoned, but he held it at bay. It would be so easy to take responsibility for Monroe's actions. He used to think it was a parent's job to do that. But his son was a grown man and needed to speak for himself. "If you didn't want to be a part of it, why did you?"

"At first, I was afraid of disappointing all of you. You, and Dawdi especially, acted like you were counting on my help. But then, when I knew I wanted something different, a different life . . . I didn't know what else to do." His voice turned tentative. "I, well, I didn't have any other skills. Not ones that were useful. Do you know what I mean?"

"*Jah*. Maybe I felt that way at times as well." He swallowed his pride and continued, knowing he needed to tell the truth not just for Monroe's sake but for his own as well. "I did things opposite. I went out on my own and tried to be a successful farmer. I failed at that. I had no choice but to join your grandfather. But it's also true that he was glad for my help."

Letting his words sink in, Stephen propped one foot over an opposite knee. "What happened today?"

Monroe's stoic expression crumbled. "Esther and I were joshing each other, just like we've always done. I went too far when I dared her to taste the moonshine. You know that."

"Is that really what happened? Did you think it was the new batch?" He held his breath, not even sure what he wanted to hear. It would be so easy if Monroe said he made an honest mistake. Stephen knew Sheriff Brewer had a soft spot for Monroe.

If Monroe said that he honestly thought his sister sipped untainted liquor, that he was just as shocked as anyone when Esther started not feeling well, then his boy would never be charged with anything. He and his father could take the brunt of the responsibility and the blame.

But would Monroe be able to live with that?

His son clenched his fists on his knees. Looked straight ahead. Then spoke quietly. "We were playing around, but I knew it was tainted, Daed. I made sure it was just a small amount."

His heart was breaking. "Son—"

"*Nee*, let me finish." His voice quickened. "You might not ever believe this, but I didn't want to hurt Esther. I really didn't. I just wanted to scare you and Dawdi enough to stop."

That was it? *That* was his excuse? "There had to be another way, Monroe."

When Monroe turned his body to face him, pure scorn filled his expression. "What other way? Mommi died! The sheriff came out to speak to the whole family. Noah told us that other people around the county were getting sick. But still you were in denial. And Dawdi? Did Dawdi even care? I don't know."

"We weren't sure . . ."

"*Nee*! You didn't *want* to be sure. You wanted to keep making money, to act as if you didn't know any better." He laughed darkly. "I think Dawdi would also keep pretending to be completely ignorant of anything that was happening in the English community. He would continue to be a clueless Amish fellow, too ignorant to understand the evils of the English ways."

"Don't talk like that."

"Don't speak the truth? Or don't hurt your feelings?"

He didn't know how to answer, mainly because he feared it was both. He didn't want to hurt anymore. He didn't want any of them to hurt anymore.

But it was time to face the truth, even if it hurt them all even more. "I don't know what to do now. The sheriff still has your grandfather in custody. And Esther isn't completely out of the woods yet."

"We have to be honest with both ourselves and with the sheriff."

"But what if he takes you into custody again?"

"Then I will face the consequences." When Stephen was about to protest, Monroe reached out a hand. "You have my back, Daed. Don'tcha?"

Stephen wrapped his hand around his son's, not caring that it was now bigger and stronger than his own. "Always."

"Then you can accept me and still love me, even if you don't understand what I've done or why I did it."

"I can," he whispered, thinking that was what Jesus did for them. He loved them even when He didn't understand their actions.

His son looked at him carefully, nodded as if he was pleased. "*Gut.* And then tomorrow morning, you can dismantle that still."

"I will do that. *Ich leevi dich,* Monroe. I will never stop loving you. And I will make sure our family is never in the moonshine business again."

Monroe blinked, then his expression cleared. "If you can keep that promise, then we're gonna be all right, Daed."

Feeling shaky, Stephen got to his feet. There were so many things he wanted to say. Apologies for the mistakes he'd made. Confessions about how difficult his life had been after Jean went to heaven. How lost he'd felt when he'd faced the truth about his financial failures.

But now wasn't the time to reveal that. Maybe it never would be. He'd always believed that it was a father's job to be strong for his children, not burden them with his weaknesses.

He pressed his palm on Monroe's shoulder, taking comfort in the span of powerful muscles he felt, then walked back inside the hospital. No matter what was in their future, Monroe was going to be able to bear it. He was strong. Stronger than he'd ever been.

And, maybe, so was he.

Stephen had no idea what the sheriff or the Lord had in

store for any of them next. All he did know was that both he and his son were going to be brave enough to handle whatever came their way. Because of this, they would shield the people they cared about from its ugliness.

And if that wasn't possible? Well, they would die trying.

CHAPTER 32

August 4

Sadie didn't know if she'd ever felt more trapped. "I don't understand why you are here," she told her father, taking care to not call him that. Weeks ago, he had forbidden it. Now? She knew he wasn't her father at all. Not where it counted. Not in her heart.

"I've been keeping my eye on you."

"How?" They hadn't talked at all.

"Your uncle has been giving me regular reports. Just because we sent you away, it didn't mean we didn't care about you, daughter."

The news disappointed her. She'd hoped that Stephen was different, but maybe it had been too much to ask. He'd taken her in as a favor to his brother. Why wouldn't he agree to spy on her, too?

As that realization sank in, Sadie stared at her father. He looked so gruff, so sure of himself. Demanding.

Like everything she didn't want to be. And with that

knowledge, she realized that she no longer feared her father like she used to.

She still loved him. At least, she thought she did, but she didn't want anything to do with him. Not anymore.

And why would she, anyway? He'd abandoned her. He'd valued his reputation over her well-being. Sadie knew she'd never choose to live anywhere near him ever again. As far as she was concerned, he was simply a part of her past that she needed to push away.

But she decided to keep silent. Though she might not now have the same fear of disappointing him, it didn't mean she felt able to knowingly set off his temper. Perhaps if she waited long enough, he would leave.

As one minute turned into two, and eventually into six, she watched her father become increasingly uncomfortable. His brow furrowed, he opened his mouth, obviously intending to say something. Then for whatever reason, he closed his mouth again.

But if looks could kill, Sadie knew that would have already happened. Though there was no need, she curved her hands around her belly protectively. Vowing once again to never treat her baby like this. She wanted her son or her daughter to trust her. Even if they weren't best friends when grown, she hoped he or she would always trust her.

After shifting restlessly again, he said, "You're being mighty silent. Don't you have anything to say to me?"

"*Nee.*"

He scowled. "That is no way to speak to your father."

"But you aren't my father. Not anymore."

"Of course I am."

"*Nee.* You gave up that designation, don't you remember?"

"You are being ridiculous."

"I don't think so. But no matter what you are to me, I'm afraid I don't have any other way to speak to you anymore. Take it or leave it."

"You've forgotten everything I've taught you."

"*Nee*, I haven't. I'm not trying to be disrespectful. I just simply don't have the words that you are wanting to hear."

"I taught you to stay silent."

She lifted her chin. "I remember those lessons well. And just now, I was silent. But you didn't care for that. Therefore, I'm not sure what you want."

His stunned expression would have been comical if she didn't have years of memories where she had tried so hard to be everything he had wanted, but she'd still failed. Now she realized that there was nothing she could have done right in his eyes.

It was really too bad that she had to be cast out from her family in order to see just how ugly their family dynamics really were. Now she understood why the Lord handled things the way He had. She *needed* to get away, but her inherent desire to please would have never allowed that to happen.

She also realized that if she'd never left, she wouldn't have met her Kentucky cousins. That would have been such a loss.

And then there was Noah.

Noah had become so dear to her. If she hadn't met him, Sadie knew she would still be searching for love and happiness. She'd needed him to understand what love was.

And she'd needed his—another—family to understand how a real family acted.

Or maybe she had only to join her cousins' family, she realized. Stephen, Willis, Monroe, and Esther were certainly not perfect. But they did their best for her.

Even more importantly, they didn't expect her to be perfect, either. Finally, she understood what God's love really
was. It didn't come with conditions or favors or sacrifices.
He didn't want her to be perfect or obedient or demure. He
wanted her to be the person He'd intended for her to be.
Sadie. Eager, imperfect, trusting Sadie, who liked sewing but
not cooking. Who liked helping others when she was able
and who sometimes stayed off to the side when she was over-
whelmed.

Her father cleared his throat, bringing her back to the
present.

"When we get home, I see I'll have to remind you again
about the proper way to act."

She shook her head. "*Nee*, Daed. You won't. Because I
won't be going back to Millersburg with you."

His voice softened as, for the first time, it seemed he was
aware that she was nestled in a hospital bed. "But you must,
Sadie. You can't survive on your own."

"I'm afraid I'm going to have to."

"All right. I admit that we should have believed you from
the start. Is that what you've been waiting to hear?"

"I am glad to hear that. But that doesn't change my decision.
I'm better here."

"Poor and in Kentucky."

"That may be the case. But at least I'll feel like I've got a
chance. No matter what, I know I won't be able to survive
back in that farmhouse, living under all those rules and
punishments. Never again. I certainly would never subject
my baby to the life I had."

"The life you had?" he repeated. "Sadie, you had everything."

"I did have a lot of comforts," she agreed. "But I also had

nothing. I learned how to do chores and mind my manners and fear your wrath. I learned to accept being ignored and belittled. I learned to not expect anything from you except pain."

He lurched to his feet. "Don't say any more."

"But of course I will. Father, don't you understand? I finally grew up. I'm no longer only worried about pleasing you or avoiding your temper. I have responsibilities and plans. I now have my own way of doing things."

"You are still a child. You don't know what you're talking about."

Well, there was her answer. No matter what she'd hoped to accomplish with him, he was letting her know that he wasn't going to change.

So she needed to do the changing. Pointing to the door, she said, "I want you to leave, Father."

His expression turned thunderous. "*Nee.*" Then, to her shock, he reached for her arm and gripped her tightly. And then yanked her up.

The monitor that had been attached to her stomach was pulled away, and along with it, the reassuring beeping and whooshing that she'd been listening to went silent.

Almost as if he had taken her lifeline away.

Everything in her cried out as he tugged on her forearm again. "*Nee!* Help!" She twisted against his grip.

And then inhaled sharply when he slapped her hard.

"You will be silent!" he yelled, pulling on her arm.

Her door opened just as she cried out again . . . and she heard a bone snap. "My arm!"

Her father turned sharply, held his hands up, saying, "I did nothing," as he became aware of the presence of a witness.

Pain was shooting through her arm, but it was nothing

compared to the sudden cramping that started again in her belly. "Help me!" she called to the nurse.

"Oh my heavens!" the nurse said around a gasp before calling out down the hall. "Assistance! Code four!"

More people rushed in. Including Noah.

"Sadie," Noah called out as he tore across the room. She could practically feel heat from his glare as he took account of everything that was happening. "Call for security," he ordered another of the nurses as he positioned himself between Sadie and her father.

"Noah, be careful," she whispered.

Noah simply stood in front of her like a stone wall and spoke to her father. "You need to step back and calm down, Mr. Detweiler. You are causing a scene and hurting Sadie."

Instead of complying, her father just looked even more wild-eyed. "Get away from her."

"That ain't going to happen," Noah said as he edged closer. "I'm not going to leave her. Not now, not ever."

"Father, please listen to him," Sadie cried. "Noah is a good man. He—"

"You are ordering me about?" he roared.

Looking as if he had completely lost all control, Sadie watched in terror as he lunged forward, obviously meaning to strike her. Crying out, she shrank back, wishing she was brave enough to fight him, but a lifetime of his abuse had left a mark on her.

She could hardly stop shaking, let alone fend him off.

Besides, she had her baby to take care of.

Just in time, Noah gripped her father's arm and held it off to the side. Her father wheezed in pain, but Noah's face remained immobile. "You will not touch her again," he stated firmly. "Not *ever* again."

Sadie was crying in earnest now. All of it was just so horrible. Esther's collapse, the knowledge that it was her relatives who had been poisoning the community. Now her father was attempting to harm her yet again.

When was it ever going to end?

Her father groaned again and suddenly shrunk back, as if all the fight had just left his body. Then he turned in alarm as two security guards strode in. It was as if their sudden appearance finally filtered through his angry haze. He froze.

"What have *I* done?" he asked. "Sadie, you must talk to them. Tell them—"

"*Nee*, Father," she said. She couldn't bear to listen to anything he had to say.

"Please escort this man from the premises," Sadie's nurse said crisply.

The security team grabbed her father's arms. He didn't put up a fight. Instead, he simply stood there, looking around at each of them with a confused expression.

"Hold on," Noah said. "Sadie, do you want to press charges? He hurt you."

"*Nee*. He just needs to go." He had hurt her, but vengeance wasn't going to make anything better or change how things were between them. All she wanted was for him to leave her in peace.

"You heard Sadie," Noah said, still not looking away from her. "Get him out of here." After the guards left, another nurse approached Sadie's opposite side.

"My stars! Let's get you settled and put back to rights."

"*Nee*, first I think you'd better find a doctor . . . Karen," Noah said to the nurse. "I'm fairly sure her wrist is broken."

After glancing at Sadie's wrist, the nurse scurried out. As

she opened the door, a cacophony of voices creeped into the room. It was obvious that her father's presence had created quite a bit of commotion.

Noah got up and closed the door firmly before sitting on the bed right beside her. Thankful for his reassuring comfort, Sadie collapsed against him. Noah murmured soothing words as he curved an arm around her shoulders and pulled her into a hug.

Sadie closed her eyes, exhaled, and allowed herself to find comfort in his arms. Yes, she was in pain, and her future was definitely uncertain, but she was so relieved that she had Noah to hold on to at that moment.

From the comfort of Noah's arms, she felt as if she were peering at everything through a veil of fabric. Then the reality of what had just happened hit her hard and she began to panic.

Her heart began to beat erratically. She felt out of breath, as if she'd been running a long distance. But more disturbing was the way her head was pounding. Every word her father had said was repeating in her brain, and she felt like she was going to be reliving that moment, when he'd twisted and ultimately broken her wrist, for days if not longer.

Needing to calm down, she gazed at the completely silent baby monitor. She needed to see and hear its reassuring cadence, and tugged on Noah's sleeve.

"Hmm?" he asked, brushing a kiss on her brow.

"*Noah*, can you turn the monitor back on? I *need* to see the baby."

He shifted to see where she was pointing. "Ah. Of course." He got to his feet. Then, as if he'd done the very same thing dozens of times before, he found the sticky pads that had been affixed to her skin, checked the cords they were attached to, and straightened the sheet over her lap as he lifted, with a tender expression, Sadie's gown so that her protruding belly was showing. He carefully placed the connectors on her skin and checked the monitor display.

Seconds later the reassuring pulse was back on the screen. Sadie leaned back in bed—"She's okay . . ." The babe was fine.

Blue eyes brightened. "The doctors found out that you're going to have a girl?"

"I don't know for certain. I just feel like I am."

"You can ask the doctors if you want," he said with a smile.

It was another reminder that what was happening was her business and her decision. She could decide whether she wanted to find out the sex of the baby. Not Harlan. Not her parents, not even the doctors and nurses. "Maybe I will ask them," she said.

As she was settling against the pillows with an exhausted sigh, Noah leaned closer. "Any minute now they're going to wheel you out and work on your arm. You'll feel better soon."

Belatedly, she realized that they already had put some kind of mild sedative in her IV. "Okay," she said, feeling drowsy.

Noah was still staring at her intently. "Sadie, before I have to leave you, listen for a moment. Please?"

She nodded as he leaned in even closer. Taking comfort in his clean, fresh smell. In the goodness that seemed to encompass every part of him.

"I know you are hurting and upset," Noah said, "but things are going to get better."

"How can you be so sure?"

He pulled back ever so slightly so she could see the entirety of his expression.

"Because I'm going to make sure of it."

He sounded so calm. So certain. As if he wasn't bothered or worried about anyone around them or anything that had just happened.

And because of that, and because she needed to believe in somebody, she bowed forward and relaxed against him.

And found peace at last.

CHAPTER 33

August 6

Two days later, Sadie was relaxing on the sofa in the Freemans' living room. Her arm was in a cast. She'd been ordered to rest and take it easy for at least the next week.

Noah and his parents had been talking about her moving in. Now they were clear, deciding, along with the doctors' concerns, that she needed to move in with them.

Sadie couldn't find any fault with that. The truth was, she loved being at Rebecca and Hank Freeman's home. Their home was lively and full of laughter. She didn't feel alone, either. In fact, she had never felt so supported. Rebecca seemed to take Sadie's continued well-being as a challenge—a challenge that she was determined to meet easily.

Then there was the added bonus of living next to Noah and his brother Silas. Each evening so far, when he got off work, Noah came over and sat with her. He held her hand and told her stories about his days.

Sadie was also doing some planning. With Rebecca's help, she wrote some lists about things she could make for babies once her wrist healed. Tiny soft sleeping gowns, warm knit onesies for when babies were crawling. Blankets and tiny quilts made out of flannel and other soft materials.

That morning, she'd even tried, rather clumsily, being in a cast, to begin a simple crochet project. It was a tiny hat for a newborn. When she felt better and it was finished, Sadie decided she'd take it to an English doctor's office. Maybe someone there would like it enough to allow her in the future to display a few items in the office.

Of course, she didn't know if these dreams would ever come to fruition. But it did give her a lot of joy to think about making something that was pretty and useful.

Getting paid for the items would make her feel good, too. She might never get rich making her crafts, but she felt above all that she could have some control over her future, even if in a small way. She was thankful for that.

Noah came over to fill her in on his work night when there was a knock at his parents' door.

He got up and answered it.

Sadie only half paid attention to the visitor from her spot on the couch. She'd learned quickly that the Freeman family was very popular. They had visits from the *kinner*, their cousins, and all of their friends. No one had seemed surprised to meet her, or to discover that she was now living with them.

In fact, some had even acted as if they were surprised it had taken her so long to move there.

All that was why she tried to give Noah the privacy he needed to greet the arrivals. No doubt it was someone his family knew well, and she most likely didn't know at all.

"Excuse me?" he blurted.

Surprised by his abrupt tone of voice, she glanced over at him again. She couldn't see who he was talking to, but she realized immediately that it must have been someone he was uncomfortable with, because his posture changed from relaxed to tense.

His mother, who'd been standing off to the side, exchanged a glance with her. Then her eyes widened when Noah stood back and Esther, Stephen, and Sadie's mother and sister Grace entered.

"Mamm?" Sadie climbed to her feet. She looked over at Noah.

He looked resigned. Not angry. She could tell, though, he wasn't pleased about her visitors.

"Noah?" she asked tentatively, thinking she did want to see her sister and mother, but had certainly not forgotten their treatment of her. She wasn't ready for them to pretend that her being in the Freemans' home was a giant misunderstanding.

"You have some guests. Are you feeling up to visitors?"

If she hadn't already fallen in love with him, her heart might have melted right then and there. Noah was not only making sure she was all right with the visit, but he had even come up with a way for her to gracefully refuse to see them.

"I'm feeling well enough to see my mother and sister."

He closed the door. "All right," he said as he walked to her side. "But let me know if you start to feel differently."

"Sadie," her mother said as she walked to her with a smile. "I canna tell you how glad I am to see you."

"I'm glad to see you, too. And you too, Grace."

Grace bounded to her and gave her a fierce hug. So fierce that Sadie had to take a step back to keep her balance.

Noah moved nearer.

"Careful now," Rebecca said. "The doctor said you need to be taking it easy."

254 Shelley Shepard Gray

After hugging Sadie tight, her mother helped her sit back down.

Once everyone had said hello and gotten settled in various chairs and couches in the large room, Sadie spoke. "Mamm, what are you doing here?"

"The sheriff came and talked to us. A Sheriff Brewer around here called our local man and he came over." She cleared her throat. "He told us what happened with your father." Eyeing Sadie's cast, she added, "How he hurt you."

Sadie nodded. She didn't know what to say. She didn't want to defend him, but she didn't want her father to get in real trouble, either.

She looked warily at Noah.

He, as she hoped, merely shrugged. She knew what his look said—that there wasn't anything anyone could do about the situation.

After his mother offered everyone glasses of water, and his father and Melody entered the room, and all the introductions were made, Sadie was at a loss of what to do next.

To her surprise, it was Stephen who filled the silence. "It was my idea to bring them over. If I've learned anything over these last couple of weeks, it's that worrying and keeping secrets doesn't help anyone at all. If anything, it only makes things worse."

"I agree," Rebecca said. "So, what is happening with Monroe?"

"Right now the police and a judge are trying to figure out if they want to press charges against him." He rubbed his neck. "Obviously, the still has been dismantled. We've been fined, but that may be all that happens. They seem to believe we had no idea that treated wood shavings flew into the still and made the concoction poisonous." He shrugged.

"I don't know, though. What the Lord wants to happen will, I suppose."

Sadie knew there was much more to the story, but nothing that her uncle was going to feel comfortable talking about at that moment.

Gazing at her mother, she said, "Why did you and Grace come here?"

"We had to see your father, of course. But I wanted to see you, too." Looking awkward and maybe even a little shy, she said, "I wanted to tell you in person that we would like you to come home."

The whole room tensed. Sadie wasn't sure what the "right" response should be. All she could do was speak from her heart. "Mamm, I love you. I love Grace and the rest of my siblings, too. But that place isn't home anymore. I can't go back."

Her mother frowned. "Is it because of Harlan?"

"*Nee*. It's because I wasn't happy there. Don't pretend that you don't know how Daed treated me."

"He's gone now. When he gets let out, some of his cousins are going to take him in. He's not going to move back home."

Sadie knew her mother probably believed that, but she also knew that her mother had willingly turned a blind eye to many cruel things her husband had done. There was little chance that she would ever kick her husband out for good.

Sadie now knew better than to argue that point. Her mother was never going to listen. She preferred to live in her make-believe bubble and pretend that they were the most respected Amish family in the area.

But even if they were still that, Sadie knew that wouldn't be enough for her.

"Mother, this is home now."

"In this house?"

"Maybe. I feel happy here. Safe here." Looking at Noah, she added, "I feel loved."

"But the baby. Sadie, you can't raise it on your own."

"I would have, Mamm. I was willing to do anything to keep my baby safe."

Standing by her side, Noah said, "I've already told Sadie that her baby is going to be mine in my heart. She's not going to ever have to do anything alone again."

Her mother gaped at him. "You'd be willing to do that?"

"Of course."

"But it isn't yours."

Her mother looked so very confused. That made Sadie realize just how wrong everything had been in her childhood home. "Mamm, Noah's love for me and this baby is as pure and right as Jesus's love for us. As comforting as God's grace is for me. Noah accepts me for who I am."

Her mother glanced at Noah. Her expression wasn't condemning, it was unsure. She really didn't understand how to love without reservations.

"Mamm. Even though I'm going to live here, I'd still like to know you."

"I'll see—" She immediately stopped herself. "I mean, I want to know you, too, daughter. No matter what happens, I want to know you."

Noah reached for Sadie's hand, gently squeezed it, and smiled.

Later that night, long after her mother and sister left and Noah's parents went to sleep, he held her close in his arms. They kissed and cuddled and he placed his hands on her stomach, laughing as he felt the slightest quiver.

Then she'd relaxed against him.

"You seem happy."

"I am. I'm no longer fearing the future. I've learned that whatever God wants to happen, I will be able to handle it."

"Because He is so good."

Looking into his eyes, Sadie nodded. "Yes. Because of that, but also because of you, too. I love you, Noah."

He stretched out and curved an arm around her. "I love you, too." After he kissed her softly, he shifted on the couch. "Now, let's go to sleep."

"Right here?" She giggled. "You're not going to leave?"

"Nope. I've found that right here by your side is the best place for me."

Maybe she should have been the voice of reason, but at the moment, she couldn't think of a single reason to say he was wrong.

And so she shifted, cuddled closer, and closed her eyes. Night had come and morning loomed.

The next day was sure to be bright.

EPILOGUE

Six Months Later

Knock, knock," Silas called out as he opened the kitchen door and walked inside. "Everybody awake and decent?"

Looking at Noah's aggravated expression, Sadie giggled. "At least he mentioned knocking. That's something new."

Her husband rolled his eyes as he got off the couch and headed toward the kitchen. "Are you ever going to start knocking at the front door, Silas?"

"Probably not."

As the brothers continued to banter back and forth, Sadie looked down at three-week-old Joshua. "The more things change, the more they stay the same, little one," she murmured. "It will serve you well to remember that."

The baby looked into her eyes and yawned.

She brushed a finger along his soft cheek and smiled. "You are right. It doesn't matter if things change or not. What is, is, *jah*?"

"What is 'what'?" Silas asked as he entered the room. To her surprise, her sister Faith was on his heels. Noah, looking like a cat who swallowed a canary, brought up the rear.

"Oh, nothing," Sadie replied. "I was just chatting with Joshua about life."

Silas reached for his nephew. "It's good we came over, then," he said as he easily pulled the baby into the crook of his arm. "That's a mighty heavy conversation for a Friday afternoon. Faith and me obviously need to hang around for a while and lighten things up."

After reaching to hug her sister, Sadie said, "When did you get here, Faith? I didn't know you were coming down this weekend."

Glancing shyly at Silas, she said, "Daisy mentioned that she had plenty of room and that she was hosting a barbecue tomorrow, so I brought down Emma. Silas and I met and started talking."

"Emma is here, too?" Emma was a year younger than Faith.

"She's at my house with Melody," Silas said. Looking mildly annoyed, he added, "Those girls thought we should wait until closer to supper to come over."

"But not you?" Noah asked.

"Of course not. Once Mamm and Daed and all the women get around Josh, I never get to hold him. I figured I might as well get my chance now."

"Do you mind sharing your *boppli*, sister?" Faith asked. "He is mighty special."

She shook her head. "Of course not. He's blessed to have such a doting family."

Smiling at Silas, Faith nodded. "He does indeed have that."

Feeling the need to stretch her legs, Sadie said, "Would you two mind watching him for a little bit? I think it might be nice to take a little walk."

"You sure you want to do that? It's really cold out."

"I know, but there's snow on the ground. Noah, would you mind going for a brief walk?"

"Not at all."

Feeling like a little girl anticipating a few minutes of freedom, Sadie slipped on her boots, cloak, and mittens and followed Noah out the front door.

After he closed it behind him, he reached for her hand. "Truth, now. What made you want to come outside? Was it really the snow?"

She laughed. "Partly. I do love a fresh snow, but it's too cold for Josh."

"And, what else?"

"Maybe I want to spend some quiet time with my husband of six months."

"I like spending time with you, too." He smiled as they walked down the sidewalk. "But . . . I'm thinking that ain't the only reason."

"Well, I thought maybe Silas and Faith might enjoy a few minutes alone together. They seem to have hit it off."

"I was thinking the same thing. Right or left?"

To the right was the end of the cul-de-sac. To the left were his brother's house and his parents'. "I think maybe right. If we go left, we'll probably get more company."

"That's a good possibility. Mamm will look out the window, wonder where Josh is . . . then run over to 'help' Silas and Faith."

Pleased that they were thinking along the same lines, she simply walked along by his side. Liking how fresh and clean the air felt . . . and how light her spirit felt.

For a while after her father tried to hurt her and all three men in the Stauffer family had been put on probation for their parts in making and selling the poisoned moonshine, it felt like a dark cloud had settled over all of them. She hadn't known how to help any of her relations. Not even Esther, who was working at Bill's Diner now.

But amazingly, the Lord had provided. Stephen and Daisy married quietly and moved into her home. Monroe had left the faith but rented a small apartment nearby and was working construction for Silas.

And Willis? Not surprisingly, he was having the most difficulty adjusting to his new way of life. He now fished a lot and frequented the library, reading several books a week. Though shadows filled his eyes, he also seemed less gruff. He'd even surprised them all by coming to the hospital to see Josh after he was born.

As they rounded the corner of the cul-de-sac, Noah said, "I go back to work full-time tomorrow."

"I know."

"It's twelve hours." He looked uncertain. "I told Mitch I was ready, but if you aren't, I can tell him that I need to only work—"

"Don't say that. It's time you got back to your job, Noah. You do good work and the team needs you." Smiling as they approached their house, which they'd moved into just two months ago, she said, "I'll be fine."

"You really will, won't you?"

She nodded. She now had everything she'd always wanted. A home where she felt safe and happy, friends and relatives she loved and enjoyed being around—and a wonderful man at her side along with a baby who was as much his as hers, thanks to Harlan formally relinquishing all rights.

"With so many blessings, how can I not be?" she asked simply.

When he merely squeezed her hand in response, she knew he understood. Sometimes one's heart was so full that words weren't needed.

Insights,
Interviews
& More . . .

Meet
Shelley Shepard Gray

IN MANY WAYS, my writing journey has been like my faith journey. I entered into both with a lot of hope and a bit of nervousness. You see, I didn't get baptized until I was in my twenties and didn't first get published until I was in my thirties. Some people might consider those events to have happened a little late in life. However, I feel certain that God knew each took place at exactly the right time for me.

To be honest, these days I rarely stop to think about my life before I was a Christian or a writer. I simply wake up, drink my coffee, and try to get everything done that I can each day! I feel blessed to be a part of a large church family and a busy career. But, every so often, someone will ask why I write inspirational novels. Or why I write at all.

Then I remember how it felt to knock on a minister's office door and tell him that I wanted to be baptized. And how it felt the very first time I wrote "Chapter 1." Both felt exhilarating and nerve-wracking.

Perhaps you are a little bit like me. Maybe you, also, developed your faith a little after some of your friends or family. Maybe you, also, began a new job in a field

that you didn't go to school for. Maybe you started on a journey where you weren't even sure you were going to be a success or even fit in.

Or maybe, like me, success wasn't what you were hoping to attain. Maybe it was a matter of following a power bigger than yourself. If so, I'm glad I'm in good company. I'd love to know your story, too.

Now I have been a Christian for almost thirty years. I've been a published writer for about half that time. Both journeys have not always been easy. Both have been filled with ups and downs. Yet both have given me much joy, too. I'd like to think that anything worth having takes some hard work. It takes some time to grow and mature, too.

And because of that, I am comfortable with the fact that I'm still on my journey, one morning at a time.

With blessings to you,
Shelley Shepard Gray ∽

Letter from the Author

Dear Reader,

I have to admit that some of our friends get a little worried when they go out to dinner with me. While everyone else talks about their coworkers, the commuting they do for their jobs, or the latest escapade their kids have been doing, I talk about my books.

Sometimes this isn't a problem. Everyone liked hearing about my research for baby pygmy goats when I was writing *A Sister's Wish*. But when I'm writing a novel like *Her Fear*? Well, even my husband felt a little burst of trepidation now and then. Yep, for the last three months I've been asking people what they're afraid of.

I know. Not the most soothing of dinner conversational choices.

To be honest, the discussions have been very interesting and sometimes really entertaining. We've talked about spiders and snakes. Clowns and enclosed spaces. But some of the conversations have veered toward the serious, too. Too serious and personal to list here.

As for me? Thanks to a mishap at the mall when I was five, I'm a little afraid of escalators. I'll get on them, but it takes me a while to take that first step. And, yes, when my kids were teenagers, I think my hesitancy used to embarrass them terribly. Now that they're adults? Well, they usually just stand by my side and let me know that if something happens they'll help me out.

And that, I think, is ultimately what this novel was about. Not just about my characters' fears but also whom they can lean on in times of trouble. As you might imagine, the people they love and their faith provided the most comfort.

I hope you enjoyed the book. And, if you happen to every so often stop and think about what you're afraid of, please know you're in good company. I hope and pray that you, too, feel someone's guiding hand, even if it's just to help you on and off a pesky escalator.

Wishing you many blessings and my thanks,

Shelley Shepard Gray ∾

Moonshine in Kentucky

From the Folk Song, "The Kentucky Moonshiner" *(traditional)*

> *"I've been a moonshiner goin' on seventeen year,*
> *I spent all my money on whiskey and beer.*
> *I'll go to some holler and set up my still,*
> *And see you a gallon for a two-dollar bill."*

While *Her Fear* is a work of fiction and I did not base it on any specific Amish community, there is a long history of individuals making homemade moonshine in the state of Kentucky. According to the numerous articles I've read about this subject, Kentucky has been known to be a place for moonshine and homemade liquor since the early 1800s. The practice became more widely known after the Civil War. Some families started distributing their homemade liquor during Prohibition.

While some folks might own a still (or a distillery purification system) such as for water purification, it is not legal to operate one in order to make alcoholic beverages. According to the Kentucky Revised Statute, Section 244.170:

"No person shall buy, bargain, sell, loan, own, possess, or knowingly transport any apparatus designed for the unlawful manufacture of alcoholic beverages."

If someone was found guilty of this, the still would be seized and the person would be charged with a Class B misdemeanor.

What about the Amish?

The Amish have a decentralized system when it comes to what is allowed and not allowed. There isn't something written down regarding drinking alcohol like there are in some other religions. That said, you would be far more likely to find an Amish man or woman drinking a cup of coffee or a soda than sipping wine or opening a can of beer. However, in some Old Order Amish communities, it is permissible to have a celebratory toast with homemade wine or cider from time to time. The New Order Amish are much more against this practice.

While doing research for *Her Fear*, I read a number of quotes from people who said they knew a few Amish men who operated a still. I have no reason to believe this happens very often. ✎

There Really Are Amish Firemen and EMTs

One of the biggest misconceptions some people seem to have about the Amish is that they are against technology. That really isn't the case. For example, if you ever visit the Sugarcreek library you'll see just as many Amish residents at the computer terminals as you will English. Most of the Amish who want to use the computer from time to time to look things up on the Internet certainly know how to do that. They just don't have computers in their homes.

That is the difference, I think. Most Amish don't want technology to run their lives. As someone who works on a computer all day long in my house, I can absolutely identify with the desire to keep some distance from Twitter, Facebook, and emails!

This belief that technology can be valuable, if utilized in an appropriate matter, is one of the reasons an Amish man or woman might become a firefighter or an EMT. Another driving factor is a need to give back and to be an asset to their district, county, or town. As in any community, firefighters and other first responders put their lives on the line to help others. The Amish firefighters and EMTs I read about felt strongly about helping the men and women in their community. One man I read about became a firefighter after the local fire department was called when his barn caught on fire. He wanted to give back and help others.

Just like every other emergency medical technician, an Amish EMT will complete the coursework and go through hundreds of hours of volunteering in order to be certified. There are even some classes available for the Amish men and women to complete online in case attending college is not an option.

When I first imagined my hero as an EMT, I envisioned that his knowledge of Pennsylvania Dutch would come in handy. It turns out that many Amish firefighters and EMTs are valued for their knowledge of both English and Pennsylvania Dutch. They can communicate easily with an Amish man, woman, or child who might be in distress. ▶

There Really Are Amish Firemen and EMTs *(continued)*

What made me smile the most during my research was reading the quotes from the Amish men and women who both volunteer or are paid firefighters and EMTs. They are proud of their ability to help others and are glad that the Lord has given them gifts to enable them to work hard in extreme situations. One man also mentioned that when his unit is called out to fight a fire, he is considered simply to be a firefighter, not an *Amish* firefighter. I could certainly appreciate that!

I'm so proud to be writing books about the Amish in different occupations that showcase their bravery and commitment to their community! I hope you enjoyed *Her Fear* and will enjoy my November release, *His Promise,* in which my Amish hero is a firefighter. ∽

Questions for Discussion

1. Though *Her Fear* was a work of fiction, I tried to incorporate a number of themes in the novel that anyone might experience at one time or another: grief, uncertainty, hope, and acceptance. For Sadie, all of these emotions are linked together. Has there ever been a time in your life when you've experienced a number of these emotions as well?

2. The Stauffer family was very different from Sadie. Do you think this was a good or bad thing? How might have her experiences with them been different if they were a more traditional family?

3. Almost every character in the novel isn't quite what they seem at first, even Stephen and Daisy. Why do you think the timing was right for them to begin their friendship?

4. What did you think of Noah and his choice to become an EMT?

5. Was there a character that you would like to read more about?

6. What obstacles do you think Sadie and Noah will encounter during their life together?

7. I loved the following Scripture verse from Hebrews that guided me through the writing of this novel. *We can say with confidence, "the Lord is my helper, so I will have no fear. What can mere people do to me?"* (Hebrews 13:6). What does it mean to you?

8. *Do what you can with what you have where you are* (Amish Proverb). How might this proverb relate to a situation that has happened in your life?

Read on

A Sneak Peek from the Next Book in the Amish of Hart County Series

Coming November 2018 from Avon Inspire!

I will be filled with joy because of You. I will sing praises to your name, O Most High.   Psalm 16:11

Prayers go up, Blessings come down.
                                    Amish Proverb

"It's SNOWING AGAIN," Grace King said to Snooze. "If it keeps up, we're gonna have a white Christmas. Won't that be something?"

Snooze, the appropriately named five-year-old dachshund, opened one eye, stared at her for a few seconds, then darted under his favorite quilt. Grace knew he wouldn't reappear for several hours.

He was truly the most unsocial dog she'd ever sat for, and that was saying a lot. She'd taken care of a variety of animals during her three years as a professional pet sitter. From pampered felines to retired greyhounds to ornery parrots, she'd even once looked after a science teacher's iguana named Sam. With every animal, she'd managed to find something to connect with the pet. Sometimes, all it took was a special treat or a couple of games of fetch. Or, in Sam's case, fresh flies.

Snooze, all fourteen pounds of stubbornness, was starting to be her most difficult client. No matter what she did, the little wirehaired dachshund didn't want anything to do with her. It was frustrating, but at least she knew the reason.

Snooze was pouting.

He missed his family and was extremely displeased that he was having to spend Christmas with her. *Only* her.

Grace knew exactly how he felt.

It wasn't supposed to be this way. When Mr. and Mrs. Lee had booked her back in September, they'd kindly told Grace that she should feel free to have any of her siblings or one of her girlfriends keep her company while she lived in their big house for two weeks.

Imagining quiet evenings spent on their soft leather couches in front of their fireplace with her best friend, Jennifer, or one of her sisters, Grace had jumped at the chance. She was the second oldest of six children and while she loved, loved, loved them all, they were a noisy and intrusive lot. They got excited, talked loudly to everyone, and were constantly in each other's business.

And at Christmas? Well, suffice to say that her mother got a little too enthusiastic about the holiday. Daed often teased her about forgetting that she was Old Order Amish and therefore should want a plain and simple Christmas. Though they didn't have a tree or string lights from the roof, her mother strung Christmas cards down the banisters, lit cranberry-scented candles from morning till night, and even sang Christmas carols to herself when she didn't think anyone was listening. And then there was the baking. And the wrapping. And the dozen holiday projects in various stages of completion scattered all through the house.

It was a little bit overwhelming for Grace, who enjoyed the quiet almost as much as she enjoyed being alone with a good book.

Grace had planned to use the Lees' beautiful, roomy and, yes, quiet house as her Christmas escape. She'd planned to attach Snooze's leash to his collar and take him home for a few hours every day so everyone could play with him. Then, when they ▶

were both tired, she would usher him back to his fancy house where they could revel in the peace and quiet.

But almost as soon as she said good-bye to Mr. and Mrs. Lee and got snubbed by Snooze, the Lord rearranged her plans.

Mamm's parents contracted a bad case of the flu. They were so weak, the whole family—well, everyone except her—journeyed up to Ohio to Mommi's and Dawdi's *haus* for the holiday.

Then Jennifer and her family decided to travel for the holiday as well.

So now Grace was having to spend Christmas alone with an unsocial dachshund who would rather sleep under an old quilt than have anything to do with her. To make matters worse, none of the books she'd brought with her caught her interest. Neither did the puzzle she'd placed on the kitchen table.

It seemed she was pouting, too.

After staring out the window again, then surveying the sparkling clean and far-too-quiet sitting room, Grace came to a decision. She needed to stop feeling sorry for herself. It was only day two of her fifteen-day job. Something had to be done.

"Snooze, let's go for a little walk."

The dog stuck out its tiny brown nose.

"I see you thinking about it. Come on. It will be fun."

Snooze grumbled when she scooped him up in her arms but didn't try to escape. Feeling encouraged, Grace threw a scarf around her neck, stuffed her feet into boots she'd neatly placed by the door, grabbed her black cloak, and stepped outside.

After closing the shiny black door behind her, she sighed in pleasure. The Lees' front yard was a winter wonderland. Rolling hills covered in white, clumps of trees and bushes arranged in artful arrangements, and a lovely stamped concrete walkway leading to the large entryway. A couple of squirrels were chattering in the distance, and a pair of bright-red cardinals perched on a black wrought-iron feeder. It all looked like something out of a picture postcard.

"You surely have quite a home, Snooze," she murmured.

When the little dog squirmed, she smiled. "*Jah*, I bet you are ready to do your business." Kneeling down, she gently placed him on the ground, half ready to pick him up within a minute or two. He seemed like the type of animal who didn't like getting his paws cold.

Sure enough, Snooze gingerly walked a few steps and paused. The squirrels in the distance chattered again. He raised his head toward them.

Then, in a startling, lightning-fast move, he barked shrilly and took off running down a hill.

Seconds later he was out of sight.

"Snooze? Snooze!" Feeling an odd combination of both shock and panic, Grace ran after him, the hem of her dark-green dress and apron brushing against the snow and soaking her stocking-covered legs.

"Snooze! Come back!" Down the hill she went, following tiny footprints like a detective. Frantically calling out his name.

But he didn't answer.

After about twenty yards, the cloak that she'd never fastened fell off her shoulders. She left it on the ground, too afraid to look anywhere but at the paw prints in the snow. "Snooze! Snooze, come here, wouldja?"

But still there was no answer.

And then, to her dismay, there were no more tracks to be found. She could only surmise that he'd gone into the woods after one of those pesky squirrels.

Standing there in the cold, the hem of her dress soaking wet, her cloak on the ground, and her head bare except for her white *kapp,* Grace forced herself to face the awful, awful truth.

She'd just managed to lose her only companion—and her only responsibility—for the holiday.

"Snooze!" she yelled out again. "Please, please come back!"

Tears filled her eyes as she stepped forward; she was simply going to have to start wandering through the woods, all while praying that some fox or other wild animal hadn't taken hold of the dog.

"Snooze!" Her feet crunched on the blanket of snow and pine needles. She reached out and moved a branch out of her path, really wishing she'd put on mittens. ▶

A Sneak Peek (*continued*)

Squirrels scampered overhead, a hawk circled in the distance. Just as she pulled another branch out of her way, another scraped her cheek.

The snow continued to fall, large flakes sticking to the branches surrounding her, clinging to her wool dress.

And still, there was no sign of the dog.

The tears that she'd tried to quell began trickling down her face. "Snooze? Here, pup."

She stopped again. She was now surrounded by trees and had no idea which way to go. No idea how to tempt one disagreeable dachshund to return to her side.

Just as she was about to call his name again, she heard a loud rustling off to her left.

With a cry of relief, she turned toward the noise. Then screamed.

The man whom she'd just spied through the tangle of branches rushed toward her.